Great Sexpectations

www.sarahbegg.com

ALSO BY SARAH BEGG

Great Sexpectations

SARAH BEGG

Laura the Explorer Book 3

A catalogue record for this book is available from the National
Library of Australia

ISBN: 978 0 9876415 2 6 (paperback)

www.sarahbegg.com

For Linden

1

At a gorgeous outdoor cafe table, surrounded by autumn leaves and the smell of roasting coffee, the man I loved sat gazing at another woman.

She wore a relaxed floral beach dress, and her enviable golden-caramel hair fell in loose waves down to the tips of her perfect shoulderblades. I could see her eyes devouring the menu, and she bit her kiss-swollen lips, a sure sign of someone looking for a huge, indulgent breakfast after a night of no sleep and lots of sex. Spent, presumably, with the man opposite her.

I wanted to be sick.

Lucas, the guy I had finally admitted to being in love with, gazed at Holly with ... wonder? I couldn't quite pick the look. Perhaps it was curiosity. He appeared to be trying to work out a puzzle, like he was wondering how he'd managed to get so lucky as to have that stunning girl out to breakfast with him.

Shifting my weight, my shoulder scratched along the exposed brick wall that I was peering out from behind.

"Laura, I don't think this is healthy," the voice of Kalina, my flatmate, said, standing beside me.

I startled, whipping around to face her. "I didn't know they'd be here!" I protested.

"Well, they are. And I'm hungry. So, are we getting breakfast or not?"

I cast my eyes around the laneway, feeling panicked. The place was buzzing with people—hardly surprising for 10 am on a Sunday morning. We were in one of the trendiest backstreets of Manly, where street art, flowers and cafes surrounded the community library. All my favourite cafes were located here, and Kalina and I had planned to get breakfast at one of them.

Although, that was before I'd spotted Lucas and Holly and dragged Kalina behind the wall.

"We can go somewhere else if you want," Kalina offered. "Let's please just make a decision?" On cue, her stomach grumbled loudly.

"Sorry. I'm being ridiculous, aren't I?"

"Yep." Kalina gave me a look, which meant "you know what I think of this". And I did. Because we'd been having the same discussion almost every day for the last month.

"Okay. It's fine. Let's go to the furthest one over there and hopefully they won't see us."

"Great!" Kalina's relief was palpable as she stepped out from behind our wall, striding over towards the chosen cafe before I had time to change my mind. I pushed my sunglasses up my nose and followed her quickly, keeping my face averted.

Please don't see me, please don't see me, I chanted in my head. Surely, he wouldn't since he was preoccupied with Holly. Even if I'd stopped and done the Nutbush right next to his table, he probably wouldn't have noticed me, anyway.

I slid into my seat at our cafe, realising that if I turned my head slightly to the right, I could still clearly see Holly and Lucas. I could see them talking. I could see them laughing. I could see her bare foot, gliding up and down across his calf beneath their table.

"Is this okay?" Kalina was watching me warily.

I snapped my gaze to her. "It's great! Let's order."

"Uh-huh," Kalina said suspiciously, closing her menu. Then she narrowed her eyes at me. "I thought you were fine with him being back together with her?"

"I am!"

"If you like him that much—"

"I don't! I mean, we're friends, that's it. Just friends."

"Laura, you need to *tell* him how you feel."

"There's nothing to tell."

"He's an idiot for getting back with her."

I pursed my lips, shooting another glance at them. That was a mistake.

"She's ... the girl he's always been in love with," I said reluctantly. "Evidently, he still is."

Even though she'd broken his heart and turned him into a suspicious, mistrusting, woman-hating guy for a while. That was before I'd ever met Lucas. I knew that he'd been with Holly for years, that he'd even proposed to her. But she'd freaked out and said she didn't think she could marry the first guy she'd ever slept with. She'd wanted to go out and date other men, and it had seriously messed him up.

But now they were a couple again.

"Well, if you see yourself as nothing more than friends with him, then it's all irrelevant. You should be happy for him."

"Exactly," I said. "He deserves to be happy. I want that for him."

"Uh-huh."

"Oh, shut up."

I could feel her staring intensely at me still, that annoying, knowing glint in her eyes, even though I was keeping my own gaze fixed determinedly on my menu.

A waiter came by and took our order then, and though I fought hard to hang onto my menu (an excellent means of camouflage), he managed to pry it out of my grip. He walked away, leaving me with nothing to hide behind.

"See, I still can't work out what actually changed for you." Kalina leaned her elbows on the table, drawing closer to me. "I mean, you definitely had decided after Byron Bay that you were going to declare your love for Lucas—"

"I *don't* love him."

"—but then, you just changed your mind. And now you've given up."

"You *know* what happened."

Kalina waved a hand, dismissively. "You saw him kissing Holly, so what?"

Oh God. It was even worse when said out loud. I'd arrived back from Byron Bay, love singing in my heart, had raced to find him and throw my arms around him, and tell him that I knew what I wanted now and it was him ...

But just like in a tragic movie, I'd been too late. I'd arrived outside his bar, looked in through the glass window and seen him inside with Holly. I'd watched, horrified, as she'd leaned into him, her face tipped up, and he'd bent his head down, his lips finding hers.

Neither of them had seen me standing there, my heart breaking in the moonlight.

"You can't just say 'so what' like it's nothing." I glared at Kalina. "What was I meant to do? Barge in there, wave my arms around and say, 'Hey, I'm over here! I know I've been stuffing you around for ages, but now that you've moved on I'm finally ready to give it a go?'"

Kalina rolled her eyes. "Sometimes you've got to fight for what you want, Laur."

"We don't do that, remember? We don't cheat on people or be the cause of someone else's relationship collapse. It's an unspoken rule that I'm sure you made up, but now I'm speaking it out loud."

"There can be exceptions."

I gave her a look.

After a moment, she huffed, "Fine. You're right. Fuck, it's hard having morals sometimes."

I couldn't help but smile. Kalina was an inspiration to single girls everywhere. In fact, she'd been one of my biggest inspirations ever since I met her and she nicknamed me "Laura the Explorer". She hated games of any sort, would always say exactly what she thought and be completely up front with what she wanted. Ever since arriving in Australia from London a couple of years ago, she'd absolutely refused to "do" a relationship, and though she'd never been short of men in her life since then, she'd stuck to her plan and had enjoyed a near-constant rotation of casual flings.

Of course, that seemed to have come to an end now. Two months ago, Kalina and I drove up to Byron Bay to rescue Ben, our flatmate, from his nutcase of a girlfriend. Not only did I learn a lot about myself on that trip—and a lot about what, or rather, *who*, I now wanted—but Kalina met a guy who managed to shake her aversion to boyfriends. Owen had been staying at the same house we rented, though at the time he'd gone by the name Echo and was secretly undercover investigating this huge scam organisation in Byron (that's a whole other story). But while we'd been there, Kalina and he had really hit it off. And now that his freelance job had wrapped up, he'd moved to Sydney to be close to her.

It was totally adorable. And she was absolutely smitten, I could tell.

"What *are* you going to do, then?" Kalina asked. "You can't avoid Lucas or keep hiding behind walls every time you spot him. We live with his brother."

"That won't be a problem. Before the bar, Lucas didn't come around to our flat at all. I didn't even know he was Ben's brother for months, remember? And now that the bar has closed and everyone has gone on to other jobs, there's no reason for Lucas to keep coming round to our place. He's probably too busy hanging out with Holly, anyway," I added darkly.

Kalina eye-balled me with an expression I couldn't quite decipher. It was kind of calculating. A bit unnervingly calculating, if I was being honest.

Time to change the subject.

"So, how's your job hunting going?" I asked with forced brightness.

Her eyes narrowed slightly, like she didn't want to indulge my diversionary ploy, but she rolled with it like a true friend would.

"No news yet," she said with a shrug. "I sent out a bunch of résumés last week, but haven't heard from any of the organisations."

Kalina, who I'd begun referring to in my head as the international woman of mysteries, had shocked me last week when she'd disclosed that she was a qualified social worker and used to work with youth outreach programs back in London. Ever since I'd known her, Kalina had worked as a bartender in Manly, working or partying by night and sunbaking or shopping by day. She'd never shown any interest in having a day job, and I suppose I'd kind of just assumed that being a bartender was the only career she'd ever wanted.

But since returning from Byron Bay, it seemed I wasn't the only one who'd changed my outlook on life. Kalina hadn't wanted to return to her old bartending and partying lifestyle—possibly because Owen had just moved to Sydney and she was very much enjoying hanging out with him most evenings.

"I still can't believe you're a social worker and I never knew that," I said.

She shrugged again. "I just wanted a change when I came here. New life, new start and all that. But now I'm getting too old to be working night shifts."

It was my turn to roll my eyes. "You're twenty-six, you goose. And as your senior, I think I can safely say that you are still quite a way from being geriatric. Now I, on the other hand, *am* turning into an old lady."

Kalina snorted. "Well, you *are* going to hit thirty before me."

"Not for two years!" I quickly retorted. Although, in all honesty, I was starting to get a bit freaked out by that fact.

The waiter came back with our cappuccinos then, depositing them on the table before disappearing.

"So, are you excited to start your new job tomorrow?" Kalina asked me, tearing open a sugar packet and dumping it into her coffee.

"Yeah. Although … well, it's a bit weird."

"Have they still not answered any of your questions?"

"Nope. It's all rather vague and cagey. But I have been sent a location for tomorrow, which is in Mosman, so I definitely have a job. I just don't know the first thing about it."

A few months ago, Ben hooked me up to meet Celeste, an Australian film producer, who hired me to be the assistant location manager for a new film shooting in Sydney. For months, I'd been really excited about starting the job. But then the date kept getting pushed back. We should have commenced filming weeks ago, but Celeste called me literally the day before we were about to begin and told me the whole thing had been delayed by a week. And then that happened again, and again, and I would have been really worried except that Ben seemed to think it was all totally normal in the film business. And although he might have been all laidback and carefree about it, I was starting to feel a little alarmed by my rapidly decreasing bank balance. I'd already been living off my savings for close to three months; any more delays and I'd need to ask Mum and Dad for a loan. Something I *really* didn't want to do, since Mum already thought I was heading off the rails and that I was going to end up a homeless trolley lady with cats for children.

"Surely, Ben can help out," Kalina suggested. "He's worked on films before."

"Yeah. I'm counting on it, at this point."

A shadow fell across our table, and I looked up, expecting to see the waiter with our breakfast. Instead, I found my gaze crashing into unfairly mesmerising sky-blue eyes, tousled sandy-blond hair and a chiselled jawline that made me think the Hemsworths had a long-lost brother.

"Oh—hi!" I squeaked, right as Kalina said, her voice way too fake sounding, "*Lucas*, fancy seeing you here!"

Lucas frowned down at us, like he suspected he'd just interrupted us talking about him, which given our weirdly chirpy responses wasn't an unreasonable deduction. And to be fair, if he'd walked over ten minutes ago, we would have been.

"Hey," he said, his eyes still assessing each of us with suspicion.

"Erm, what are you doing here?" I asked, belatedly realising how unfriendly that sounded.

He frowned at me in a way that was one-hundred-percent

accusation. "I thought I'd come say hello so you couldn't avoid me again."

"What are you talking about?" I gave a weird trilling laugh and refused to glance at Kalina, who I could sense was watching on with a mix of glee and smugness. "I haven't been avoiding you," I added innocently, blinking up at him like I was Bambi.

"Really? I could have sworn I saw you yesterday, but you seemed to just turn around when I waved and run in the other direction."

While Lucas spoke, he grabbed a chair from the vacant table beside us and pulled it towards our table. When he sat down between Kalina and me, my senses were teased with the scent of salt water and a touch of something else that was just *him*, and it was all I could do not to lean in closer and take in a huge drag of air like a smoker after a twelve-hour flight. The smooth curve of his biceps sticking out below his t-shirt sleeve was so close to me that I could practically feel the heat coming off him, and I had to fight hard against the sudden urge to pull his arm against my chest and rub my boobs against his bare skin.

"Did I?" I choked out, sounding oh-so-fakely surprised. "I didn't see you. I probably was just out walking and then remembered that I forgot something back at the flat. Actually, yes, now I remember. I'd put toast on, then forgotten about it and gone out, then realised and worried it might have caught fire, so I had to rush back."

"Laura's been getting confused lately," Kalina added helpfully. "She can't decide what she wants."

"Thank you, Kal." If my eyes had laser beams attached, they would have destroyed her retinas.

"So, you're back together with Holly?" Kalina turned to Lucas, staring innocently up at him. "Is she here with you?"

I suddenly expected to see Holly hovering behind his shoulder like some creepy wraith, but there was no sign of her. The table they'd been sitting at down the laneway was now occupied by an older couple and their excessively drooling Saint Bernard.

"She's gone shopping," Lucas replied casually. "Hey, I wanted to ask you both—how's Ben doing?"

Hmm. Did he just *deliberately* change the subject?

"He's ... okay," Kalina said. From her hesitation, I knew exactly what she was thinking. What do you say about someone who just found out their first real relationship was all a lie and that the girl was only pretending to be in love with you to try to steal your money?

"He seems to be dealing alright," I added, meeting Lucas's eyes.

That was a mistake.

Christ, how could they be so blue? Even now, with his brows pulled down slightly in concern and a frown crossing his face, my brain was unhelpfully imagining what it would be like to crush my body against his and kiss that mouth and breathe him in and feel his arms around me.

Just as I'd done that once, all those months ago, in the store room of Los Perdidos. I'd kissed him and he'd kissed me and it had been amazing, except for my dark and shrivelled heart, which had panicked and sent me running away.

Well, my heart wasn't dark and shrivelled anymore. It was whole, and beating, and I was pretty sure it was beating for *him*. Stupid heart. It didn't seem to have registered that Lucas now had a girlfriend, which meant he was definitely *not* in love with me. Which meant that, just like I'd told Kalina, I simply needed to *not* be in love with him, anymore.

A plan that would be much easier to execute if he didn't happen to be sitting right beside me, causing my heart to palpitate and my thighs to squeeze together and my lips to nibble on themselves.

I shot my attention back to Kalina and tried to remember what I was saying.

"He's better than okay, actually. All things considered." I raised my eyebrows at Kalina as if I was passing the conversational football to her.

"He's going out a lot," Kalina supplied. "Hanging out with his friends, which is good. Why do you ask?"

Lucas sighed, sounding frustrated. "I've been trying to make time to see him, but he keeps blowing me off. I feel like I'm going to have to corner him just to get him to talk to me."

"You should come around this afternoon," Kalina said. "We were all planning to have drinks on the lawn."

I stopped breathing for a moment, mentally screaming at Kalina to rescind that offer. I didn't want Lucas coming to our afternoon drinkies! That went exactly against what I'd said to her earlier about avoiding him, although ...

Oh.

Oh.

She met my gaze, a deceptively innocent challenge twinkling in her eyes.

Of course. She was meddling. And she didn't give two shits about Lucas seeing Ben. She wanted him to see me.

"That ... yeah, okay. I'll make time." Lucas's hand came up to knead the back of his shoulder. My eyes darted to the way his forearm bunched on his biceps and made both muscles bulge deliciously. Again, I had that urge to rub my breasts—my *naked* breasts—against his bare skin. Let his arm with its light dusting of hair graze against my nipples ...

Christ. *Friends, Laura. Friends.*

"Great!" Kalina said brightly, looking as triumphant as if she'd just convinced him to come to her fancy-dress Eurovision party. "'Bout four, yeah?"

"Sure." Lucas's gaze slid to me and I did my best to match Kalina's enthusiastic smile. But in my head, I was frantically reassessing what I should wear to our casual lawn drinks and then cursing myself for even thinking about it because Lucas had a girlfriend and probably couldn't care less if I looked hot or not.

"Cool," I found myself saying. "You should bring Holly, too."

ARGH!

Did I seriously just say that? What was *wrong* with me?

Lucas clearly thought there was something wrong with me, too, judging by the confusion that washed across his face.

"Okay. I will."

"Perfect." I turned my snakelike smile onto Kalina, as if she was a mouse who thought she'd just outsmarted me, but now she could see that I was hellbent on sabotage and completely prepared to eat myself.

And honestly, she could have looked a bit sheepish, or disappointed or something, but instead she just gave me this level stare, a tiny smile touching the corners of her lips. As if she thought I'd just laid down a challenge, and she was ready to accept it.

Well, game on.

2

Later that afternoon, Kalina, Ben, Owen and I dragged our two beanbags, a picnic blanket and a whole lot of beer and wine down to the grassy nature strip at the back of our apartment building. It overlooked one of the small walking tracks to the beach, and there we sat in the afternoon sun, drinking and relaxing.

Kalina and Owen were smooshed together on one of the beanbags, her legs draped over his, and if I'd only just met Kalina I never would have guessed at her former aversion to boyfriends. The two of them just seemed to fit together, in a way that was both adorable but that also sent weird pangs through my own chest if I watched them for too long.

"What do you think will happen tomorrow?" I asked Ben, since he was also starting work on the film job with me. Ben was an audio engineer, and he'd worked on other movies before this one, so I guessed he'd have a pretty good understanding of the process.

"What do you mean?" he asked, cracking open another beer.

"I mean, how do you think the day will go? I don't know anything about the film, except that it's called *Trigger*. And tomorrow we're working at a house in Mosman, so will we be filming already? Or is it like a kick-off meeting day where they'll go through everyone's job roles and stuff?"

"There'll definitely be filming. With these sorts of jobs, you're expected to just show up and start work straightaway."

"Shit. But I have no idea what I'm meant to be doing."

Ben shrugged like he thought it was no big deal. "You'll work it out. Celeste wouldn't have hired you if she thought you couldn't manage it."

I chewed on my lip, feeling only slightly reassured by this. "Are you *sure* you don't know anything else about the film?" I asked Ben for about the millionth time.

He rolled his eyes. "No more than you do. I just turn up and start recording."

I made a little huffing sound and returned my attention to my beer. My non-alcoholic beer, because I was being responsible like that.

Months ago, I found it impressive how relaxed and blasé Ben was about all the jobs he did, but now that I was going to be on the same job I thought it was highly irritating. I mean, who just turns up for a job without knowing anything about it?

Ben, apparently. And also me.

"Don't stress about it," Ben said, watching my face. "Just think about the money you're going to get paid."

I huffed a laugh. "Yeah, that's the main thing I'm latching onto at the moment. If they'd delayed one more time ..."

"Yeah, I know, right? As it is, I'm going to be back to back with my next gig."

That was a surprise. "What next gig?"

"My next contract," Ben said, as though I should have known such a basic detail. "I've got some corporate contracts after this."

"Oh," I said stupidly. "I didn't realise you had anything else planned."

"Of course. I've got the next six months lined up."

I almost choked on my beer. "Six *months*?"

"Haven't you thought about what you're going to do after filming?" he asked me, now looking slightly concerned. "The *Trigger* job only lasts six weeks."

"Of course!" I lied. "I mean, I just haven't got anything, you know, *locked in*. I'm still weighing up my options. Seeing if, well, seeing what happens, I suppose ..."

I trailed off, realising I was about to say, *Seeing if I get offered another film job*. But I was too embarrassed to admit that to Ben, mainly because I didn't want him to correct my current dream. Celeste might have been a little evasive with the details of this film project, but I was still envisioning all the glamour and excitement of working on a movie set. And, sure, maybe I'd been imagining myself being the best damned assistant location manager Celeste had ever hired, and that I'd make myself indispensable to the whole crew, and by the end of filming they'd all be saying, "I don't know what we'd have done without Laura Baker here. We definitely won't be able to make a good movie without her around ever again."

"Fair enough." Ben shrugged. "I guess you'll probably go back to your marketing stuff after this, right?"

Like hell I'd ever go back to Tiger Finance.

"Maybe," I said, matching his shrug.

But, oh God, would I have to? I had a sudden vision of me back in Cara's office, her long acrylic nails clicking on the desk as she watched me grovel with that deadpan expression of hers. Although, hang on, I thought Cara had left Tiger Finance, too. So, who would I have to grovel to?

My thoughts were distracting me so much that I almost didn't notice the two people approaching until they were practically upon us.

"Hey, guys," came a sunshiny-warm female voice, and I immediately hated the new arrival for having a nicer voice than me.

But of course I was going to hate her, because she was Holly and she'd stolen Lucas.

Alright, not *stolen*. He was never mine.

Repeat, he was *never mine*.

Reluctantly, I lifted my gaze to take them both in. Lucas looked as drool-worthy as ever, with a baseball cap shading his eyes while drawing attention to his jawline and mouth, which was totally kissable, but I couldn't think about that because it was really inappropriate and he was off limits.

Holly looked like she'd tried way too hard for drinkies on the nature strip. A gorgeous geometric-print maxi beach dress (*I wonder where she got it?*) skimmed over her slender figure, while also enhancing her bigger-than-mine cleavage. And that hair was *really* unfair. It would take me hours with my GHD to achieve those casual curls, but she'd probably just stepped straight out of the sea and had natural salt-water beach waves. I wasn't positive she was wearing makeup, but was anyone's skin *really* that glowy without it?

I realised everyone else had got to their feet to greet Lucas and Holly, so I quickly followed suit. Lucas gave me a swift, friendly kiss on the cheek that was sudden and over way too quickly, and then Holly was before me, baring her perfect white teeth at me, her arms outstretched for a hug.

"You must be Laura!" she said warmly, enveloping me in her skinny-but-toned arms.

I bet she could do proper push-ups, the bitch.

"Yes, hi!" I managed to say, returning her hug and surprising myself with just how friendly I could sound.

"I've heard so much about you," Holly said, her arms still wrapped around me. God, she even *smelled* nice. I really had to up my perfume game.

Like, remember to put it on in the mornings.

"Really?" I squeaked out, wondering what Lucas had told her about me. Would he have mentioned that we'd kissed once? Unlikely, considering this hug I was getting.

"Yeah!" Holly finally released me, pulling back just far enough so that she could stare right at me while she spoke. "The way you and Kalina went up to Byron Bay to find Ben? That was so sweet of you. And I can't wait for us to be friends."

Kill me now.

"Me too!" Oh God, I was gushing like a pro. A really fake pro. "It's so great that you're with Lucas, and so nice to finally meet you. I've heard so much about you, as well."

Like how you broke Lucas's heart and nearly destroyed him.

But glancing around at the group, I wondered if I was the only one still holding a grudge against Holly? She sat gracefully down on the picnic blanket beside Kalina and Owen, pulling out some bags of chips and a packet of Tim Tams, and earning a delighted squeal from both Kalina *and* Owen, who promptly ripped open the salt-and-vinegar bag.

Lucas and Ben were standing a little away from our picnic area, but it looked like they were having a private brotherly kind of talk. So reluctantly, I sat down next to Holly.

"It's been an age, hasn't it, Kal?" Holly was saying. "Are you still working at The Pony?"

"I thought about going back, but I'm ready for something different." Kalina punctuated her sentence with a *crunch* of a chip.

"I've been applying for jobs for the past week."

"Cool! What sort of jobs?" Holly asked.

"Social work, mostly. I used to do youth work in London a few years ago, so I'd like to get back into that."

"Oh, get out!" Holly said. "I'm working at Follow the Rainbow in Manly now."

"No way!" Kalina sat forward with excitement. "I applied for a job there! What are you doing?"

"I'm one of the project coordinators. I could definitely talk to HR, though—you'd be great working for us."

"Seriously? That would be fantastic!" Kalina's smile was ebullient, and she turned to Owen, whacking him on the leg a few times as if to make sure he'd also heard.

"See?" Owen drawled. "Told ya it'd be a piece of piss." He kissed her on the forehead, oblivious to her confused and slightly horrified expression.

"Aww, so how did you guys meet?"

As Holly continued talking to Kalina and Owen, I sat there on the other side of her, doing that thing where you're listening in but at the same time feeling like a total interloper who's not actually part of the conversation. It didn't help that Holly was facing Kalina and Owen, which meant I was sitting kind of behind her like some loser pretending to be part of the cool group. The three of them chatted away and the longer I just sat there being ignored, the more uncomfortable I felt. Eventually I got up and went to rummage in the esky, even though I didn't really want another drink.

I also pretended I had very important things that needed checking on my phone, opening and closing my email app, then WhatsApp, then skimming the headlines on a news website, and finally opening Instagram before closing it again because of how pathetic I was being.

Pasting a bright smile on my face, I turned back to the group. Lucas and Ben had joined us, and Lucas was now sitting where I'd been next to Holly on the picnic blanket. Ben was in the other beanbag, and beside him was that big patch of dirt because we hadn't brought anything else to sit on. They were all mid-conversation, big smiles on their faces, and not a single person was paying any mind to me.

Ridiculously, I felt my throat close up like I was about to cry.

"I'm just going to go grab something from upstairs," I muttered to Ben, who nodded absently at me as I passed.

I walked away from them, back up to the building, swallowing and blinking and wondering why I was feeling so upset. When I turned back to see if anyone had noted my departure, all I was presented with was five backs, chatting together and laughing. Kalina was squealing as Owen poked her in the side, and Holly had snuggled up against Lucas. Ben sat like the king of the castle in his beanbag, commanding the surrounding area. They looked like the cast of a TV show, five friends enjoying the afternoon together, Holly wedged right in the middle.

And there wasn't any space for me.

3

Heading upstairs, I had the sudden urge to call my old work bestie, Rose. But then I remembered that she'd gone to France to meet her boyfriend's family and it would probably be the middle of the night over there. I decided to call Mum, just to hear her warm and comforting voice, but when I dialled the home line, it was my younger sister, Elle, who answered.

"Yo, sis!" she said. "How's it going in your new hood?"

"It's fine. How's it hanging at the family pad?" I responded, my language maturity immediately regressing. Elle was twenty-one—a good seven years younger than me—and despite having recently spent close to a year travelling through South America with her best friend, Marrika, she didn't appear to have matured in the slightest.

"It's fab! I thought I'd hate being here alone, but I'm freaking loving it."

For a second I had no idea what she was talking about, and then I groaned inwardly as I realised my error. Mum and Dad had just set off on their big holiday. They'd bought a second-hand caravan that they'd found on Gumtree (I didn't know Mum and Dad had even *heard* of Gumtree) and they were doing this big drive up to Port Douglas and back, stopping off in basically every scenic coastal town along the way. At least, that was their plan. I was still highly sceptical about Dad's ability to *drive* the caravan, let alone Mum's ability to have a shower in that tiny cubicle thing it had going on. But they seemed really determined to do it, especially since their friends, Trish and Phil, also had a caravan and the four of them were going as a convoy. I wasn't sure two caravans counted as a convoy, but Dad seemed to like saying "going on convoy!" so I hadn't mentioned it.

"Oh God. If you're throwing any parties, just don't tell me about it," I said to Elle.

She barked a laugh. "As if! I'd need you to come around and help me clean up."

"Ellie!"

"Kidding! Jeez, settle down. I'm not going to trash the house."

I sighed. When I'd been living at home, even when I'd had to temporarily move back after my marriage ended, I'd always had to pay board to my parents. Elle, I was quite sure, had never been asked to pay a cent.

"Besides," Elle continued, "I'm way too busy now. Plus, I'm saving—Marrika and I are moving out together as soon as Mum and Dad are back."

"Cool. Where are you thinking?"

"Pyrmont," she answered instantly.

"You're not tempted to come to the beaches?"

"Nah, too far from the city. We want to do our own *Sex and the City* thing."

I couldn't help laughing. It amazed me just how many generations of women cleaved to *Sex and the City*. I'd devoured all six seasons on DVD when I hit university, and I was pretty sure Elle and Marrika had watched them when they were still in high school.

"Speaking of boys, you got anyone special yet?" I teased her.

"As if! I'm not settling down for a looong time. Not until I'm in my late twenties, at least."

I rolled my eyes, kind of loving that she thought she could control these things. Then again, maybe she could.

"How about you?" Elle asked, suddenly sounding serious. "Are you dating anyone?"

"Nope." Gosh, that came out very abruptly. "I mean, no. Not currently."

"Oh, Laur. You'll meet someone again."

Why did she sound so compassionate and caring?

"I don't—I mean, I'm not looking for anyone at the moment. I'm just like you. Exploring the world and the men in it."

Elle erupted with a roar of laughter. In fact, she laughed for such a long time that I was tempted to hang up.

"Why is that so funny?" I eventually managed to ask.

"I'm sorry," she sniffed, clearly trying—and failing—to get her laughter under control. "I just can't imagine, well, *you* doing anything other than seriously dating."

"Hey! I'll have you know that I've—" *Slept with a Tantric sex instructor. Gah! No, can't tell Elle that.* "—been with a number of men in the past year."

There was silence down the phone.

"You still there?" I asked.

"Yeah. Just … weird visuals."

"Don't visualise things! Why would you visualise that?"

"You're the one that said it!"

"Elle!"

"Okay, fine," she paused. "Well, good for you. I'm very happy that your vagina is happy."

"Argh!" Younger sisters were the *worst*. "I'm going."

"Alright, love you."

"Love you, too. Bye."

I hung up and flopped down on my bed, this time with a smile on my face. Elle might be younger than me, but for the first time in my life, I felt like we finally had a bit more in common.

4

It was the day! My very first day of work as an assistant location manager for the film production of *Trigger*! I was super-excited and nervous and pumped and honestly feeling like I was high on painkillers or something because it was also not even 5 am in the morning and I was driving across the Spit Bridge on my way to Mosman.

And surprisingly, there were quite a few cars on the road already, all beaming headlights around in the dark. Did people seriously get up this early for work every day? I wondered if they all had exciting jobs like I did. I didn't even mind the early start—it wasn't like I'd got any sleep last night, anyway—and I was already feeling so productive! *I should do this every day*, I thought. It was strangely satisfying, knowing that I was already on my way to work and most people were still asleep in bed.

Or in the passenger seat beside me, also asleep.

"Ben!" I half shouted, glancing over at him.

"Hmph," he grumbled in response.

"Aren't you excited?"

He didn't reply, but I caught one eye open a crack and staring at me like I was mental.

"Come on! We're going to work on a *movie*."

He yawned, but at least he sat up a bit. "Yay?" he said weakly, rubbing his eyes and sounding not at all enthused.

"Alright, I get this isn't exciting for you. But *I'm* excited."

And nervous, as my tummy was communicating to me. Oh God, *please* don't let my tummy get upset on my very first day of my new job. I could have some serious nightmares about shared toilets with no ventilation and no air fresheners available.

I remembered this advert I saw once for a product called "V.I.Poo", where you could spray it over the toilet water and it trapped all the smells in there while you did your business. I remembered thinking, who on earth would go out carrying V.I.Poo spray in their handbag?

I kind of wish I had some V.I.Poo on me now.

But it was fine. A few deep breaths had my tummy sorted out in no time.

"It'll be good to meet the rest of the crew," Ben said finally. "The director is a real up-and-comer, according to Celeste."

"You do know more about it!" I slammed on the brakes, having almost rear-ended the car in front of me in my shock. I ignored Ben's wince. "Tell me everything you know. Immediately."

"We'll be there in five minutes," Ben replied, his eyes on the GPS.

"Spill. Now."

He sighed. "Amity. I think that's her name. Young but talented. That's about all I can remember."

"Has she directed anything before?"

"Don't think so. Probably some short films. But not a feature length."

"Amity," I repeated, imagining someone calm, cool and collected. She'd patiently show us all how to create a beautiful, exciting film, and I'd naturally become indispensable to her while I …

While I was …

Hmm. I still wasn't entirely sure what it was I'd be doing. How did one actually manage a location?

"Do you know who the location manager is? Who my boss will be?"

"No idea, sorry. Celeste often works with the same people, though, so it could be Fred. I've worked with him before—he's pretty cool."

"Fred. Excellent." Already, I was feeling doubly optimistic.

The GPS led us to an impressive stone house a few streets back from the Mosman high street, which had a beautifully maintained English-country-style garden at the front. Leafy creeper vines painted themselves up the front of the house, and beneath an enormous oak tree was a rambling rose garden, illuminated by the bright streetlights from the road. Finding a park nearby, I helped Ben get his audio equipment out of the car and together we made our way up to the house.

I could *hear* the mayhem before we even pushed open the door. People were shouting, squealing, laughing and shrieking. I could practically hear the hum of movement from within, as if I was standing beside a beehive.

Ben didn't bother knocking, and as soon as the door swung open, the cacophony escalated.

I stayed behind Ben as we made our way down the hallway, my tummy doing its very unhelpful gurgling thing again. I had no idea who I was looking for, but I felt immensely grateful that I was with Ben. We passed smaller bedrooms and sitting rooms as we made our way further into the house, and glancing inside them I saw a makeup artist working on a girl in one, and another girl steam-ironing a rack of clothes in another. The hallway ended and we stepped into the kitchen, the source of most of the noise.

Six people were gathered, all shrieking and yelling over the top of each other—and over the sound of the kettle, which seemed to be boiling nonstop—and I was relieved to recognise Celeste among them. The producer looked just as fabulous as the first, and only, time I'd met her; dressed in a flowy, animal-print top and white jeans. I was a little stunned that she was also wearing platform sandals, despite the fact that she had to be in her seventies. Her short blonde hair was spiked up on top, and she was wearing her signature red lipstick and tortoiseshell glasses and looking far more put together than anyone should look at 5 am.

Although, basically everyone in the room looked way more alert and with things than I was expecting. The others in the group were a good two, maybe three, generations younger than Celeste; none of them looked much older than me. And they looked *cool.*

One girl had shoulder-length blonde hair that was dyed in a rainbow ombré, fading from pink to red to purple and then blue at the tips. Two guys both looked like they'd stepped out of a *GQ* magazine, albeit one featuring young and trendy bar tenders in the city. One was covered in tattoos and had a perfectly styled beard—I'd bet a hundred bucks he was regularly given beard oil for Christmas—and the other had a preppy-cool thing going on with a neck scarf and a crisp blue shirt with a parrot print on it.

Two more guys stood with the group. One was tall and lanky, and looked like he couldn't possibly be out of high school. The other had rich olive skin and dark hair, was tall and toned and was a likely suspect for a soccer player.

"Hey—where can I set up?" Ben asked the group without preamble.

Immediately, six pairs of eyes were upon us.

"Ben!" said almost everyone at once.

"And Laura," Celeste added, beaming at me.

"We're over here," the lanky guy said to Ben, coming forward and holding out his arms for the stuff I was carrying.

"Er, thanks," I said, handing the equipment over to the guy, who I decided had to be Oliver, Ben's boom operator.

"Laura here is our location manager!" Celeste said excitedly to the rest of the group, moving to my side and putting an arm around my shoulders.

I didn't have time to correct her, because immediately the girl with the rainbow hair was stepping towards me, her arms outstretched.

"Laura! It's so great to meet you." She went in for a hug, and I managed to quickly hide my surprise and return the hug.

"I'm Amity," she said. "And we're *so* excited to have you with us."

She was the director? Wow. She looked the same age as me, but with a *much* stronger sense of her own identity. Aside from the rainbow hair, she resembled someone who had just stepped out of a Japanese anime cartoon; she was wearing low-slung cargo pants and boots, a crop top that highlighted her tiny waist and she had a nose stud.

"This is Will, our production manager." Amity indicated the *GQ* guy wearing the parrot shirt and scarf.

"Rory, our cameraman." The guy who looked like a soccer player nodded, and I was momentarily caught by his alluringly rich chocolate-brown irises. *Ooh, hot guy alert.*

"And this is Troy, our leading man," Amity finished, indicating tattoos-and-beard guy.

"Hi." I managed to nod to each of them.

"So! Laura, we were just discussing what we're doing today, and we've decided to do the beach scene."

"Er ..."

"The weather's gonna be shit for the rest of the week," Will said, peering at his phone. "But today is perfect."

I glanced around, panicking already. Was I supposed to know what they were talking about? Oh God. I was likely going to need the bathroom in a minute. But it would be fine. I just needed to find my boss and they could tell me what was going on.

"Where's the location manager?" I asked. Four faces all stared blankly at me. "Fred?" I added, a bit desperately.

"Ah," Celeste said from behind me, and it was amazing how much meaning came across in that one tiny word.

Actually, was "ah" even a word? Or just a sound?

Anyway, whatever it was, the way Celeste said "ah" was like when you turned up to a party with a 750 ml bottle of Smirnoff and the host said "ah" right before telling you that, actually, everybody was doing Dry July.

Celeste took me gently by the elbow and led me slightly apart from the group. The others watched us for a moment, all looking somewhat confused, but then they quickly resumed their conversation, which Ben and I had interrupted.

"About Fred," Celeste said, turning me around to face her. "He's had to step down—family commitments, I'm afraid. But the good news is, you've been promoted! You are now *Trigger's* location manager."

My stomach made its discomfort *very* known.

"I'm ... what?"

"Yes, I've had to slim down the crew quite a lot, unfortunately. Budget and all that. But don't worry, you'll be an absolute star, I'm sure of it."

"But ..." Oh God, I could feel the panic rising. I dropped my voice before speaking as quickly, and urgently, as I could. "Celeste, I don't know what I'm doing. This is my first job on a film. And I don't know the first thing about the locations, or about the movie, or about anything! You haven't given me any information!"

"Haven't I?" Celeste frowned, but she seemed entirely unconcerned by what I was saying. "I was sure I sent the script out to everyone. Well, not to worry. You'll soon pick things up. Just do everything Amity and Will ask you to do—they're the ones really in charge of all this. Now, I *must* go find Phoebe and clarify some things she wanted in her contract. So, if you'll excuse me."

My mouth hung open as Celeste walked away. Was she serious?

Desperately, I looked around for Ben, but he was busy unpacking all sorts of cables and something that looked like a DJ deck and talking to Oliver. The four others in the kitchen were still speaking, although now I noticed that there was a whole lot of paperwork on the counter top, and Amity and Will were talking excitedly and referring to a few documents.

I was half tempted to just walk out of the house. To just turn around without saying anything to anyone and walk back down the hallway, back across the rose garden, back to my car and then drive myself home and get back into bed.

But I couldn't do that. I hadn't even started, hadn't even *attempted* the job yet. Even though I had no idea what the job was, Celeste seemed totally confident that I could manage it. So I could. I'd just have to bluff my way through things until I worked out what the fuck was going on.

Taking a steadying breath (*Settle, stomach, settle*), I moved back towards Amity and the others.

"Er, hey," I made my presence known to them. "So, what were

you saying about the location today?"

Amity glanced up at me in relief. "Right. The weather. So, today's weather is perfect for the beach scene, which I know wasn't scheduled for today, but we've just made a call that we're going to shoot that this morning."

"Of course." I smiled confidently, as if I knew exactly what she was talking about. "And, er, which scene was the beach scene, exactly?"

"Scene seventeen," Will responded. When he clocked my startled look, he frowned. "Don't tell me you haven't seen the script, either?"

I shook my head. "Sorry. Although I'm relieved I'm not the only one in the dark here?"

"Argh, I knew there was more she'd forgotten!" Amity said, slapping her hand against her forehead.

"I'll send it now." Will had his phone out and within moments I heard my phone buzz with an incoming email. "Check scene seventeen, while we round everyone up. We need to leave for the beach in half an hour to make it while the light is still good."

5

An hour later, I wasn't feeling any more enlightened.

I'd sat on a couch in the lounge room and frantically skimmed over the script on my phone, growing more and more confused about it. As far as I could tell, the film was a bit like *Memento* crossed with *Inception*, with a whole lot of jumping through into different realities. I kind of wanted to ask Will if there was a marketing pack or at least a blurb about the film, because I had no idea what genre we were even working in.

But I filed that dilemma away for later in the day. Because I'd barely got my head around scene seventeen—where the main character, Haven (played by the young actress I saw having her makeup done) was being chased by the main guy (tattoos-and-beard man), although it wasn't really clear why he was chasing her or what he wanted with her. It was set on a beach at sunrise, and so ten minutes ago we'd all jumped into cars and driven down the road to Balmoral Beach, and now we were hovering around in a big flock and I wondered how anyone knew what they were meant to be doing.

"Action!" Amity shouted from the stone ledge above the sand.

Well, perhaps I was the only one who had no idea what I was

supposed to be doing.

I decided to simply freeze and watch as Phoebe Winters, the actress playing Haven, started stumbling along the shoreline, her white cotton dress bunched up in her hands, and looking, in my opinion, like she was drunk. Behind her, tattoos-and-beard man, aka the actor Troy Davidson, was scowling and loping after her, limping heavily and with makeup applied to his face that made him look like he'd just been in a cage fight.

Rory, the hot cameraman—I mean, the cameraman (who was undoubtedly rather hot)—was sitting on the stone ledge, filming them both stumbling past. All the other members of the crew, including me, were just loitering around on the nearby grass, and I wondered if I was the only one who felt rather confused.

"Cut!" Amity called. "Let's go from the front. Rory, Ben, Oli— down here, please!"

I watched as Ben and Oliver sprang into action, swinging down onto the sand. Oliver was carrying a huge boom microphone, and Ben was holding his laptop. They both had headphones on and cables connected to what looked like walkie-talkies on their belts. Rory also swung down off the ledge and moved to the shoreline so he could film the actors from the front. Further down the beach, there was an extremely overweight man waddling down to the shoreline, and I wondered how Rory was going to avoid getting him in the background of the shot. Should someone ask the man to not swim there?

Oh God, was that what *I* was meant to be doing?

I glanced uneasily at the people around me. The remaining crew members—Charlotte, the hair and makeup artist; the girl from wardrobe whose name I couldn't remember; and Will, the hot *GQ* guy/production manager—were standing with me, but they were all preoccupied on their phones. Further afield, other members of the public were gathering to watch us.

Maybe it was my imagination, and let's be honest, I had zero experience to compare this to aside from my own imagination, but it felt like this filming thing was a little … disorganised. I wished Celeste had joined us at the beach so I could ask her what was going on, but she'd stayed behind at the house.

"Okay, guys, let's try up on the grass," Amity called out, and then we were all on the move. The whole group followed Amity as she strode along through the park above the beach. She was looking around as she walked, her head turning every which way and her rainbow ponytail flicking about behind her like some amazing bobbed unicorn tail.

"Will!" she shouted. "What do you think about here?"

Will and Rory moved forward and began pointing and talking quickly, gesturing around at the trees. Amity obviously didn't like what they were saying because she gave a little shake of her head and started striding off again.

I glanced around at the rest of the crew, trying to catch someone's eye, but everyone was just watching Amity intently and moved to follow her as soon as she set off. Even Ben wasn't looking my way, as he was talking to Oliver and tapping his headphones.

What am I doing here?

The thought floated through my mind as we walked. I felt like I'd arrived at some weird early-morning boot-camp session that I had no memory of signing up for. I had no idea what I was meant to be doing and I suspected that if I simply turned around and walked off in the other direction, not a single person would even notice.

We came upon the large white rotunda in the centre of the park, and Amity seemed excited about this. Quickly, she directed Phoebe to go and stand up the top, and she had to have told her to look wistful or something, because then Rory was below her, the camera pointing upwards as Phoebe stared off into the distance.

Will moved up to stand beside me, and after frowning down at his phone for a moment or two longer, he put it away.

"Hey," I said quietly, catching his attention. "Is there anything I'm meant to be doing?"

Will seemed surprised. "No, not currently. We're just trying to get the wide shots in."

"Right." My eyes snagged on a woman chasing her toddler across the grass behind the rotunda, which I was sure would definitely be in any wide shot the camera was currently capturing. "Shouldn't we be filming when there's nobody else here? I mean, couldn't we have got the park closed for an hour or something?"

Will shot me an incredulous look. "No way we could afford that. That would take our entire locations budget in one whack."

"Oh. Er, right."

Will grinned. "Don't worry, we can make it work. I'm doing all the VFX and post. Plus, this is one of the only spots where we have to contend with members of the public."

I was about to ask him for more information regarding our other locations, since he seemed to know more about what we were doing, but Amity suddenly appeared in front of us.

"Will, can you grab camera two? Laura, do you mind giving him a hand?" She smiled at me, and the tiny gem in her nose stud glinted in the morning sunlight.

"Sure. Let's go." Will nodded to me and then, to my shock, he started *running* back across the park to where we'd left all the cars.

Blimey. I was wearing comfy flat sandals, which I'd thought would be ideal footwear for today, but I hadn't realised running would be on the cards. Plus, even if I had been wearing gym gear, running was *not* my forte.

I made it to Will's car a good minute behind him, clutching my side and breathing as hard as if I'd just attempted the Balmoral Burn.

"You right?" Will asked me, as he unzipped a large carrier case in his car boot.

"Oh, fine," I gasped, waving my hand, dismissively. "Just warming up."

"There you are!" came a shout from nearby, and I spun around to see Celeste power-walking towards us on her platform sandals, her silky top billowing out behind her like a fabulous cape. "How is it going?"

I let Will answer that question, since I wasn't sure I was capable of doing so.

"Good so far," he replied, emerging from the boot with another large camera. He handed me a bag that was heavier than it looked, and peering inside I saw a mess of battery packs and cables.

"Excellent." Celeste rubbed her hands together in delight. "Lead on, then! I've come to watch the action."

We walked (thank God) back to the rotunda, where Rory was now filming Phoebe walking slowly down the stairs. Troy, the other actor, was having his makeup touched up by Charlotte, and Ben and Ollie were standing off to one side, looking at things on their phones.

"Amity dear, how is it going?" Celeste called, wasting no time as she strode in amongst the group.

"Hey, Nan. It's going great." Amity beamed back at Celeste.

Hang on a second.

Nan?

Oh my God. It suddenly made sense. The lack of organisation. The sense that nobody quite knew what they were doing. Was this just some hobby project that Celeste was funding for her granddaughter? Was this even a real bloody movie we were making?

I suddenly felt ill, as actual panic began welling up inside me. The only thing preventing me from having a full-blown meltdown right then was how unconcerned every other member of the crew seemed.

Was I seriously staking my career on a low-budget, family-hobby film?

Blinking rapidly, I realised Amity was still speaking.

"—the wide shot of Haven. And then we'll get both cams going when he chases her through the meadow."

"Fabulous, darling!" Celeste said, beaming around at everyone. "You're all doing a fabulous job."

I felt slightly numb as the group set off again, moving further down the park to find another spot to film. I was trailing at the back, my shoulders hunched over, wondering what I was doing there. This was nothing like I'd imagined the job to be.

Job—ha! Could I even call it that? Aside from now carrying a bag of camera batteries around, I didn't even have a job to do.

The idea that this could turn into a career seemed suddenly laughable. Amity, Will, Rory—they were little more than film-school graduates. I'd been imagining working somewhere like Universal Studios, with security guards and trailers, and well, *professionals*. Not tramping around a park with a bunch of amateur film buffs.

Oh God, was I being too harsh? Had I really thought that a big, professional film production would hire someone completely inexperienced like me?

I felt like crying.

"Excuse me?" came a deep male voice from behind me.

The group had stopped up ahead, and Amity was directing

Rory and Will on where to position the cameras. I spun around and came face to face with a man wearing dark sunglasses and a khaki uniform with *Ranger: Mosman Council* emblazoned on the badge on his chest.

"What's going on here, then?" he asked me.

My immediate, visceral reaction was dread, and I wondered what lie I should come up with about what we were doing. But then I realised that, actually, as the location manager this was my first real responsibility. I could answer him.

"We're shooting scenes for a new feature film," I told him, giving my most confident smile.

"Is that right?" He frowned. "Have you got a permit to film here?"

My smile froze in place. "Of course we do! Let me just go and find out where it is."

Shit. This was exactly the sort of thing that I should be across, but I wasn't across any bloody thing. But someone here would know where the permit was. Will or Celeste knew what was going on, they just hadn't shared any of the details with me.

I hoped the ranger would hang back and wait for me to go find out about the permit, but he stuck to my side like a bad smell as I walked towards Celeste.

"Action!" Amity shouted up ahead of us, and then Phoebe and Troy were running across the grass, Rory and Will following after them with the cameras.

"Celeste, hi!" I said in a low voice, coming up beside her. "The council ranger here wants to see our filming permit?" My eyes slid uneasily to the ranger as I spoke, who looked like he hadn't cracked a smile since sliced cheese was invented.

"Does he, then?" Celeste said, her own smile dropping as she eyed the man. "Just one moment, please."

She moved towards Amity and spoke quietly to her, and a moment later Amity was waving Will over. Ranger man stayed beside me, like he'd realised that I was meant to be the responsible one here.

It would be fine, I told myself, wondering why the sight of Celeste, Amity and Will all huddled together and speaking urgently was making me feel uneasy. I glanced at the ranger again.

"Lovely morning here, isn't it?" I said inanely with a smile.

Behind his sunglasses, which had transparent lenses, his eyes narrowed at me. And then, just when I thought that surely my bad vibes about this job and this whole morning had to be overrated, there was a loud and simultaneous shout from both Amity and Celeste of: "RUN!"

My heart literally stopped.

In horror, I watched as every member of the crew suddenly picked up and bolted across the grass, heading away from the ranger and also me, who was still standing beside him in shock.

My eyes met his. The tiniest thinning of his lips was the only warning I got.

FUCK!

I sprang backwards as he tried to grab my arm, and then I too was running across the park, my sandals slap-slapping uncomfortably as I tried to run while cradling a heavy-as-fuck bag of pointy camera batteries to my chest. Ahead of me, the crew was darting up towards the footpath, and ridiculously all I could think was, *Where the fuck are we running to?* The cars were in the other direction.

I was too terrified to look behind me to see if the ranger had given chase. All I could think was: *Run like the wind, Laura! RUN LIKE THE WIND!*

Oh God. Why wasn't I a faster runner? Everyone else was so far ahead of me, and if anyone was going to get caught by the ranger, I just knew it would be me. Up ahead I spotted Celeste, running like a cheetah in her platform sandals with her silk top streaming out behind her, and I thought I might cry-laugh at the sight of a woman in her seventies running faster than me. Christ, I hoped she wasn't going to have a heart attack.

Actually, I hoped *I* wasn't going to have a heart attack.

I could hear footsteps thudding behind me, and with a half-sob I launched myself across the road, forcing an oncoming car to slam to a stop in a loud squeal of brakes.

Fuck!

I saw Celeste disappearing up a side street in a whorl of animal-print silk and I ran after her, no idea what would happen if the ranger followed. Was I about to be arrested? Was I about to get Celeste arrested? Shit, should we have all split up and run in different directions?

My heart hammered in my chest as I ran up the street, my feet thumping painfully on the pavement in my ridiculous sandals that had absolutely no arch support. I had no idea if the ranger was behind me or not, but either way I knew I had to stop running in a minute. My lungs were on fire and I could taste bile in my throat.

"Here!" A hand with red fingernails reached out from behind a van parked on the side of the road, and then Celeste was pulling me off the footpath and behind the vehicle.

I slumped over, dumping the bag of batteries not quite gently on the ground between my feet, and grasped my knees with my trembling hands.

Celeste patted me on the back as I stood there wheezing, like I'd just had nothing more than a coughing fit.

"There now!" she said brightly after a moment. "Nothing like a bit of excitement on a Monday morning!"

I stood up slowly, knowing my mouth was hanging open as I gaped at her.

Celeste was peering around the side of the van, not a single hair of hers out of place. Then she turned to look at me with the most radiant smile, absolutely full of exhilaration, her eyes shining with glee. And she clapped her hands together and started *laughing*.

6

I was furious and upset and ashamed. This job that I'd pinned all my future hopes and dreams on, this job that I'd been looking forward to for the past three months, this job that I'd thought was going to kick-start an amazing career for me, was an absolute joke. Even the pay, which would only just barely cover my rent, made so much more sense now. I'd justified it to myself that it would be like doing an apprenticeship—the low pay would be offset by the fact that I'd be learning so much and getting started in a new industry. Now I just wanted to laugh at how deluded I'd been. I'd make the same amount of money working at Maccas.

I could feel tears burning in my eyes, but I couldn't decide if they were angry tears or tears of despair. Trying to keep them at bay, I clenched my hands around the steering wheel until my knuckles turned white.

"Well, that was an interesting first day," Ben said from the passenger seat.

My lips thinned until they were nearly nonexistent. Somehow, miraculously, I'd made it through the rest of the day. After we'd regrouped far away from the beach and the ranger, we'd then all driven to a secluded public garden area nearby and repeated the morning's process, though thankfully without any more rangers. I didn't bother asking if we had a permit to film at the garden. I'd just kept my mouth closed, followed the group around and quietly contemplated the resignation letter I was going to write to Celeste.

This was *not* what I'd signed up for. Granted, I wasn't really sure what it was I'd signed up for, but I could not imagine spending the next six weeks having daily repeats of today's incident. What the hell was I even learning? How to run in sandals and avoid doing things legally?

Now that I was alone with Ben again and we were driving back home towards Manly, I suddenly realised that I was furious with *him*.

"You could have warned me," I snapped, punching the air-conditioning settings down to try to cool the heat from my face.

"About what?" Ben asked, sounding baffled.

"*Seriously?* You didn't think today was an absolute joke? Or is running away from park rangers your usual thing?"

"That wasn't normal, sure, but it wasn't a big deal."

"Not a big deal? Not a BIG DEAL?" Dear God, I was sounding hysterical. "I had no fucking idea what was going on all day! I thought I was going to be an assistant on a huge movie production, not told on day one that, guess what, you're now the location manager, and by the way, nobody is going to bother telling you what that even means. What the hell am I doing here? They have no use for me. I honestly can't see any reason to go back tomorrow and have that enormous farce repeated all over again."

Ben was silent, and when I cast a look over at him, I found him staring at me in complete shock with his mouth open.

Shit. Maybe I'd overdone it.

"Look, I'm sorry," I said, trying to sound calmer. "I know you got me the job. But I ... I really don't think they need me at all."

"Why would you think that? Laura, it was just day one, and it was all done on the fly because of the weather forecast for the rest of the week."

I scoffed. "Amity is Celeste's granddaughter. Did you know that?"

"So what?" A hard edge entered Ben's voice. "She's lucky that as a filmmaker she has a grandmother who happens to be a producer. That might give her an advantage over other directors trying to get started, but it doesn't mean she doesn't know what she's doing. Celeste wouldn't green-light something that wasn't worthwhile. Trust me, I know her."

I bit my tongue, feeling the tears threatening again. Great, now not only was I upset, I was acting like a total jerk, too. Of course Amity was probably talented. What did I know about directing films, anyway? It was totally unfair of me to be unkind towards her simply because she was lucky enough to have some stellar family connections.

"I just think ..." I could feel my throat tightening, but I forced out the rest of the words. "It's not what I thought it was going to be."

Ben sighed. "Yeah, that happens sometimes. A lot of the time, actually. I've learned never to have any expectations about an upcoming job until I get there. So long as the pay's right, then that's all that matters. I just turn up, do what they tell me to do and go home."

I choked out a laugh. "Your lack of excitement makes so much more sense now."

I could feel Ben looking at me again, but I kept my eyes firmly fixed on the road, willing the tears to disappear rather than spill down my cheeks.

"Is it really not what you were expecting?" Ben asked me.

I made a sound that was a bit like a hiccough. "Honestly? I don't know what I was expecting. I guess it just wasn't that."

"Why don't you give it a chance? Tomorrow we're back at the house, doing the scenes that were originally planned for today. Things will be a lot calmer and easier. No park rangers allowed."

I snorted a laugh, and appreciated Ben's attempt at a joke.

"I really don't think they need me," I said again, but it felt flat even to my own ears.

"They do. Trust me. These guys, they're all trying their hardest to create something meaningful. Something that people will connect with. I've worked with most of them before, and it's a big deal for Amity and Will especially, being in charge of their own film. Plus, Celeste wouldn't have hired you if she didn't think they'd need you."

I raised an eyebrow and shot him a sideways glance. "When did you get all wise and knowledgeable?"

He laughed. "I've just spent too much time working with creative types like them."

When we arrived home there was no sign of Kalina, and I assumed she was out for dinner with Owen. Ben had a quick shower then headed out to meet up with his mates, so I soon found myself standing alone in the silent apartment.

Or rather lying flat on my bed, staring up at the ceiling and wondering if I could be bothered making myself some instant pasta for dinner. It wasn't like I could afford anything better.

Sighing, I sat up and pulled my laptop towards me again. It was still open on the same jobs advertisement site that I'd pulled up twenty minutes ago. The homepage, though, because I hadn't got any further.

I looked at it again, at that search bar inviting me to enter a keyword and begin my job search. Slowly, I typed in "marketing", but couldn't bring myself to hit "enter".

Because I knew what results I'd get. Coordinator-type jobs for financial institutions. Social media work for industrial companies. Obscure-sounding positions that seemed vaguely interesting on screen but would in reality just be a whole lot of data wrangling.

I deleted "marketing" from the search field and stared at the empty box again.

What the fuck did I actually want to do with my life?

Slamming my laptop shut, I wrenched my hands into my hair and let out a small scream.

What was I *doing*? Was I seriously back to square one, having a career crisis all over again? I *had* a job. A badly paid, short-term job, sure, but a job nonetheless. Was I really going to be one of those people who bailed on their commitments? Was I really going to call Celeste to tell her that, actually, I wouldn't be back?

I felt sick all over again. If it wasn't for Ben, I probably would bail. But Ben was going to go back tomorrow, and I wasn't sure I could bring myself to hang him out to dry by not showing up. He'd vouched for me to Celeste, convinced her to give a totally inexperienced newbie a start in the film business. It would reflect terribly on him if I quit after my first day.

I decided I needed the pasta.

Dithering about in the kitchen, I dumped the packet of dried pasta and powdered flavouring into a bowl, then added milk, butter and water. I'd just put it in the microwave when my phone began ringing with Michael Bublé's "Come Dance With Me", heralding my mother calling.

"Mum, hi!" I said, trying to inject as much cheerfulness into my tone as possible while I stared at the microwave bowl slowly rotating.

"Laura, darling, hi! How was your first day?"

Argh. Sometimes I wished my mother had a worse memory than she did. But of course she remembered that I was starting my new job today. It was all she'd been asking me about ever since I left Tiger Finance three months ago. In fact, it was slightly irritating just how many times she'd said the words, "So, *when* is your new job starting?" like she thought I'd been making the whole thing up. I knew she was just worried about me and worried that I'd thrown away a perfectly good career. And knowing what her thoughts were made tears spring to my eyes.

I couldn't tell her it had been a disaster, more likely to stump my career and hurl it backwards by a few years. I didn't want her to know that I'd been wrong and that once again I had no idea what I was doing with my life.

"It was great!" I managed to sound surprisingly positive as I dashed the tears away from my face. "Really fun. I had such a good day."

"Oh, I'm *so* glad. And you're learning a lot, then?"

I learned that you needed an expensive permit to film at Balmoral Beach.

"*So* much. I'm learning, just, everything. The people are really nice and everyone is so professional. It's a really great opportunity for me. It's going to open so many doors."

Dear God, what was I saying? Sugar-coating it much?

"Oh, Laura, I'm so relieved! You know, your father and I were worried about you for a while there. We were sure you were making a terrible mistake leaving your old job. But if you've found something you love, then all the better! You can do anything you set your mind to, I know you can."

I felt my face crumpling. "Thanks, Mum."

Luckily, Mum didn't seem to hear the despair in my voice.

"And you know Ellie's really found her feet with work, as well!" she went on excitedly. "I'm not sure *exactly* what she's doing, but the company she's working for in the city sounds wonderful. They have a full cafeteria with free food every day and doughnuts on Fridays! I gather she's making inroads, and has already been promoted up from a junior!"

"I got promoted too," I heard myself saying petulantly. "I'm not just an assistant location manager. I'm *the* location manager."

"Really? How wonderful! You'll be all set for a career in Hollywood next."

I stifled my urge to scoff. Swallowing, I decided it was best to change the topic. "How's the trip going, then? Where are you at the moment?"

"We're at South West Rocks, and it's fabulous here! Your father's bought himself a stand-up paddleboard to match Trish's one and he and Trish have been out on the river almost every day. Phil offered to take me out in the kayak, but between you and me, he's not very stable in it. I saw him capsize yesterday, so I think I'm much safer on the shoreline."

I tried to picture my father on a stand-up paddleboard, racing his friends along a river, but wasn't sure I could adequately do the image justice.

"You'll have to send me some photos," I said instead.

"Oh, they're all on Facebook! Haven't you been following us? I put some selfies up yesterday of me with a koala."

"Er, right. I'll have to check it out."

To be honest, I hadn't been on Facebook in a while. My feed there was full of old high school and uni friends posting photos of their children, or distant relatives reposting depressing news articles with long-winded paragraphs about their religion and how they were "praying" for the victims.

I spoke to Mum for a while longer about her trip, but rang off once my pasta was ready. And then I sat at the kitchen bench, finding with every mouthful that a plan was starting to form in my mind.

Maybe I *could* still make this job work for me. Success, after all, was in the eye of the beholder. And as a former marketing and PR professional, I was a pro at smoke-and-mirror tactics to make something seem more exciting and impressive than it really was.

If I went back tomorrow, then maybe I could shape the job into what I wanted it to be. If nobody could tell me what my job was all about, then I could create something for myself. And like Ben said, I could be part of creating something meaningful.

And if all else failed, I'd at least be able to put some vague bullshit on my résumé about working on a film for a few months.

Facebook Alert
Cath Baker added 58 photos to the album "Port Macquarie"
Trish Stephens Commented:
Tally-ho! Onward, my friends!
Elle Baker Commented:
Dear God. What is Dad wearing?!

Tinder Alert
Laura, your matches are waiting ♡
>>App "Tinder" successfully uninstalled

New Email
Subject: Call times for tomorrow
Trigger filming day 2 (Tuesday)
Location: Mosman house (see address below)
Call times for all crew and actors as per below:
  Locations: 4.45 am
  Hair and makeup: 4.45 am
  Wardrobe: 5.15 am
[message clipped]

Amazon Shopping
Are you still interested in *Career Checklist: How to Find a Job You Love*?

7

The next morning, I returned to the Mosman house.

I'd spent a good few hours last night watching everything I could find online about being a location manager, which I knew I probably should have done before actually starting the job, but I'd honestly thought I was going to have some on-the-job training and a boss who could tell me what to do. Although reports of the job varied from travelling the world in search of the perfect spot for a shoot, to doing low-level grunt work (apparently, some location assistants nicknamed their job "traffic, trash and toilets"), I'd decided my role had to fit somewhere in the middle. So, rocking up for my second day of work, I was feeling marginally more prepared.

And luckily, it seemed I wasn't the only one who thought yesterday had been a bit of a shambles.

Will came over to me as soon as I walked into the kitchen. He looked like another iteration of a *GQ* model, wearing skinny jeans, combat boots and a cool retro-tweed blazer over a dark, low-vee t-shirt. In fact, a quick glance around the room at the other crew members present and I realised they *all* looked like they'd stepped off the pages of some cool fashion shoot for an artsy magazine like

Frankie. I could just imagine them all living in trendy, inner-west suburban Sydney suburbs like Balmain or Newtown.

I was really letting the team down in my basic jeans, Converse and a t-shirt I was pretty sure I bought at Big W. To be fair, it was a cute t-shirt.

"Laura, hey," he said. "Look, sorry about yesterday."

I was so stunned that I wondered if Ben had said something to him.

"I know this is your first job," he went on quickly. "And we're basically throwing you in the deep end. So, I just wanted to have a chat with you about what we need you to be doing."

"Great!" I said, the relief practically falling out of my mouth. "Because I was really feeling left in the dark about, well, everything. I had a read of the script last night," (at least, I'd attempted to read it but ended up thoroughly confused), "but I have no information about the locations."

"Ah, so you haven't been sent a login for StudioBinder yet?"

"Er, no. I don't know what that is."

"Okay, come with me."

I followed Will into the adjoining dining room, where laptops and paperwork created a sea of mess across the eight-seater dining table. He sat in one of the chairs and opened a laptop, and I took the seat next to him so I could watch on.

"Whose house is this, by the way?" I asked, while he logged in.

"It's one of Celeste's," he said, not looking up from his computer. "We're using this as our main base for the whole production, and shooting as many scenes as we can here."

"Oh, right. So are there many other locations?"

He glanced at me in surprise. "We've really told you nothing about this job at all?"

"Nope." I smiled grimly.

"Damn. Sorry about that. Yes, there're a few other locations, and you'll find all the info for them in here. Do you know what your main duties are each day?"

"Er … is it traffic, trash and toilets?"

Oh God, please let me be wrong.

Will laughed. "I like that. But seriously … well, yes. But a lot more than that, too."

"Great," I repeated, not feeling as enthused. I was kind of hoping the trash and toilets part was a joke. But then, I supposed, someone had to do it and who else besides the locations manager?

"We also need you to look after catering on some days. And I'm about to show you where all the locations info is saved, so we'll get you to take over managing that as well. It's all pre-organised, all the locations we're using, so you basically just need to reconfirm details with each place before we shoot there and then be the point of contact on the day."

"Sure," I replied, feeling positive again. *This* was much more like what I'd been expecting.

"But," Will added, "as it's a small crew, there will be other things that come up, and everyone is expected to pitch in and help out when required."

"No worries. What sort of things might come up?"

"Oh, anything really. Last film I worked on, I ended up being an extra in multiple scenes."

I blinked twice. He'd ended up *in* the movie? How cool was that! I hadn't even thought of that as a possibility, but I'd definitely be down for a cameo. Maybe even a speaking role.

I could just see it now, there'd be this crucial scene where the actor didn't turn up, and Amity and Will would look at me and say,

"Yes, Laura would be perfect!" and they'd quickly put me through hair and makeup and I'd step in front of the camera and it would turn out that I was a total natural at acting and everyone would be so impressed and then I'd get Nicole Kidman phoning me up and asking me to be in her next movie and—

Oh shit, Will was still speaking.

"—lighting to camera work. Just whatever's needed really."

Did he just say I might do camera work? How cool was—

"Well, I'm your girl," I said, before my imagination could run off with me again. "Whatever needs doing, I am happy to help. Just call me Girl Friday."

Will stopped typing and looked quizzically at me. He was pretty cute, I decided. Not in a drool-worthy hot kind of way, but in a slightly nerdy, smart kind of way. The type of guy you wouldn't realise you were attracted to until you were twenty minutes into an absorbing discussion about how chocolate was made or where the comedic line was. "Do you *want* to be called Girl Friday?" he asked with a small tilt of his head.

"No! Not actually. It was just, you know, an expression."

"Right." He looked off into space for a moment before shaking his head. "It's a funny one, though, isn't it? Makes you realise how culturally inappropriate it is nowadays."

"Eh?" Oh God, what had I said that was culturally inappropriate? Were we not referring to Fridays anymore?

"Girl Friday. Like, reminds you that women used to just be these minions that ran around the office doing everything and anything their boss—usually their *male* boss—asked of them. It's very *Mad Men.*"

"Oh! Yes, good point. It should be more of a ... *They* Friday now?"

Hmm. That didn't sound right.

Will raised an eyebrow. "Is that your pronoun?"

"Er, no. I don't think so."

"You don't *think* so?"

"I haven't thought about it." I held up my hands. "I mean, I'm just the normal—wait, not *normal*—er, regular—no, no, *not* regular—um, *old-fashioned* kind of girl. Like a girl-girl. A she! That's it. A she/her."

That took me way too long to remember the pronoun thing. Suddenly, I had a vision of Will scowling at me, standing up from the desk and flinging his arm out to point at the door, demanding I leave immediately with my backwards, intolerant ways.

I wasn't intolerant. At least, I didn't think I was.

Oh God, was I? Did referencing Girl Friday make me some sort of cultural monster?

My panic spiral dissipated when I saw Will laughing softly.

"Hey, chill," he said, giving me a reassuring smile. "You don't need to define yourself at all. We're just—" he spread his hands out wide "—ourselves. And if you hadn't guessed from reading the script, that's what this film is all about."

Was it? I wasn't sure I got that from the weird chasing scenes and the obscure conversations I'd read.

"About the script," I said. "I have some questions."

Will's smile grew. "Fire away."

"So... can you explain what the movie's actually about?"

He laughed again, and I decided that I quite liked Will. And his laugh. Plus, he had nice hair. It was light brown and thick on top but shaved down the sides, like how all the hot guys wore their hair in *Peaky Blinders*.

"It's about the questioning of one's identity," he said. "See, Haven keeps getting pulled into different timelines where she is a different expression of herself. And Troy's character reflects what she's experiencing—sometimes he is her enemy, other times her lover. Other times he's *her*."

"I think that's where I got lost. That scene where he's suddenly wearing her clothes."

Will nodded. "It's hard just reading the script without any context, or without being able to *see* what's happening. But by the end of the film, Haven realises she has to channel all of her personas into one life in order to break the triggering cycle."

"And the actual *triggering* part of it? What's that about?"

"It's like when you have this really vivid dream that you forget about the next day. You wake up with no memory of it, but then you'll be doing something really ordinary, like peeling a banana, and *wham*! This sense of deja vu hits you and your mind is suddenly thrown into that dream and you can remember it exactly. That's what happens each time Haven is triggered, only it's not a memory that hits her, she's literally transported into the dream world, or rather into the alternate reality."

I wanted to ask more questions, but Amity shouted from the next room that they were ready for a take and Will stood up.

"Stay in here for a while if you want to read over stuff," he said to me as I also made to get up. "But if you can get lunch organised in a few hours that would be great. The food's already pre-bought and in the fridge—I can show you a bit later if you like."

"Thanks, that would be great."

The StudioBinder platform turned out to be a goldmine. Within the *Trigger* project, the script was overlaid with every single piece of information to do with each scene, from the locations information and mood boards, to the actors and crew required, call times, costumes and any other notes that were needed. There was so much information to wade through that I was slightly overwhelmed. I'd have to tackle it in chunks, I decided, and knew that I needed to be across absolutely everything by the end of this week.

When I ventured out to get a coffee around eleven, I did a quick clean-up of the kitchen as well—because, you know, location manager—and then I found myself heading outside to where the crew was filming in the back yard. Clouds were threatening overhead, but so far it hadn't rained, and apparently being overcast was actually perfect for outdoor filming.

For a property in Mosman, this place had an enormous garden. And it was spectacularly overgrown yet surprisingly tame, like some real *Secret Garden* shit. At first glance it looked like a wilderness, but when you looked for long enough you saw form and design going on.

I headed up the back as silently as I could, since I couldn't tell if they were mid-take. The crew members all had their backs to me, but as I approached I could see the scene they were shooting, and I knew it was going to look beautiful on film.

Phoebe was sitting on a garden swing that hung from the branch of a grand old tree. She wore a floaty pastel dress and had flowers in her cascading curls, her feet bare. Behind her stood Troy, looking like he'd just stepped off the set of *Bridgerton* in a Georgian-era waistcoat and pantaloons. Behind them, a leafy hedge made the perfect background. Except that ...

Hmm.

I blinked a few times, squinting at the hedge. It wasn't as thick as it initially looked, and through the branches I could see the house next door. In fact, I could see right into its open-plan living room, which currently had two people in it. Two people who were *engaged in oral sex on the couch.*

I glanced around in alarm at the crew members beside me. They were so focused on our actors that I wasn't sure anyone else had clocked the neighbours. But based on where Rory was standing with the camera, and what direction the camera was pointed …

Gingerly, I edged around the group until I was standing in the same line of sight as Rory, albeit far behind him. How could he not have noticed? How could nobody have noticed? Right there, not fifty metres away, was a naked man sitting in a power pose, with a girl kneeling between his legs, her head bobbing up and down.

The second Amity called "Cut!" I edged forwards and cleared my throat.

"Er, hey."

Rory looked up in surprise.

And *damn* if he wasn't a hottie. He had a Mediterranean vibe going on, like the kind of hot local you'd see striding out of a seaside villa in Santorini. And those eyes, those dark chocolaty eyes beneath dark brows, just had that kind of *zing* to them that made my lungs temporarily forget how to work. Instantly, I wanted to be lying by a pool somewhere tropical with him, snuggled together on the one sun lounger with me able to run my hands over what would be (as far as I could tell) some very toned, muscular abs.

But anyway. This wasn't the time or place for such thoughts. Even if what I was about to point out to him was in a similar realm. "I just wanted to check if you were catching the performance in the background over there?"

"The what?" Rory looked to where I was indicating, and I waited one, *two* ...

"Well, shit," he said.

"Yep." I laughed awkwardly. "Those two are certainly having a good morning."

Rory shot me a look, like he wasn't sure if I was joking or not, before a conspiratorial grin crept over his lips, and, dear God, those shiny teeth and the cheeky sparkle in his eyes did flippy things to my insides.

Rory checked the sight in his camera, and when he muttered a curse I knew that he'd discovered he was recording the sex show in the background.

"Bugger," he muttered. "I wonder how long they've been there?"

For a moment we just stood there, watching them. The girl was apparently done with the blow job, because she crawled up onto the couch, presented the guy with her butt, and then he was kneeling behind her, hands on her hips. They were turned so we had a full view of them now doing it doggy-style on the couch.

"And to think we were worried about dogs barking," Rory said, and I burst out laughing.

"Let's go again," Amity called out, but Rory waved her over.

"Slight problem," he said, pointing towards the house. "We've got background extras."

Amity looked as well, and I saw her do a double-take when she clocked the two naked interlopers. She seemed alarmed at first, but then she started laughing.

"Seriously?" she said. "At eleven am on a Tuesday? I feel kind of jealous."

I wasn't sure I'd heard her correctly.

"Should we switch positions?" Rory asked, and I wasn't sure I'd heard *him* correctly until I realised he was referring to the camera.

Amity scrunched up her nose, looking around at the garden with a critical eye. Then she shook her head. "I liked the house just visible in the background. The empty house."

There was a pause, and then I found both Amity and Rory looking at me. A hopeful smile was pinned to Amity's face.

"Er, yes?" I asked, not sure I was liking the gleam in her eyes.

"Laura, do you think you could go over there and ask them to stop?"

I couldn't have heard her correctly.

But shit. This was exactly the sort of thing a location manager was meant to deal with, wasn't it?

"Okay." I nodded confidently. "I—sure. I can do that."

Rory nodded encouragingly at me, which I wasn't sure helped or not. By this point, the rest of the crew as well as the actors had cottoned on to what was happening in the house next door, and they were all standing around giggling and watching like it was some free sex show.

"You've got this, babe. You can do it," Amity said to me.

My eyes moved back to the house, where the girl was now lying spread-eagled on her back, the guy above her thrusting as enthusiastically as a piston.

"Should I wait until they're done, at least?" I asked. "Before knocking on the door?"

"I mean, they don't need to *stop*," Amity said. "But it would be nice if they'd move to another room so they're not in our shot. Unless they want to be in the movie, which I don't really mind, to be honest. We'd just have to get them to sign a waiver."

I had no idea if Amity was joking or not, but I was seriously doubting my ability to get this couple to stop doing anything.

Interrupting them mid-sex seemed like a terrible idea, and I had a sudden image of everyone standing here in the garden, watching as I chased two naked people around the lounge room with a broomstick, the *Benny Hill* theme song playing in the background.

"You'd be happy having them in the film?" I asked hopefully, playing for time and willing the dude to just hurry up and finish. I mean, really, how long could this go on for, anyway?

"Oh yeah," Amity said, sounding delighted.

"It's nothing compared to what we're shooting next week," Rory added.

That had my attention tearing away from the couple. I stared at Amity. "Are we filming a sex scene?"

"You didn't know?" Amity frowned, looking mildly concerned. "God, Celeste *told* me everyone was on board."

Oh wow. We *were* filming a sex scene.

"Oh, it's fine," I quickly said. "I mean, it's not a problem. I was just surprised."

Amity's gaze turned serious. "You sure that's not a problem? I don't want anyone feeling uncomfortable on set. And some people, I know, are a little ... prudish with that stuff."

A weird laugh came out of me, like a hyena having a coughing fit.

"Well, not me." I gave her my most confident smile. "In fact, I'll be so comfortable with it that I might as well be in the scene. Although, er, not actually *in* the scene. I just meant that as an expression."

Amity clapped her hands together. "I knew I liked you!" And then she was giving me a surprise hug. A surprise hug that was really quite tight, and I felt like her boobs were pressing into my boobs way too much. "Now, back to *this* sex scene," she went on. "Do you think you can deal with it?"

I tried swallowing, my throat suddenly dry. "Of-of course," I managed to stutter out. "Absolutely. No problem at all. I'll go talk to them now."

8

"Okay, everyone, let's take five!" Amity shouted at the crew and started clapping her hands together. "Come on, let's move away from the hedge now, we don't all need to spy on the neighbours."

There was some general grumbling from the crew, as it seemed most people were well on board with staying to see the end of the show. And of course that was my cue to get moving and go deal with this problem, as per my job responsibilities.

It would be fine, I told myself. *Absolutely. I can do this.*

I left the house and immediately took out my phone to check where, exactly, I was currently and therefore what street the house over the back fence was located on. Google Maps told me it was a three-minute walk to get there, since I had to circle around the block, so I quickly set off at a jog. Honestly, who knew this job was going to involve so much running?

My phone guided me in the right direction, but I slowed down, a stitch in my side, as I neared the sex house. At least, I hoped it was the right house. Imagine if I knocked on the door and an old man answered and I told him to stop having visible sex and he dropped dead from shock at such an allegation? Or maybe a woman would answer in a bathrobe and I'd think it was the woman I'd seen, but it would turn out to be a young mother who'd now think that her husband was cheating on her or something like that.

As it happened, when I knocked on the door that I *thought* was the right house, nobody answered. I waited about ten seconds, then knocked again. Waited twenty more seconds, then knocked a third time.

Still nothing.

I called Ben.

"Laura, what's happening?" he asked immediately.

"I'm at the house. At least I think it's the right house, but nobody is answering."

"Try knocking again?"

I did as Ben asked and waited.

"Ah," Ben said. "Yeah, I think they heard it because they paused. But then they just kept going."

"Damn it. They're just ignoring me?"

"I think so."

"Well, what am I supposed to do? I can't do anything else, right?"

Frustrated, I banged on the door again, much harder now.

"Did you just knock again?" Ben asked.

"Yeah. Why?"

"The dude's coming, I think."

"As in … he's doing his sex-finishing move?"

"No. As in, he's coming to the door."

My eyes widened, just as I saw a shadow looming on the other side of the decorative stained-glass door panel. I quickly hung up on Ben and shoved my phone into my back pocket just as the front door was flung open.

"WHAT?" shouted a very enraged and very naked man.

I mean, a stranger might have assumed that he was wearing underwear behind the pillow he was holding in front of his crotch, but I knew better.

"Er, hi!" I squeaked, taking a quick step backwards. And also taking in the view of the man, who, if he was not quite so terrifying right now, I would be very much appreciating his toned body. Like, *damn.*

"So sorry to bother you," I quickly said, trying to ignore the sound of "Living on a Prayer" blasting from a stereo within his house. "But the thing is, we're filming a movie next door, and er, the hedge is a bit on the thin side."

"Eh?" He looked at me like I was insane.

I kind of felt like I was. I cleared my throat and tried again.

"We're filming up against the back hedge, which is very thin, which means we can see you having sex inside your house. And, like, it's getting filmed. Accidentally. Totally accidentally."

I watched as his face morphed from confusion, to incredulity, to something I couldn't quite identify, but it was definitely hostile.

"You're fucking filming me?"

"No! I mean, not on purpose. As I said, we're shooting a movie, but we just realised that you and your, er, wife, were in the background. Accidentally. And so we just wanted to ask you to stop so you're not in the footage. I mean, you don't need to stop! God, I'd never try to tell you to do that. But if you could maybe just move to a different room?"

He stared at me for a beat, and I honestly thought he was finally understanding what I was asking. And really, it wasn't such a bad request, was it? It was for his own good. And the woman he was with, whom I was about ninety percent certain was *not* his wife. Now that I'd highlighted the situation to him, he could calmly and reasonably put on some clothes and perhaps take his girlfriend off to a different room.

But apparently, he didn't agree.

"GET THE FUCK OFF MY PROPERTY!"

Argh!

I practically jumped away from him and that scream might not have been entirely in my head. For a second, I just froze and stood staring at him, aghast. He was flexing his arm muscles and I realised that if he wasn't currently holding a pillow against his naked crotch it might be entirely likely that he'd chase me down the street. As it was, I decided to simply turn tail and run away, as if I was, in fact, being chased by a naked, scary but objectively rather attractive man.

In the two and a half minutes it took me to run back to the Mosman house, I'd half convinced myself that it wasn't so bad. I mean, sure, that guy looked like he wanted to throttle me. But in reality, surely now that he was aware of the situation, he and his girlfriend (?) would move away from the camera's direct line of sight. I mean, nobody *wanted* to make a surprise sex cameo in a movie, did they?

I arrived back to our own back garden, panting, hoping to see that filming had casually resumed. But much to my alarm, everyone was still staring at the hedge like there were possums doing some interpretive dancing in the branches.

Joining the crew, I felt my heart sinking. The dude was having sex again. But now, he'd actually thrown open the big glass doors of his living room, so that we all had a completely uninterrupted view of them. Plus, he'd also turned the music right up, and now Journey's "Don't Stop Believin'" was blasting across his garden and right through the hedge. It added a definite performative aspect to the whole thing, and I wondered if he was expecting us all to pull up deck chairs and start cheering him on.

Rory spotted me. "I'd ask how it went, but, well ..."

I grimaced, moving to stand beside him. "He ... did not take my suggestion so well."

Amity joined us. "Okay," she said. "In hindsight, we probably should have just let them finish. What happened?"

I gave them a brief rundown of my encounter with Shouty Sex Man.

"So, shall we just wait it out now?" I asked.

Rory shook his head. "Even once they finish, this dude will make a point of pissing us off for the rest of the day. Maybe even all week."

My stomach dropped. Oh God, I'd made it worse, hadn't I? My first real job as a location manager and I'd stuffed it.

Noticing the anguish on my face, Rory said, "Hey, don't worry, I have an idea. Let's go see him again."

"You want to go *back* there?"

"Yeah." He grinned. "Come on. Can't hurt to try, right?"

I was pretty sure the look I gave him implied otherwise, but regardless, I soon found myself jogging along next to Rory as we headed *back* to the sex house.

"I didn't know this job was going to be so active!" I panted as I struggled to keep up. Rory was clearly a lot fitter than I was, if his lack of heavy breathing was anything to go by.

"We need to get the scene finished before the light changes too badly! Otherwise, we'll have to shoot it all again."

"Oh shit! I'm so sorry."

Rory slowed to a walk then, looking at me in confusion. "You don't need to be sorry. This isn't your fault."

I laughed at that, a laugh that came out like a hacking cough because I was struggling to breathe. "Isn't it? You've probably realised that I'm not really a location manager by now."

He just shrugged. "This is your first job on a film, isn't it? You'll get there. It's only day two, after all."

"Thanks. I hope so."

"Any help you need, just ask me or any of the crew. We're all happy to help."

"Oh—thank you. That's really nice."

We arrived back at the sex house and both stopped on the footpath, staring at it like it was some alien spaceship. "This is it," I said unnecessarily.

Rory chuckled. "No wonder that guy's such a douche."

He nodded to the car parked in the carport, which I hadn't really noticed before. I mean, cars were great and all, but as far as I was concerned, they were just a means of transport. But some people, guys especially, could be *really* into cars. Like, abnormally obsessed with washing and polishing and primping the thing, like it was somehow a reflection of their penis size.

Shouty Sex Man was definitely one of those guys, if the vintage yellow Mustang was anything to go by. It had a black racing stripe painted across its bonnet and the whole thing shined to within an inch of its life.

And considering he had a house in Mosman and didn't look a day older than thirty, I surmised that Shouty Sex Man was either one of those sadistic financial guys or a deadbeat living on his parents' dime. Possibly the latter, given he was having a marathon sex session mid-morning on a Tuesday.

"So, what's your plan?" I asked Rory.

"Bribery," he answered instantly, and shot me a grin. "Bribery is always a good option."

I followed him up to the front door and stood slightly behind him while he knocked. We could hear the music blasting from this side of the house, and I wondered if Shouty Sex Man would even hear it this time.

I decided to phone in backup.

"Ben? What's going on in there now?"

"Er … we're all just wondering that, as well."

"What do you mean? Can they hear us knocking?"

"I don't know if they can hear you, but … I'm not sure if we need to call an ambulance."

My eyes met Rory's and I knew he'd heard the word "ambulance" coming from the phone. I pulled it away from my ear and hit the "speaker" button.

"What's happening?"

"Well, I think they were trying to show off and be a bit acrobatic on the bar table. But, like, the girl fell off."

"Shit. Is she okay?"

"I don't know. They've disappeared behind the counter and we can't see anything. And the music is still going, so we can't hear anything, either."

There was a rustly crunching sound from the phone and then it was Will's voice coming down the line.

"Guys? I don't know what the hell's going on next door, but if you're there then I think you should go down the back and see if they need help. The girl might be seriously hurt."

I knew my eyes were as wide as saucers as I stared at Rory, my phone held up between us like an offering. Oh God, had Shouty Sex Man accidentally killed her? This was like the plotline of some domestic thriller. Except instead of being *The Girl on the Train*, I was going to be *The Girl from across the Hedge*.

"We'll check it out," Rory said.

He tried the door handle, but unsurprisingly, it was locked.

"Round the back," I suggested, heading for the side of the house that wasn't blocked by the carport. There was a tall wooden fence there, but in the middle was an arch-shaped gate. Finding the small hand opening, I reached through to try the latch. But all I felt was a padlock.

"Gate's locked," I said, to both Will on the phone and Rory, who had followed me.

"I've got a bad feeling about this, guys," Will said. "There's still no sign of them since they disappeared behind the bench. I'd try to get through from here, but the hedge is too old and solid."

"Should we just call an ambulance?" I asked, looking up at Rory to see what he was thinking. He was staring at the fence, considering it. Then he turned to me.

"We'll climb over."

"*What?*"

"It'll be easy. I'll go first."

I watched, slightly horrified but also rather impressed, as Rory used the hand opening in the gate as a foothold, placing his right foot in it, then jumping so he could grab the top of the fence with his hands. As if it was the easiest thing in the world, he hoisted himself over the fence and disappeared on the other side.

"Your turn," he called. I could see him just slightly between the wooden fencing, an unmistakable grin on his face.

"Right. Sure. Easy." I dubiously eyed the fence.

"Don't hurt yourself, Laura!" Will half shouted down the phone. "We don't have—"

I ended the call and stuffed my phone into my back pocket. I knew I could do this. I mean, if Rory had made it look so easy, then how hard could it be?

After some awkward scrambling and an inelegant side roll over the fence, I landed (rather surprisingly) on my feet on the other side, and Rory was there immediately steadying me with his hands on my back.

"You good?" he asked me, his hands lingering around my ribcage, deliciously firm.

"Yes," I replied rather breathily.

He dropped his hands, and as I turned to look up at him, I found we were standing extremely close together. Like, kissing kind of close.

"You good?" I managed.

For a second he stared down at me, and from the look in his eyes I found myself wondering if he also had the sudden, inexplicable desire to kiss me. I stopped breathing, waiting, and kind of hoping that he would.

But then he shook himself, like he was realising where we were and what we were doing, and with a grin he stepped away. "Yep. Let's go."

Despite the fact that the music was still blaring, now with a cover rendition of Michael Jackson's "Smooth Criminal", which seemed ironic, we were unmistakably *creeping* down the garden path. I wasn't sure if that was because the pathway was totally overgrown and it was definitely spider town, or because we were quite seriously trespassing on someone's property right now.

And Shouty Sex Man seemed, from my brief encounter earlier, the kind of guy who'd take a very personal approach to dealing with trespassers. I just had to hope Rory was as strong as he looked and could take him on. And possibly that the hedge was not as thick and gnarly as Will had implied it to be, because I was not above doing a dive through there if the need arose—especially since I was pretty sure that Shouty Sex Man would *not* follow me through in the nude.

Remembering the hedge, I was suddenly extremely aware of the audience on the other side. As we crept our way to the back of the house, passing by a tiny shed thing that housed the garbage bins, I realised it was almost impossible to see the film crew from here. Which might explain why Shouty Sex Man hadn't taken my request seriously.

We were nearing the corner of the house, still creeping along like we were in a bad spy movie, when the music suddenly stopped.

Rory and I both froze. He glanced back at me, and I shrugged. Then I felt a buzz in my pocket signalling an incoming message.

Quickly pulling out my phone, I read the text that had just arrived from Ben.

Abort! Girl fine. GET OUT!

Alarmed, I grabbed Rory's arm and showed him the text. "We should—"

Two things happened then before I was able to complete my whispered suggestion.

The first was that Shouty Sex Man suddenly stepped out onto the grass, not ten metres away from us, and still extremely naked. He was facing the hedge, which saved us from being immediately spotted, and also gave me a prime view of the *Where's Wally* tattoo on his butt cheek.

The second thing was a loud and highly unconvincing bird call that came from the direction of the hedge, which sounded less like a real-life cockatoo and a lot more like a human shouting, "CA-CAW!"

"What the fuck was that?" came a woman's voice, and a second later the girl, who had draped a bathrobe around herself, stepped out onto the grass next to Shouty Sex Man. I wasn't sure if I was relieved that she was safe and well or terrified that in about two seconds they would both turn around and discover Rory and me standing here staring at them, on the very trespassy side of the locked garden fence.

"CA-CAW! CA-CAW!" came again, and luckily Rory seemed a bit more in tune with his counterparts over the hedge, because he used the distraction to grab me and drag us both the few steps back and behind the small bin shed.

There we crouched, and I felt like all my senses were heightened. Which wasn't so great smell-wise, considering we were squatting right next to the bins.

"What the fuck's that?" the woman asked again, sounding less curious and more angry now.

"Fucking neighbours. Hey you!" Shouty Sex Man yelled. "Yeah, I can fucking see you through there!"

For a moment I thought he was talking to Rory and me, but considering he hadn't charged down the garden path and punched me yet, I guessed he was referring to the crowd on the other side of the hedge.

Rory and I were squished together, the skin of our arms and shoulders touching, and I turned my head and met his eyes. Despite the dire and definitely criminal situation we were currently in, Rory's lips twitched, and I found I had the almost irrepressible urge to laugh. Panicking, I pressed my left hand firmly over my mouth and used my right hand to fire a message back to Ben.

Help! Need distraction!

A second later, we heard Will shouting through the fence, "Hi there! Sorry to disturb you guys!"

"What the fuck do you want now?"

"No biggie, we just had something really, ah, important to share with you both."

I peeked out from behind the bin shed until I could see the

back of Shouty Sex Man, standing legs akimbo and hands on hips confronting the hedge like it was a wall he was about to knock down. I couldn't see the girl anymore, but I decided it was time we took our chances and ran.

Grabbing Rory's arm, I pulled him as silently as possible back out to the pathway and we half ran, as cat-like as we could, back to the fence.

"I think you'll find that my colleague has been trying to get your attention at your FRONT DOOR," Will was saying, loud enough that Rory and I could still hear.

We looked at each other in alarm.

"Here," Rory said, knotting his fingers together and holding his hands out for me to use as a foothold.

Without arguing, I let him boost me back over the fence, where I landed a lot less gracefully and much more painfully on my butt.

"If that bitch has come back again—" I heard from Shouty Sex Man, and if I wasn't feeling quite so panicked I might have been rather indignant and offended by that. I was *perfectly* polite considering he'd been the one dressed in just a pillow.

But a second later Rory dropped to the grass beside me, and after I'd let him hoist me to my feet, I pushed him not so gently towards the front door.

"Quick! You do the talking!" And then I dived behind a bush.

I probably didn't need to move quite so fast, because there was a good half-minute there where I was trapped amongst the brambles and Rory was staring at me from the front doorstep and laughing. But then the front door opened and he instantly switched to cool, calm buddy mode.

"Hey, sorry to bother you, mate," Rory said, and from my hiding place I couldn't see if Shouty Sex Man was still naked or not. "But we're trying to do some filming next door and we were hoping you could turn your music down? I'll buy you a case of beer for your trouble."

I held my breath, waiting for the moment when Shouty Sex Man told Rory to fuck off. But he didn't.

"How long?" Shouty Sex Man asked, in a very calm and reasonable-sounding voice.

"Just a few hours. Nothing major."

"Yeah, alright. A case of beer, was it? It better be good stuff."

"Yeah, of course. We really appreciate it. And if you could stay away from the back garden for a bit, just while we're filming outside, that would be really helpful."

Silence for a beat. Then, "Throw in a bottle of whisky, too, and you've got a deal."

I felt outrage then, absolute outrage, and if I wasn't currently hiding behind a bush and at very real risk of stabbing myself on some sharp branches, I'd have jumped up and told this arsehole where to go shove his whisky bottle.

But all Rory said was, "Sure, mate. If you help us out, I'll get you something nice."

There was a grunt, I thought, from Shouty Sex Man, which I supposed was an agreement. Then I heard the door shut and Rory was standing beside my bush.

"See? Easy."

I took his outstretched hand and let him hoist me to my feet once more. For a moment we stood close together, grinning stupidly at each other, and I could feel my heart still racing with adrenaline. My hand remained in his, but neither one of us made to let go.

He was breathing as heavily as I was, which I thought odd considering how cool and collected he'd just sounded speaking to

Shouty Sex Man. His eyes were locked on mine, and a smile danced across his lips.

I realised it wasn't the adrenaline making my heart beat fast. And I had the sudden and very real urge to just grab Rory and kiss him like our lives depended on it. But sanity prevailed.

"We should get back," I said, then tipped my head towards the house. "Before he sees me."

Rory kept staring at me, a hungry expression in his eyes like he also wanted to pull me close and devour my mouth with his. His hand briefly tightened around mine, but then he let it go. "Yeah. We've got a movie to shoot, after all."

We jogged back to the house together. Maybe it was the thrill of what had just happened, or the fact that I was jogging beside Rory and finding it hard to think of anything other than *him*, but I barely even struggled. In fact, I felt energised and exhilarated and like I should most definitely enrol myself in a half-marathon.

And then we were back at the house, then in the garden, and a huge cheer went up from the crew members as we rejoined them.

"Jesus Christ!" Ben said, clapping me on the back. "That was terrifying!" But he had a huge grin on his face.

I laughed, and found myself catching Rory's eye again. Something passed between us, and I knew that for our short adventure together we'd become slightly more than just colleagues.

9

"What do you think of this one?" came Kalina's voice, followed by the sound of a curtain being drawn back. "I don't know if it's retro-chic, or just a bit *Sound of Music.*"

I quickly pulled the grungy Led Zeppelin t-shirt over my head and assessed my own reflection in my fitting-room mirror. Should it be tucked *into* the biker pants?

Deciding on a front tuck, I pushed back my own curtain and stepped out to see Kalina in the hallway of the H&M fitting rooms. We looked at each other silently and then both burst out laughing.

"I'm sorry!" I told her. "But you look like Dorothy from *The Wizard of Oz*!"

"*You* look like you're off to play fan-girl at a Metallica concert!" She cackled.

Oh, I didn't mind that description, actually. But no, I was too old for that stuff. Definitely.

"God, these are *so* not us." Kalina had turned to eye herself in one of the mirrors again. "But why is it so hard to find nice work clothes? It's all either corporate suits or see-through tops that are way inappropriate for the workplace."

"Well, I have no idea how to look cooler. All the crew members have this effortless style going on, and I've been wearing the same jeans all week."

It was Saturday and my first day off since filming began. I'd made it through an entire week of filming at the Mosman house, and could now say with about ninety-percent confidence that I knew what I was doing. I'd worked my way through all the available information in the StudioBinder project; had nailed how to do the catering; and had even found myself starting to not only enjoy, but actually look forward to work each day.

There was just one tiny issue I'd found in the locations information, namely that there didn't seem to be a location for some of the crucial scenes near the end of the film. But it was probably just that someone hadn't correctly uploaded the documentation, and as soon as I remembered to ask someone about it, I was sure it would all be sorted out.

Meanwhile, Kalina also had started her new job this week. I was trying not to let it bother me that Holly had kept her promise and had put in a good word for Kalina at Follow the Rainbow, the youth charity company she worked for in Manly. I mean, it was lovely for Holly to do that, absolutely stellar to help Kalina get a job there. But now it meant that Kalina and Holly got to work together every day, and that made me feel … a little bit weird.

But I was being silly. There was absolutely no reason for me to have an issue with Holly. She was lovely, apparently, a really nice person. Why shouldn't she and Kalina be friends? I should be friends with Holly, as well. We should all be friends.

All big … happy … friends.

"You ready for a coffee yet?" Kalina called from back within her dressing room.

"Yes," I mumbled, the t-shirt coming off with a sizzle of polyester static through my hair. Argh! When had clothes shopping become so difficult?

We left H&M soon after, both of us with carrier bags of clothes (I mean, who could go past those low prices, right?) and headed to our favourite coffee shop in Warringah Mall. After ordering at the counter, we flumped into chairs outside in the mall, acting like we'd been shopping for hours rather than the forty minutes it had actually been.

"So, you've barely told me anything about your job," I said to Kalina, watching her clean the smears off her sunglasses lenses with her t-shirt.

"What do you want to know?"

"Everything. Spill. I want all the goss."

Kalina shrugged. "Well, it seems great so far. I've been put in this team that's organising an LGBTQ-plus ball in a couple of months' time."

"A ball? Really?"

"Yeah. It's one of the community outreach programs to encourage inclusivity in the area. I haven't met any of the youth involved yet, but I think that's happening on Monday."

"Right. And the actual workplace. What's that like?"

"It's great! The office is really modern, and it's so close to all the shops and the beach."

"And, er, how about the people? What are they like?"

Oh God, to my own ears it sounded really obvious that I was fishing for intel on Holly. But I wasn't sure whether Kalina noticed.

Or maybe she did, but she was withholding so I'd have to ask directly about Holly.

Twisted woman.

"Really nice. The whole team pops down to the pub around four on Fridays, so it's all very social."

Our coffees arrived then, and there was a pause in our conversation while the waiter placed them down in front of us. I took a nice long sip of frothy cappuccino and sighed with satisfaction.

"It's so funny that we both ended up starting new jobs in exactly the same week, isn't it?" Kalina said, stirring sugar into her coffee. "What are the odds?"

"I know, right?" Oh dear, I could feel it coming. Unable to abort the situation, I added, "And you're now working with Holly! How weird is that?"

"Yeah." Kalina's eyes were suddenly pinned to my face. "Are you okay with that?"

"Me? Of course! Why wouldn't I be! I mean, she got you the job, didn't she?"

"Yeah, but well, it's not like I really work *with* her. I mean, we're on totally different projects."

"Of course. You're right. It's not weird at all."

We fell into an awkward silence, and I suddenly found the plants growing along the pillars *very* fascinating.

"So, what's she like? At work?" I finally asked.

Kalina sighed. "She's quite nice, really." When she clocked my crestfallen face, like a true friend she added, "But she has this one pair of heels that she leaves under her desk and they smell kind of manky."

It shouldn't have made me feel better, but oh! How it did.

"What's *Ben* like at work?" Kalina asked, looking at me quite intensely now. "Does he seem, you know, okay?"

I pulled my thoughts away from imagining Holly's stinky feet. "He does seem okay. At least, he acts very professionally. He's pretty quiet at work, but then that might just be because there are so many loud personalities on set. Are you still worried about him after what happened with Amy?"

"I *wasn't* worried," Kalina said, "because I honestly think that working and not thinking about girls is probably good for him right now. But Lucas called me yesterday to talk about Ben."

"He did?" I tried to ignore the fact that my voice had just risen by an octave. There was also an unpleasant sloshing feeling passing through my stomach, which might have been due to Lucas choosing to call Kalina instead of me to talk about Ben. I mean, he knew that I was the one working with Ben on *Trigger*. So if he wanted to ask about his brother, surely I would have been the better choice?

But, whatever. His decision.

"Yeah. He reckons Ben's avoiding him and not returning his calls. Do you think something's happened between them?"

"I can't imagine what. I mean, aside from Ben basically ditching his job in Lucas's bar and running off to Byron Bay, but if anything it should be Lucas pissed at Ben over that."

"That's what I thought. But who knows—guys are weird. Maybe Lucas is just imagining it."

"Well, the *Trigger* job is pretty demanding. We've been doing ten-hour days all week, and apparently, that's what I'm meant to expect for the whole production. Maybe Ben's not avoiding Lucas, he just doesn't have time to call him."

"Hmm." Kalina frowned at her coffee, sounding very unconvinced.

To be honest, I wasn't very convinced, either.

"How about we both try to talk to Ben next time we see him," I said. "See if we can work out what's going on."

"I haven't seen him in days, so it might be *you* talking to him next time you're at work."

"Okay. I will." But the thought of that discussion made me feel a bit weird inside.

"He asked about you, too, you know," Kalina said, eyeing me over the rim of her coffee cup.

"Who did? Lucas?" It felt like Pegasus was lifting off through my ribcage.

"Yes, Lucas."

"Oh." I casually picked up my own coffee cup, trying to look like this information didn't affect me at all. "What did he say?"

"He just wanted to know how you were." Kalina was still staring at me.

I went for a sip of coffee and managed to spill it down my chin and onto my jeans.

"And what did you say?" I asked, frantically patting the wet spot with a serviette.

"I said you were up to your eyeballs in film-crew dick and having a wild fling with an actor."

"Kal!" My hand slipped mid-wipe and I ended up punching my thigh much harder than one might expect for such an innocuous action.

"Kidding! I told him he should ask *you* how you were doing."

"Oh. Well ... that's better."

But as much as I loved Kalina for prodding Lucas in my direction, I knew it was hopeless. He had Holly now, and though he may have asked about me to be polite I was pretty sure he wouldn't be wasting his time wondering about me.

10

The second week of filming included the highly anticipated sex-scene shoot, and despite it being a "closed set", there were a hell of a lot of people at the Mosman house that day. Aside from the four extras, who were completely comfortable wandering around the house in their underwear, there were additional crew members for lighting and cameras. Even Celeste, who'd been scant on the ground all last week, arrived at the house before shooting began, an enormous flask of coffee in hand and an eager smile on her face.

Not that I was entirely sure the "closed set" label was really needed, since this particular sex scene was really pushing the limits of what a sex scene was. I mean, if Troy's character was dressed up like a wolf and Haven was made up like a dominatrix, I wasn't sure how R-rated this could possibly get.

"So, let's run through this again," Amity said, moving in between Phoebe and Troy. "Only *after* she runs the cat-o'-nine-tails across your pelt, do you submit and stop pawing at her."

The set was at the back of the house, in the large glass-walled conservatory. From what I understood of this scene, Haven had trigger-jumped into a reality where her sexuality was so pervasive and domineering that it was what kept her in control of the situation.

I just wasn't entirely sure about the relevance of the wolf man. Or the four sexy extras, languishing on various pieces of furniture in the background.

"And when I straddle him, is it my bum towards the camera?" Phoebe asked, demonstrating how that might look. I was impressed by how confident the actress was, but I supposed the tiny black lace G-string she was wearing wasn't so terribly different to the Brazilian bikinis popular on Manly Beach nowadays.

Popular with teenagers, at least. I did not even want to contemplate the level of hair removal and fake-tan requirements to pull off one of those myself.

"We'll do a take like that, but then shift the camera around for a frontal take, as well," Amity said. "Rory, how's that looking?"

"Good from here," Rory answered, sounding completely unaffected by the fact that he was shooting a half-naked actress pretending to have sex with a guy dressed like a wolf. For a moment I let my eyes linger on him, appreciating the pull of his t-shirt across his back muscles as he stooped to peer through the camera lens. I remembered how strong he'd felt when he'd hoisted me off the ground last week, and that look in his eyes when we'd stared at each other for a little too long.

Funny, I thought, that there were two almost-naked and definitely attractive male extras not ten metres away from me, yet my eyes didn't want to stray from the fully clothed cameraman.

"Okay, guys, can we clear the room of non-essentials, please?" Amity called out. "We're going for a take."

Feeling disappointed that I had no good reason to stay, I shuffled out of the room along with the hair and makeup artist and the girl from wardrobe. Ben got to stay, naturally, since he was in charge of the sound recording. Walking out, I remembered that I'd promised

Kalina I'd try to talk to him about his brother this week—something easier said than done. We had different start and finish times most days (because I was the location manager, I had to arrive first and leave last), so we weren't ride-sharing to work anymore. Plus, break times were so busy and everyone hung out together, so there wasn't a good opportunity for me to bring up personal stuff with my flatmate. I was sure I *could* find an opening during the day, but there was always so much going on with the film production that I honestly kept forgetting.

I made my way back to the kitchen, which was far enough from the conservatory that we were allowed to speak quietly in there without disturbing the filming. Celeste was just finishing up a phone call when I entered, and she smiled at me and patted the bench beside her, indicating I should sit on the vacant bar stool.

"How are things, Laura? *Loving* the boots, by the way."

I beamed as I sat down, my eyes dropping to my new combat boots with the aqua laces, one of the cool accessories I'd bought while shopping on the weekend. I wasn't *quite* rocking the same urban style that the crew members were pulling off daily, but I was starting to come close.

"Everything has been going really well," I told her. "We've got our first on-location day next week and I've been putting together the travel and parking guides for the crew. Although—while I remember—I haven't been able to find the location information for scenes thirty-five to forty. Do you know where we're meant to be filming those?"

Celeste scrunched up her face in thought. "I remember Fred mentioning something about that, about trying to get approval at a farm. I thought it was all sorted, but now that I think about it … hmm. Leave it with me, Laura. I'll make some calls."

"Okay, thanks. It's still a few weeks away, but I want to make sure we have something booked in."

Celeste patted my hand where it rested on the bench. "You're doing a wonderful job so far. I knew you'd be a great hire."

"Oh, thanks!" I said, unable to hide my surprise. To be honest, I was pretty much just winging it most days and relying heavily on Will to tell me what to do.

"I mean it, Laura," Celeste continued. "I know this is a strange project to work on. Quite different, really."

I nodded slowly. "It certainly has an … interesting script."

Celeste threw her head back and burst out laughing. "Oh my, yes, that's one way of putting it. Although, I do *love* the bestiality involved."

I felt my mouth drop open and I couldn't quite hide my shock. Celeste was old enough to be my grandmother, and as far as I was aware, everyone of that generation—everyone of my parents' generation, even—would rather die than talk about anything to do with sex. Let alone sex with a wolf man.

"Of course it's not actual bestiality," Celeste went on. "But how freeing the world is these days! My friends and I were real trailblazers back in our time, but there's so much more acceptance now."

I was fascinated by this discussion. Totally and utterly fascinated.

"What sort of trailblazing did you do?" I asked, leaning forward with interest.

"Oh, everything. Sex, drugs, you name it. We were having orgies before anyone even knew what the word meant."

My mouth was on the floor. Literally.

Okay, not *literally*. But it might as well have been.

Celeste sighed happily, as if lost in her own glowing memories of group sex. "Well, now," she turned back to me. "You're single, aren't you, Laura? How's your love-life going?"

"Er, yes. And it's going … slowly."

If by *slowly* I meant it had stopped at a station and wasn't showing any signs of moving again, then sure. But God, talking to Celeste was making me feel strangely guilty. Like, why wasn't I out there having group sex? I was single. I was in the prime of my life (even if I'd found a scarily white hair on my head the other day). Why wasn't I taking advantage of this and dressing up like a dominatrix to whip a beast man?

I mean, a man. Just a normal, liked-to-be-dominated man.

As if reading my thoughts, Celeste patted me on the hand again. "If you want my advice, then *live* while you're young, darling. You've got no commitments and the world is at your feet. Oh, how I miss making love to everyone I could. I still do sometimes, mind," she added with a wink. "My good friend Glenys is sometimes a bit more than a friend."

I was out. On the floor and tapping out.

Celeste sighed reminiscently again and got to her feet. "Well, I'd better be off. Lots to do today. Let Amity know I've left, would you, love?"

She leaned in and kissed me on the cheek, and I clocked a definite scent of whisky in the air. Eyeing the enormous coffee flask Celeste collected to take with her, I realised her coffee was of the definite Irish kind.

"Thanks, Celeste," I said, then quickly added, "and if you could check about those scenes for me?"

"Sure, sure. Bye now." Celeste threw me a wave over her shoulder as she left the kitchen, and I hoped she'd at least remember that part of our conversation.

I was tempted to try to sneak back down to the conservatory

to see if I could watch some of the filming, but decided I should probably get morning tea sorted in case they decided to break soon. There wasn't usually an official break until lunchtime, but if the actors had to do a costume change or Amity wanted the camera style altered, then there'd often be crew members sneaking away to grab a coffee or a snack in the lull.

I was boiling the kettle for about the sixth time to fill up the enormous coffee urn when two of the extras came wandering into the kitchen.

"Food!" The girl's eyes lit up at the spread of muesli bars, fun-sized chocolates and mini-muffins on the kitchen bench. "Is it free? Can we have some?"

"Of course." I tried to hide my surprise at her question.

"This is great," the guy said, seeming way too enthused by the urn of coffee as he poured himself a cup. They both had bronzed, almost totally bare skin, and I had to work really hard to pretend that they weren't prancing around in G-strings. I hoped neither of them was going to burn themselves on the coffee.

"Is filming still going?" I asked, wondering why they weren't on set.

"Yeah, but we're not needed for now," the girl said, sliding onto a bar stool and biting into a muffin. "Oh my God this is *good!*"

"Last job I did the food was terrible." The guy helped himself to three muesli bars, and I wondered what he was planning to do with them all. "What's for lunch here?"

"Today we're getting sandwiches and salads from a local deli," I replied, watching as he attempted to put a muesli bar down the side of his underwear.

"You know where the food is really good?" the girl said with her mouth full of muffin. "On set of *The Unhinged*. The caterers there are amazing."

"I'm there on Thursday and Friday this week," the guy said.

"Me too! And I'm on hold for next week, as well."

"Do you guys do this kind of work often?" I asked them.

"Yeah," the girl said. "I only do extras work."

"I've had some speaking roles," the guy offered. "And I was the body double for Astor North on the last *Reaper* film he did. We're the same height and body shape, you know. I had eight weeks of solid work on that film, and I got to hang out with Astor, as well."

"Oh wow, look at the garden here!" The girl was suddenly up and peering out the window. "This place is enormous! I'm going to take a look."

Without waiting for permission, she strode out of the room, heading for the back garden, and the guy followed her. Unsure if the half-naked extras were supposed to be roaming around the house by themselves, I decided it would be best to follow them.

The air was crisp and fresh, though the sun cut through most of the chill. The extras didn't seem to notice the cold, nor did they seem to care particularly about their lack of clothing outside as they strolled around together in the garden like Adam and Eve.

I was debating whether I should try to wrangle them back inside when there was a sudden loud blast of sound that reverberated through what had to be a kilometre-wide radius, like when you turned on your car and the music was left set to deafening.

The noise—it was definitely radiating from a TV—blasted across us, then diminished quickly, before being turned right up again.

And I knew exactly where the sound was coming from.

With a feeling of dread, I ran over to the back hedge and peered through. Sure enough, there was Shouty Sex Man, only half-clothed in trackpants, lounging on his couch with the glass doors thrown wide open and what sounded like *Top Gun* playing full blast on the TV.

"Is that going to be a problem?"

I startled, having not noticed the two extras now flanking me and peering through the hedge, as well.

"Definitely." I felt the dread lurch through me. Was I seriously going to have to try to deal with this guy again? Didn't he have a bloody job to go to?

"I can shout at him," the girl said. "HEY!"

"No!" I quickly silenced her. "No, trust me, we can't piss this guy off. He'll just turn up the volume louder. You guys should go inside, and I'll deal with it."

I herded them into the house, and quickly raided Celeste's drinks cabinet. No way was I going back over to that house empty-handed.

I still had my head buried in the cabinet when I heard Katie, the production assistant, asking the extras to return to set.

"And, Laura?" She was suddenly right behind me. "Can you find out where that noise—"

"I'm on it!" I gasped, emerging with a bottle of Johnnie Walker Black Label. I didn't *think* it was particularly expensive, and hoped Celeste wouldn't mind where it was going.

"Thanks," she said, eyeing me sceptically.

I drove myself around the block to Shouty Sex Man's house—much faster than running—and was feeling cool, calm and collected when he finally answered my knuckle-breaking knocks on his front door.

"What do you want?" he snarled at me. He hadn't bothered to put on a shirt to answer the door, and there was a sly grin on his face as he eyed me, which changed to what I was sure was a look of triumph as his gaze dropped to the bottle of whisky in my hand.

The little shit knew exactly what he was doing, I realised. My hand closed tighter around the bottle, suddenly reluctant to give it to him and wanting to hit him with it, instead. But I made myself stay calm and plastered the friendliest smile possible onto my face. I was a professional, capable location manager, after all.

"Hello. So sorry to bother you again." I tried not to choke on the words. "But we're filming a movie next door and—"

"And you want me to turn the sound down?" He crossed his arms over his chest, that sly smile growing ever wider.

Oh, I *really* wanted to punch him.

"Exactly!" I kept the sunny smile fixed to my face. "Even if you could close your back doors and turn the sound down, that would be so helpful. And here." I held the bottle out to him. "As a thankyou."

He snatched the bottle and appraised it, looking almost disdainfully at it. "I suppose I can do that. It's very inconvenient for me, though. But since I'm feeling nice today ..." He shrugged.

Keep smiling. Just keep smiling.

"Thank you," I forced myself to say. "It's hugely appreciated."

Without waiting for him to say anything else, and not trusting myself to say anything else, I quickly turned and left.

Back at the house, I was relieved to find that he had shut his back doors, and the sound from his TV was now imperceptible. When I passed the conservatory, Katie smiled at me and gave me the thumbs up, which I took to mean a job well done.

And I did feel like patting myself on the back. Because I'd just successfully taken care of a location-based problem all on my own.

Maybe I could become a successful location manager yet.

11

When Friday rolled around, I was almost surprised to realise that I'd been working on the film production for two whole weeks. I was impressed by my own ability to have picked up the job—even if I did feel mostly like a grunt-work-level assistant. And I was growing quite fond of the crew. As soon as filming began, every single person became committed and professional, and I was even starting to grow fond of the weird and definitely eccentric film we were making. But during breaks and once filming wrapped up, people relaxed into jokey banter with each other, and I realised I was beginning to feel like I was friends with a lot of them.

To celebrate the end of our second successful week, Amity had suggested we all pop down to The Buena, an iconic old pub in Mosman. Most of the crew had stayed for just one drink before heading off for Friday-night dinner plans, including Ben, who had taken the car home. But I'd stayed out, keen for some more drinks and some more friends, and so it was that I found myself three drinks in and sitting at a bar table with Amity, Will and Rory.

It hadn't taken me long to work out that the three of them all went way back. They'd worked together on film projects before, and seemed to be genuinely friends outside of work. They'd been talking about making their own film since they'd been at film school, and this was their first opportunity to make it happen.

"So, who chose the script?" I asked, glancing between Amity and Will, who were sitting side by side with their shoulders touching. "And where did you find it?"

"Celeste found it, actually," Amity replied, pulling out her ponytail elastic and fluffing up her rainbow hair. "She'd already agreed to produce a film for me to direct and so she handed me a stack of about fifty scripts and told me to choose one. She said she liked the sound of all of them."

"Wow. And were they all ... similar to this?"

Will snorted. "Nowhere near. I went through them, too. I think we were always looking for something a bit ... different." He met Amity's gaze and something passed between them, a kind of secret smile. Then he turned back to me. "There were some real standard ones. Action, drama, romance. But Am wanted something meatier."

"Something more on-trend and open-minded. We were originally looking for something LGBTQ-plus, but then we found this."

"Huh." I surreptitiously assessed them all, including Rory, who was sitting beside me, and I was *very* aware of our proximity. Not that we were sitting as close as Amity and Will were, but when he got up to get the last round of drinks ten minutes ago and his leg brushed against mine, I literally became short of breath.

"So, are you ...?" I trailed off, wondering if *gay* was still the word du jour. I didn't really think Amity was—I mean, the way she was leaning up against Will made me wonder if they were a couple.

Amity smiled at me, as if understanding my unasked question. "I'm pansexual."

I nodded and made a kind of affirmative sound in my throat,

like I totally understood. But really, I was racking my brain, trying to remember what *pansexual* meant. Unhelpfully, all I could imagine was the Greek god Pan, chasing after nymphs on his little goat legs while playing the pan flute.

"And that's the one ..." I trailed off.

"It means you're attracted to the person, regardless of what their gender or sexuality is," Rory was the one who answered, giving me an easy smile. "So whether they're a guy, girl or a non-binary person, it doesn't matter. You're attracted to their personality rather than anything else."

"Right." My head was nodding up and down and I wasn't sure I knew how to stop it. Turning back to Amity, I asked, "Does that mean you've dated a whole range of people?"

She shrugged and spread her hands out wide in a kind of what-are-you-gonna-do gesture. "Dated, slept with, had a fling with. Sure. I like experimenting."

Will snorted. "If they've got two legs and two arms, Amity's probably into them."

"Hey, don't be discriminatory against the disabled. Legs and arms are not a prerequisite."

I laughed, not quite believing we were really having this conversation.

"Who's the strangest person you've ever been attracted to?" I couldn't resist asking.

Amity looked thoughtful for a moment, then leaning in, she said, "I did have a thing for a fluffer once."

"A what?" I glanced at Rory and Will, but saw they were both already snorting with laughter, as if they'd heard this story before and loved it. "What's a fluffer?"

"I met her on the set of an adult film," Amity continued with a grin. "The one and only time I've ever accepted a job in the porn industry. She was this really out-there woman in her mid-forties—totally shameless, it did not bother her to do anything. But it was her job to get the actors *ready* for filming."

"What do you mean, 'ready'? Did she have to shave them or tan them?"

Amity's smile grew wicked. "No. She had to get them *excited*. As in, turned on enough to be able to perform."

It took me a second to comprehend what she meant. When I did, my mouth dropped open. "Is that a *real* job?"

"Yep. She got paid lots of money for it, too. Every time they were filming, if the guy lost his erection it would be her job to get him going again."

"No! Tell me that's not a thing!"

"It totally is."

"And you *dated* her?"

"No, we just hooked up. For someone who was so good at her job, though, she wasn't very exciting to sleep with."

I glanced again at Rory and Will, who were both chuckling still. "This story doesn't surprise either of you?" I asked.

"Nah, we've known Am for ages," Will replied.

"Takes a lot more than a porn story to shock us," Rory added.

"Oh go on, have you got stories to top that? Are you both pansexual, too?"

I said it like I was expecting them both to laugh. But to my amazement, Rory shrugged nonchalantly and Will just grinned.

"It's all about changing the world," Will said, leaning in across the table. "Soon, the idea of being either 'straight' or 'gay' will be just a relic of the past. It starts with us, with everyone today. Feeling the need for definitions or to pigeonhole people into something that has a label is the start of division, of seeing people as 'other' and really where hate stems from. If everyone accepts that anyone can be attracted to anyone else with no caveats or barriers around it, then there's no need for traditional hates and dislikes and disapprovals. We lose the need to put a label on what any of us are."

"Right. So ... I mean, I understand the theory, and yes, it sounds very idealistic. But are you *actually* attracted to everybody?"

"Not everybody," Will said. "But I'm *open* to being attracted to anyone. It becomes about the person, nothing else."

I turned my incredulous gaze to Rory, wondering if he felt the same way. He smiled.

"It's interesting to think about," Rory said. "If you take a step back and start to question *why* you're attracted to certain types of people, you'll probably realise that you've been subjected to programming since you were a child."

"Exactly," Amity interjected excitedly. "It's like, look at now. We have these ideals of what sexually attractive men and women should look like, but even that is different to what it was twenty years ago. Can you imagine if you'd grown up in a world where you weren't constantly fed representations of monogamous relationships? Where you were surrounded by same-sex couples, instead? Do you think you'd still be attracted to men?"

I sat back, stunned and not quite knowing what to say. Around us, the pub was starting to pack out with a solid after-work crowd, and I wondered if any other tables were having as interesting a discussion as we were.

But Amity was right, I realised. I'd grown up surrounded by ideals of girl-meets-boy relationships. I'd loved Disney movies as a child (let's be honest, I still loved them), plus I'd always loved any kind of story with heterosexual romances. That wasn't to say I had an issue with other types of romances, I just couldn't remember any of them ever appearing in my orbit when I was younger. It had only been the last few years that I'd really noticed it, what with the advent of Netflix and calls for queer representation in everything. Would *I* also be pansexual if I'd been exposed to more types of sexuality when I was a child?

"Don't worry, Laura!" Amity said again, and I realised I'd been sitting there looking totally perplexed. "You can't help who you're attracted to. Nobody can. We just think that if everybody took a step back and questioned *why* they're attracted to certain types, then people might start coming up with interesting answers."

Rory nudged me on the arm, and leaning in close, stage-whispered, "You can tell we've had this discussion before."

"Yeah. Right," I said, picking up my glass again. "I guess ... I'd never really thought about it."

"That's how we're changing the world." Will winked at me. "Changing one mind at a time."

"Or hopefully lots of minds, if our film has anything to do with it," Amity added.

Our conversation topic switched to upcoming film releases as easily as if we'd gone from discussing jellybeans to smarties. Yet for the whole rest of the night, I found myself questioning things I'd never even thought about before.

Was I really supposed to be attracted only to men? Or was that totally narrow-minded? Even Celeste was more open-minded and adventurous than I was, and she was in her seventies.

I'd never been attracted to women before ... but was that just because I'd never thought to consider it?

12

"Kal, have you ever hooked up with a girl?" I asked my flatmate the next morning.

We were walking along the beachfront promenade, heading into Manly for a very late breakfast. I'd had a much-needed sleep-in that morning, and despite a mild hangover, was finding the walk in the fresh air, with the ocean breeze blowing, the sound of waves crashing and the scent of salty seaweed in the air absolutely the best thing ever.

"What the ef?" Kalina looked incredulously at me, her eyebrows rising well over the rims of her blue-lensed aviators.

"I'm just curious. I mean, you've been with heaps of guys, but have you ever been with a girl?"

"If you're propositioning me, I have to say you're too good of a friend for that to happen between us."

"No!" I gave her a push sideways. "That's not what I meant. Just, like, are you definitely straight?"

I watched her scrunch up her nose in thought. "I'm straight. But I've also been with girls."

"Seriously?" I stopped walking and grabbed her arm so she had to stop, too. Behind us, a man walking his Jack Russell terrier huffed his annoyance at our sudden halt before skirting around us.

"Yes, seriously. Years ago. Wasn't really my thing. Threesomes are pretty good, or foursomes. But otherwise, there just aren't enough dicks in the room for me."

I felt my mouth drop open. Kalina just smirked, before turning and continuing to walk.

I caught up to her after a moment.

"Wait, wait. You've had a *three*some? And a *four*some?"

"Shout it louder, Laura."

"Sorry. Just ... huh."

"What's this about?" Kalina peered over her sunglasses at me, her eyes narrowed. "Are you into a girl?"

"No. I mean ... well, no. But I *could* be. In fact, I suppose I'm wondering why I'm not."

Kalina burst out laughing. "Oh my gosh. You are adorable."

"Hey." I crossed my arms and eyed her, testily. "I could be into a girl."

"I think I've seen enough to say that you're pretty straight."

"Yeah, but maybe I don't know it yet. Maybe my mind doesn't know it."

"Is this because of your ex?"

I felt my insides recoil. Funnily enough, I hadn't even thought about Jack in regards to this. He'd pretended to be straight for the whole eleven years I was with him. Well, pretended might be the wrong word, though I didn't suppose I would ever know what was really going on inside his head. The point was, he'd convinced everyone, including himself, that he was straight until the day he decided to tell me he was gay. And now we were divorced and he was living his best, happiest, gayest life.

And now that I was thinking about it all, *straight* didn't even feel like an appropriate word. Like, if you weren't heterosexual, were you somehow bent? Who even came up with the word *straight* in the first place?

I was sure Amity would know what the modern appropriate word would be. I was probably still going around with thoughts about sexuality that belonged in the stone age.

"No, nothing to do with him," I answered Kalina. "I guess I'm just wondering why I'm only into guys. Have I been programmed that way?"

Kalina shrugged. "Probably. We're all a product of our upbringing, aren't we?"

"Are we?"

Kalina pulled a face that clearly indicated she had no idea.

"Oh, there's Owen," Kalina said, waving.

I spotted Owen jogging towards us, his shaggy beard, singlet and board shorts making the seamless transition from Byron Bay hippie to local Manly surfy.

"How're ya goin'?" he drawled, sounding like the most bogan Aussie in the world.

He gave Kalina a kiss and squeezed her bum at the same time. I rolled my eyes, trying not to gag at just how adorable they were.

"We getting coffee over here?" Owen asked, indicating one of the nearby cafes.

"Sure. You want one, Laur?"

I shook my head. "I'm dying for a BenBry hangover burger. I'll see you guys later."

As they walked away, I watched as Kalina playfully bit Owen on the shoulder and he retaliated by grabbing her and squeezing her into a bear hug while he nuzzled her neck. They were both laughing and smiling like two people who were hopelessly in love, and I felt extremely happy for Kalina even as I felt the unmistakable stab of envy.

In a blink, I imagined it was Lucas doing that to me, us the ones laughing and failing to keep our hands off each other. Another blink and I reminded myself that he probably was already doing that. With Holly.

I turned abruptly and continued my walk towards the central Manly Corso. I'd been doing really well for the past two weeks by focusing on my new job and pretending that Lucas didn't exist anymore. Because that was definitely the healthiest way to get over someone. But just being in Manly again felt like I was conjuring his presence. The sight of the volleyball nets made me remember the first time I'd ever seen him. The cafe I was approaching was the one where we'd exchanged phone numbers. And the fact was that Lucas *lived* in Manly, so the likelihood of running into him was extremely high. Maybe that was why my eyes were darting around like crazy, scanning the faces of everyone approaching in search of him.

But I needed to switch off that part of my brain. Maybe the solution to no longer thinking about Lucas was to switch over my attention entirely to *women*.

Sure, I'd always considered myself heterosexual. I'd never been interested in other women before. Though I did remember, back when I was in high school, all the parties I used to go to. Almost without fail, there would come a moment, usually late at night when everyone had had a few too many Smirnoffs, when a great cheer would sound from the group of boys sitting outside and everyone would go look and sure enough, there'd be two girls kissing.

It was a total thing back then, the party kiss. Katy Perry wrote a whole song about it. What used to bother me, though, was the fact that the girls seemed to be doing it purely for the boys' entertainment.

And I used to wonder—if all things were meant to be equal, then why was there never a cheering circle of girls with two guys kissing in front of them? Why was it so acceptable for girls to kiss each other, but so abhorrent to suggest that two guys might also like to tongue wrestle?

I supposed we didn't have Rory and Will at those parties.

But anyway. Party kissing aside, why was it that I wasn't attracted to girls? Was I truly heterosexual, or had I simply been programmed to be so since I was a child? Was Amity right and we were all really meant to be pansexual?

As I passed people on the walkway, I started to take note of who I was looking at. My eyes were usually drawn immediately to hot guys, although I did have a tendency to look at hot girls, too. Could I be pansexual and not even realise it? Or was I just wondering where they got their cool clothing from or how they got their hair to stay like that?

I forced myself to focus on a hot girl approaching up ahead. She had a great tan. Nice running shoes. A t-shirt that clung to her abs, and broad shoulders and muscles and …

Oh wait. I was looking at her boyfriend, instead.

Okay, back to the girl. Nice hair. I liked her top and the way it dipped down on the sides. I wondered if she got that from Lululemon?

Oh, shit. She passed me, luckily oblivious to my attention. Hmm. This hetero conditioning might take a bit more training to overcome. But overcome it I would, I decided. Because I could do it. I absolutely could. I was sure there must be a hidden side to myself that I'd never even known about.

Plus, it would be the perfect way to stop thinking about Lucas.

I just needed to expose myself to more representations of nonheterosexual relationships. And not in a slow-drip approach. I was almost twenty-eight—I had to take drastic action to try to challenge years of heterosexual programming.

I was going to jump straight in the deep end, I decided. I was going to switch up my thinking and explore my pansexuality.

And it would all start with some totally normal, dip-your-toe-in lesbian porn.

13

I decided to put my new plan in place that very night. Porn, after all, was a very easy, very accessible way to explore your sexual orientation. It wasn't like I was going to do anything extreme like hire a female escort, or create a profile on a queer dating app. That would be too sudden. Wouldn't it? Also rather terrifying.

But I could surely find some porn videos with some nice-looking girls involved. Exploring pansexuality couldn't be that hard.

Sitting on my bed, laptop open, I went to the first (and probably only) porn website I knew the name of. And—oh wow. I didn't think I'd ever been to a porn website myself before. I'd always just looked on over the shoulder of friends or else made Jack do it. There really weren't any controls or firewalls or anything, were there? A simple click from the Google results and I was in, the videos all just right *there* in front of me, already playing little snippet previews, which I found simultaneously alarming and yet strangely enthralling.

No wonder people got addicted to watching porn. There was so much content instantly available. And it didn't even feel all that illicit anymore, not compared to the stuff available on Netflix.

But anyway. I needed to remain focused. I was here for a specific reason, after all.

A search bar sat at the top of the site, so I typed "lesbian" in and awaited my results.

A whole page of videos appeared, and my eyes widened in alarm, a tiny scream catching in my throat. My first thought was, *dear God no*, but then I quickly reminded myself that, *yes*, this was what I was looking for. The video thumbnails were playing little "highlights" of the films, but I thought I might like something that had a bit more of a story behind it. With that in mind, I tried scanning the titles instead, looking for something appealing. Unfortunately, descriptions like "perfect fake tits", "busty stepdaughter" and "amateur lesbian threesome" weren't any more appealing.

And then ... Oh God. *Twins*? Did that mean sisters were going to ...

No. *No*, that would have to be illegal. It would be *incest*, wouldn't it?

Grimacing, I kept skimming down the page.

None of the videos looked particularly enticing, but I supposed I was there to try to broaden my mind. They might not be enticing *now*, but they would be by the end of this experiment. I was sure of it.

Taking a quick breath, I clicked on a random video and braced myself to start watching. And after a worrying advert for an adult video game, my video began playing.

There was one girl, sitting on a very white bed, wearing lingerie that honestly looked like it was from Target. In fact, it still had a label on it—the little ticket was sticking out of the side of the bra!

What kind of shoddy production was this?

But not the point. As I watched, another girl entered the scene. She walked over to the bed and they both started giggling.

Oh, *as if*. This was definitely directed by a man.

Distractedly, I wondered how many crew members were required to make a porn film? Despite *Trigger* being fairly low budget, there were still many people standing around watching the actors every time we went for a take. So, was it the same on a porn set? Would there have been a whole crew there, behind the scenes, watching these girls? And would the actors find that off-putting?

And would there have been a fluffer on this set?

Oh my God, could this have been the adult film that Amity worked on?

Alright, I clearly wasn't paying enough attention to the video. The girls had started kissing and were touching each other now. I watched for a full half-minute before I realised that I was frowning and wasn't feeling anything remotely sexual towards what was happening.

That was a bad sign. Not the adult film, though I wasn't sure I'd call it *good*, but my lack of any *reaction* was bad. I really had been conditioned to be straight, hadn't I? I couldn't even watch two girls kissing and find it arousing.

I just needed to be objective. It was time to examine my own reactions. What was it that I didn't like about the film? Both girls were attractive, so that was a positive. They both had cute, if a little cheap-looking, underwear on.

Or not on anymore, as it happened.

There'd been a sudden scene break and I couldn't help but wonder if there was a director there shouting, "Cut! New shots coming!" and the actors just stopped getting it on and started chatting together about their weekends, and maybe pulled out their phones from under the pillow to scroll through Instagram, until the crew was ready to roll again. Maybe the fluffer would have stepped in with a heater, making sure the girls didn't get cold while they waited.

Anyway, back to the film. There was another scene break and suddenly the girls were all atangle, one lying on her back and the other one kneeling over the top of her, each with their faces between the other one's legs.

Oh God, there were close-ups. I had my own hands plastered over my eyes, so I forced them back down. I should be watching closely for tips, shouldn't I? In case I ever found myself in this situation?

The two women in the film were now moaning and crying out super loudly, lapping at each other like they just couldn't get enough. I was trying to watch it seriously, but it just looked so *fake*. Not that any porn was that realistic, but still. Those exaggerated screams were far louder than they needed to be, not to mention it was slightly irritating having *two* women practically competing for who could moan the loudest—

A knock sounded on my door, accompanied by a deep male voice. "Laura?"

Fuck! Ben was supposed to be out! How had I not heard him arriving home?

I dived for the end of my bed and slammed the laptop shut, hoping like hell that my bedroom door was sufficiently thick and the moans hadn't escaped. Ben would have a field day if he caught me watching lesbian porn.

"What is it?" I called out, my voice sounding high-pitched and definitely guilty as I jumped off the bed and threw open the door.

I tried to look completely innocent as I looked at Ben in the hallway.

Except it wasn't Ben.

I couldn't help a little strangled squealing noise in my throat—like a racoon facing off with a badger—as I realised it was Lucas standing in front of me. And he had his eyebrows raised knowingly, a crooked grin on his face, as if he'd heard everything.

Shit.

Had he heard the moaning? Did he realise I'd just been watching porn?

Hopefully, he didn't think that *I'd* been making those noises, in here by myself.

I cleared my throat, trying and probably failing to look really chilled out. "Er, hello."

He crossed his arms, that grin still on his face, and I knew he'd definitely heard something.

"Busy?" he asked.

"No! I'm not doing anything. I mean, I'm obviously doing something, not just sitting here in my room doing nothing, ha-ha. I was doing … some research. For my new job. It's a bit embarrassing, I mean, I don't know if you heard anything, but that wasn't me, it was work research. Totally legitimate work research and not at all weird."

He'd barely moved. He just stood there watching me bury myself, looking thoroughly entertained.

"What are you doing here?" I quickly asked. "I mean, can I help you with anything?"

His smile slipped then. "I had to grab something from Ben. Thought I'd stop in and say hello, but if you're busy—"

"No! Not busy. I'm not busy at all."

This felt weird. He was practically in my bedroom, I was guiltily blocking the doorway, and less than a metre away from us was a laptop that, if opened, would start broadcasting porn into the room.

"I was about to get a cup of tea, actually," I continued, hustling into the hallway and closing my bedroom door firmly behind me.

"You want one?"

"Sure." He stepped out of my way then followed me into the kitchen.

I busied myself putting on the kettle, collecting mugs and tea bags, all without looking at him. My heart was racing uncomfortably, and I had no idea if it was because I was super embarrassed at having been possibly sprung watching porn by myself on a Saturday night, or because Lucas was here in my kitchen and I was making us tea like it was totally normal. Like, yeah, I regularly had cups of tea with guys I was trying not to be in love with because they were in love with someone else.

Hang on a second.

"Where is Ben?" I asked, only just realising that he didn't seem to be in the apartment.

"Out still. He lent me his key so I could come grab a charger from his room. I did knock, but there was no answer. And erm, then I heard ..."

"Work research! Honestly, that's all it was."

Lucas grinned again and I really wished he wouldn't look at me like that, like he was teasing me and we were friends and like he knew exactly what I'd been watching and he liked it.

Oh God. I was feeling a bit hot.

"So you saw Ben, then?" I said, trying to act totally normal. "Everything's alright between the two of you?"

His grin dropped off his face and he shrugged. "Eh. He makes it hard for me to act like his older brother sometimes, you know?"

I huffed a laugh. "Yeah. My younger sister can be a bit ... trying sometimes, too."

I went to get the milk out of the fridge, but as soon as I opened the door the most foully intense smell hit me.

"Argh! What is that!" I took an involuntary step backwards.

I probably should have thought a bit harder about reacting like that, because within seconds Lucas was behind me, also gagging on the absolutely putrid stench.

"Fuck. What have you got in there?" he asked.

"*Me?* None of *my* food smells like that." I held my nose, the smell so repulsive that I almost wanted to gag.

Lucas moved around me to get a better look in the very over-stuffed fridge, and if we weren't currently standing in the stink cloud of something absolutely horrifying, I might have been rather excited by his closeness.

Within moments, he was pulling out a parcel wrapped in white butcher's paper, which had soaked through with a mysterious fetid liquid.

"Prawns," he said, reading the half-dissolved sticker label. "How long have these been in here?"

"Oh my God. Ben must have bought them … over a week ago. Maybe two. Quick, put them in the bin."

"The bin?" Lucas looked at me like I was crazy. "That'll stink up your whole apartment building for the next week. Have you got a plastic bag?"

Wordlessly (I was trying to hold my breath), I grabbed a small bin bag from the roll beneath the sink and handed it to him. Lucas proceeded to seal the prawn package in the bag and then, to my horror, put the whole thing in the freezer.

"Why are they going in there? They'll stink-bomb the ice-cream!"

"No, they won't." He shot me a knowing grin. "Just leave them until bin night. You'll have to remember to take them out and get rid of them then."

"Oh. Right." I gave him an appreciative look, which was easier to do now that the smell was retreating. "Thanks."

While Lucas washed his hands in the kitchen sink, I moved around to wait by the kettle as it finished boiling.

"So, how's your new job going?" he asked me, drying his hands on the kitchen towel. "You fallen in love with the movie star yet?"

A laugh burst out of me. "Who, Troy?" I rolled my eyes as if this idea was preposterous. "Definitely not. The actors are lovely, though. And the crew. Everybody is really nice."

Lucas leaned against the bench and put his hands in his pockets, his eyes on me. I tried to copy his posture, even though his proximity was making my stomach tie itself in knots.

"You like it, then?" he asked.

I shrugged. "It's not what I was expecting. But ... yeah. I do like it."

And I realised that I did. I hadn't thought about resigning again since that first day.

"So, you think you'll make a career out of being a location manager?"

I glanced at him in surprise. "If it was that easy, then sure. But I'm hardly a location manager now—there's been barely any location-type stuff for me to do so far. Although, I did just find out that nothing has been organised for some key scenes that we need to shoot in a couple of weeks, which need to be done out in some big, open field somewhere. Which shouldn't be that hard to organise, except that there is literally zero budget left for it. So, now I have to try to find somewhere we can do it for free."

"You could use my aunt's winery out in Mudgee," Lucas offered. "That's got a lot of big, open fields as well as grapevines."

"Really?" I frowned, not sure if he was serious. "She'd let a whole film crew come and work there?"

Lucas shrugged. "Don't see why not."

"Well … that would be amazing! But, oh." My face fell. "If it's out of Sydney we'd need accommodation for the crew, and again—no budget."

Lucas scratched his chin. "How many people are we talking about?"

"Hmm … we could probably do essentials only, but even then there are at least twenty."

He nodded thoughtfully. "Shouldn't be a problem. My aunt's just finished converting the old dairy into guest accommodation. It's not even listed yet."

I stared blankly at him, not sure I understood. "You'd let the whole crew stay there? For free? I mean, I'm sure we could at least afford to pay for cleaners or something like that."

Lucas shrugged. "We could work something out. Call it a family discount."

For a second there, I thought Lucas was implying I was family, but then I realised he was probably referring to Ben.

"That's really nice of you. Will your aunt mind?"

"Nah, I'll have a chat to her."

"Well, Amity will probably need to see some photos first. Is there a website? Or do you have any pictures of the place?"

He shook his head. "The website's from about ten years ago. I don't have any pictures, but I'm heading up there tomorrow so I can send some if you like."

That surprised me. "You're going up there? How come?"

The kettle finished boiling then, so I made the cups of tea and gestured for him to follow me over to the couches. Then thought better of it and headed for the dining table, instead. It was safer.

"I've got to go help my aunt. She broke her wrist last week. Slipped over in the warehouse and fell on it, awkwardly."

"Oh, shit! Is she okay?"

"Yeah, she'll be fine." Lucas chuckled. "In fact, she kept working for the rest of the day after she did it, then drove herself to the hospital once it had become so swollen she could barely move it. The doctor told her she can't do any winery work for the next six weeks, which normally wouldn't matter, except my uncle's leaving to go on a research trip to France tomorrow."

I nodded. "So, you're going to help them?"

"I don't mind. In fact, I love it out there. I'd just planned to be here in Sydney, looking after my old clients again for a while. Still, it's only four hours away, which isn't a bad drive. I'll just be doing lots of back and forth for a while."

"Is Holly going with you?" I asked, then could have kicked myself for bringing her up. I needed to remind myself, though, that Lucas was off limits. Because sitting here chatting to him was feeling far too easy.

His eyes snapped up to mine, and I couldn't quite work out what the expression on his face meant.

"Maybe," he finally said. "She doesn't like the country much."

I couldn't hide my incredulity. "She doesn't like the country? Wine country? How is that possible?"

He grinned and something shot through my chest. "Bad experience as a kid, apparently. Bare feet and an ants' nest."

"Ah. I suppose that would put you off."

We were silent for a moment, and I prolonged sipping my tea. I knew I should change the topic. I definitely should. Talking about Holly wasn't healthy for me. And yet ...

"How are things going with you two?"

Lucas sipped his own tea, which was perhaps also a little prolonged.

"We're still finding our feet, I guess," he said eventually, not meeting my eyes now. "Seeing if this is what we both want."

I nodded, but I could feel my heart suddenly pounding in my chest, like I'd just run up five flights of stairs.

"It must be nice having her back in your life. Nice that you were able to forgive her."

Lucas met my eyes with his piercing blue ones, and we stared at each other, his expression indeterminable.

"People change," he eventually said. "She knows what she wants now."

I couldn't hold his gaze any longer. For some reason, his words felt like a direct attack on me. Just because Holly had her shit together with her fancy job in Manly and her absolutely perfect boyfriend. Holly struck me as the kind of girl who always got what she wanted. She had Lucas back, and she was becoming all chummy with Kalina. More importantly, she didn't have just any old job, she had a *career*. One that she'd chosen and she seemed to enjoy.

I, on the other hand, had no idea what the fuck I was going to do with myself in four weeks' time when my job ended.

As if reading my thoughts, Lucas asked softly, "Have you worked out what you want, Laura?"

I startled, my gaze jerking to his before skittering away. And of course, because I couldn't answer him honestly, I gave an elegant, indifferent shrug. "I'm still just enjoying living the free life. Trying different things, you know, exploring my options." I forced a broad smile for added positivity. "I've done married, and done the soulless career, remember. Now I'm just loving being untethered. Doing whatever I want each day. Not being tied down by anything."

I met his eyes, challenging him to contradict me. *Wanting* him to contradict me. Wishing he'd see the lie in my words and understand that I was bluffing.

But my words seemed to have fooled him, because he nodded. "I thought so." He drained the last of his tea. "Well, I'm glad that you're happy."

I wanted to scream, or perhaps to cry. Was I happy? I'd thought that I was—happy enough at least—but with him sitting there opposite me, looking at me like that, I felt like there was a hand constricting around my oesophagus.

"And how about you?" I choked out, the words sounding like an accusation. "Are you happy?"

"Happy enough," he said, but his smile was sad.

I didn't know what to say. I wanted him to stay. I wanted to scoot across the dining table and crawl into his lap. I wanted him to tell me that he wasn't in love with Holly, that he was in love with *me* and that I was the one who would make him truly happy.

"I should get going," he said instead, and my fantasy was shattered as I watched him get to his feet. "Thanks for the tea."

"Right. Yes, thanks for stopping in."

I trailed him at a safe distance to the front door, and watched him pull it open. But then he hesitated and turned, his eyes locking onto mine again, as if he also wasn't quite committed to the whole leaving thing. Softly, he said, "Bye, Laura."

One second passed. Two. Three.

Please don't leave, I thought.

"Goodbye," I said.

And then he was gone.

Facebook Alert
Cath Baker added 62 photos to the album "Byron Bay"
Cath Baker commented:
Getting into the queer pride in Byron!
Elle Baker commented:
WTF is Dad wearing now???

*New Email**
Subject: Call times for tomorrow
Trigger filming day 11 (Monday).
Location: Mosman house (see address below)
Call times for all crew and actors as per below:

    Locations: 4.45 am
    Hair and makeup: 4.45 am
    Wardrobe: 5.15 am

[message clipped]

Amazon Shopping
Are you still interested in *Gender Exploration: Understanding What Your Body is Telling You*?

HER App
Continue setup?

14

On Monday we were filming on location at a studio in Alexandria, which was a welcome distraction from the two burning questions I'd developed over the weekend. Two questions that I knew would need further investigation, even if I quite desperately wanted to know the answers, immediately.

First, how many of the crew were pansexual?

And second, was there any possibility of turning this job into a career?

The studio space we'd hired was part of a larger studio complex, and I knew that there was a second film crew onsite who had rented out "Studio B", one of the other spaces. It was somewhat intimidating seeing how many crew members and equipment arrived for Studio B, and it made me realise once again just how small and low budget the *Trigger* production was.

Still, I felt oddly protective as I stood in the carpark while my crew arrived, directing them on where to park and where to unload their gear. Sure, we weren't rolling up in trailers and big furniture-removal-style trucks like the other crew was, but whoever said you needed heaps of expensive equipment to make a stellar movie? Exactly.

Once the majority of the crew had arrived and I was confident that my signage could effectively direct any latecomers, I headed inside to see how things were progressing in Studio A. The actors were still with hair and makeup in the dressing rooms we'd been allocated, and everyone else was on set.

The set today, the reason why we were at this studio, was made up of an enormous green screen with a bare stage before it. The green screen would be replaced by Will during post-production, because today we were filming the part of the movie where Haven found herself up in a strange cloud land surrounded by mythical beasts.

I watched as the crew went about setting up for their first take, and wondered when would be a good time to talk to Will and Amity about using a winery in Mudgee as one of the locations. To be completely honest, I had mixed feelings about Lucas's offer, mainly because I wasn't sure I wanted to spend three whole days on the same property as him. But if we didn't accept his offer, then the fact was there was nowhere locked in to shoot those particular scenes, and I wasn't sure my fledgling skills as a location manager extended as far as me sourcing a new location in time.

Plus, if we did use the winery, I probably wouldn't even see Lucas at all. He'd be off doing his winery thing, and I'd be hanging around with the production crew. I could probably go the entire time without needing to say more than a quick "hello" to him.

"You right?" a voice said beside me, making me jump.

Ben was grinning at me, and I realised I'd been staring off into space for a good while.

"Oh—yeah, fine. How are you going?"

"We're good. Almost ready to roll."

I trailed Ben as he went back over to the wheeled table he was using for his audio setup. There was a huge controller on there that looked like a DJ deck, plus his laptop, a few pairs of headphones and about a bazillion cables.

"Your aunt's winery in Mudgee, Middlebrook," I said. "Have you been there, lately?"

"Nah, not for a few years. Why?"

"I was going to recommend it as a location for some of the later scenes. Nothing was organised and Lucas mentioned we could probably use it."

Ben looked thoughtful for a moment. "Yeah, my aunt would probably love that. It's big. Lots of open spaces."

"And Lucas is up there helping her out at the moment," I added, apparently unable to prevent myself from mentioning him again.

To my surprise, Ben kind of scoffed and rolled his eyes.

"What?" I asked him.

"Ah, just golden-boy Lucas. Always the best child."

"Is *that* what your problem is with him?" I asked, a teasing grin spreading across my face. "That he's being too helpful?"

"No! I don't have a problem with him," Ben said, but I noticed his cheeks turn a bit pink.

"Really?" I crossed my arms, still grinning at him. "Could've fooled me."

"Ah, he's just. You know. Keeps trying to lecture me."

"What about?"

Ben sighed and looked away. "About my choices in women."

I couldn't help it, I burst out laughing.

"Shut up!" Ben shoved me on the arm, but he was also smiling. "It's not funny. Lucas acts like he's such an expert, but he's the one making stupid decisions."

I stopped laughing, immediately. "You think? As in ... Holly?"

"Yeah. Like, as if my choices are worse than that."

"I thought you liked her?"

"I don't *not* like her. I just don't like how she dumped him last time. At least when I realised what Amy was doing, I left her and haven't looked back."

I patted him on the shoulder, suddenly feeling immensely warm and affectionate towards him. "And good for you. That's a much better decision. The next girl you date I'm sure you'll have your eyes wide open."

Ben looked at me like I'd just said something ludicrous. "The *next* girl? Fuck, I'm not getting involved with anyone again for a long, long time."

"Oh. But what if ...?"

"No. Nope. No way. I'm swearing off women. One-night stands excluded."

"Huh. Well, I mean, just don't rule out meeting someone else. You never know when it might happen."

Ben raised his eyebrows. "This, coming from you?"

"Fair point."

"Laura?"

I turned to find Eloise from wardrobe behind me, looking anxious. "You said we had dressing rooms A through to C, right?"

"Correct," I said. "Is there a problem?"

"C is locked, and there isn't enough space for me to set up the steamer in the other two. Can you check it out?"

"Of course!" I gave Ben a quick goodbye nod, then hurried away towards the dressing rooms, feeling a small inward thrill.

Look at me, acting like a real location manager! My confidence was definitely growing the longer I did this job.

I reached dressing room C, and after trying the doorknob found that it was indeed locked. I quickly knocked, in case anyone was currently in there, but when there was no response I pulled out the keys I'd been given that morning.

Eloise was hovering behind me, and I cast her a quick, triumphant smile as I unlocked the door and pushed it open.

I supposed what happened next was quite comical, especially because I was looking at Eloise when the door swung inward, so I had only her expression to go off. At the same time as her eyes widened in shock, I heard two gasps come from within the dressing room.

I turned, feeling my stomach plummet, and found myself equally caught in shock.

Within the dressing room was Phoebe Winters, our leading actress, half-naked and locked in a very compromising position with Charlotte, the hair and makeup artist.

It took me a moment to register what I was seeing. Instead of springing apart, they were sort of clinging together, likely to try to hide their semi-nakedness. And after a horrible frozen moment where I stared at them, and they stared back at me (and, presumably, Eloise), I quickly grabbed the door and slammed it shut again, muttering, "I'm so sorry!" in the process.

Eloise and I stared at each other like we'd just seen the Dalai Lama doing a dance inside.

"Um," I said, not sure what else to say.

"I'll, er, just use one of the other rooms, then," Eloise muttered, moving back down the hall to the other dressing rooms.

I preferred to get as far away as possible, and so returned to our studio, trying to breathe normally and tell myself that what just happened wasn't weird or unusual and that I should probably just forget what I'd seen.

I mean, sure, it wasn't like the whole crew was waiting on Phoebe to finish with hair and makeup so we could start filming. I now just wasn't sure what *finishing* with hair and makeup entailed.

"Laura!"

I jumped like I'd been hit with a cow prod.

Amity raised her eyebrows at me. "You okay?"

"Yes! Sure! Fine!" My voice had gone a little soprano there.

Amity didn't look convinced. "Have you seen Phoebe?"

"Er ..." I cast around for something to say. *Yes*, was the obvious response, but *No* seemed like a much safer bet with no follow-through questions. Although, it had the obvious downside of being a lie.

"She's, ah, with *hair and makeup*." I said it like I was speaking in code words, dropping my voice and looking around to make sure we weren't being overheard.

Amity surveyed me, not like she thought I was mental, but like she was processing the code words I was dropping.

"And by *with*, you mean ..."

I stared at Amity, my eyes still kind of wide.

Surprisingly, she just rolled her eyes then shook her head, her rainbow hair dancing around her shoulders. "Bloody actors," she muttered. "I guess I'll give her another five minutes."

My eyebrows shot up. "You're not surprised? Or angry?"

"Surprised? No. Annoyed? A little. But," she shrugged, "how long can they be, right?"

I tried not to laugh, and managed to snort instead.

Amity looked delighted.

"While I've got you for five minutes," I said, seizing on my opportunity. "I might have found a location for scenes thirty-five to forty. It's a winery in Mudgee—actually, it's Ben's aunt's winery—and we can use it practically for free. They even have accommodation there, as well."

"Have you got photos? What's the layout like?"

"I can get some photos sent through. And probably a map, too ..."

Amity was shaking her head. "Have you been there?"

"Me? No, but—"

"You'll need to do a site visit. Trust me, you'd be amazed how different things can look in real life. And we can't afford to send the whole crew somewhere that turns out to be a no-go on the day. You'll have to go this week. In fact, Friday we're back at the Mosman house again, so you could go then. Drive out there, check it out fully, get photos and video of each spot that you think will work, then we can review it and make a decision next week."

Amity was talking so fast that my brain was struggling to keep up. Or maybe it was simply that my thoughts had been snagged by the very first thing she'd said: *You'll have to do a site visit.*

A site visit meant spending time with Lucas. Because he was out there, working on the property, and he was my contact for this whole thing. I swallowed, trying to take in the rest of what Amity was saying, but my heartbeat had started thumping ridiculously loudly and it was all I could seem to hear.

"Thanks, Laura," Amity finally said, giving my arm a squeeze. "You'll be great at this."

I nodded mutely at her, but she was already striding away. And then I saw that Phoebe had finally appeared, looking calm and professional and not at all like she'd just been getting off with another girl in the dressing rooms.

It made me wonder how many other crew members were shagging in secret. And why on earth *I* wasn't shagging anyone.

15

I could do this.

I could visit the winery in Mudgee without things needing to get weird with Lucas and me.

I mean, sure, we might have spent a bit too long staring into each other's eyes and making cryptic comments over tea less than a week ago. But the fact was that he was back together with Holly, and they both had their shit together and their lives on track, and so even though I was quite possibly in love with Lucas, I had to remind myself that I was probably wrong. I mean, you couldn't be in love with someone who was in love with someone else, right? Exactly. It should be impossible. Love had to go two ways. It's like science or something.

So, I couldn't be in love with Lucas. And I just needed to stop thinking about the way my heart kept going all fluttery when I was near him. In fact, I just needed to stop thinking about him altogether. Like, *now*.

...

Or, *now*.

NOW.

...

Bugger.

"I'm so jealous. I want to go to Mudgee," Kalina complained to me via my car's speakers, as I sped down the motorway heading out of Sydney on Friday morning. I could hear her back at the apartment making her breakfast, the toaster popping in the background.

"It's not a holiday," I told her. "It's work."

"*Fun* work."

I rolled my eyes, even though she couldn't see me. "I thought your work was fun?"

"Oh, it is. It's just intense."

"Didn't you meet your kids last week?"

Kalina snorted. "*Kids* is definitely not the word I'd use to describe them. They're sixteen going on twenty-five."

"I thought they were all troubled youths. Isn't that who you're meant to be working with?"

"Some are troubled more than others. But honestly, Laura, they're all just so ... *promiscuous.*"

I burst out laughing. "Oh my God, it must be bad if even you're describing them like that!"

"I know, right? But seriously, they send not just naked photos to each other, but photos of close-ups of their ... bits! They reckon if you can't see their face in the photo, it doesn't matter."

"Ew! They don't seriously do that?"

"They do! I had to have a discussion with a whole group of them yesterday and explain to them about why they can't do that. Aside from the obvious reason, some of the kids doing it are under sixteen! It's totally illegal, and anyone forwarding on a photo like that could be done for distributing child pornography."

"Wow."

"Exactly. Still, that aside, none of them seem to care too much.

You know, I was talking to this one girl yesterday—she's seventeen—and she was telling me about how she's been making pornos with some of her friends."

"*What?*"

"I wish I was joking. But they're all so open about it nowadays, that they don't even see it as a big deal. Honestly, if you were to go on a porn website, you'd be shocked by how young homemade porn actors are."

Oh my God. Had I inadvertently watched some of Kalina's youths on the porn site the other day? But no, surely not. Those girls were at least … twenty.

Suddenly, I felt a bit queasy.

"Anyway, this girl was telling me about how four of them filmed a group scene the other day," Kalina went on. "They had a great time, apparently. I spent at least an hour trying to convince her never to publish that video, but she honestly couldn't see a reason not to. Her entire aspiration for her life seems to be to become a porn star and earn money through an OnlyFans account."

"Holy crap. How times have changed."

"Don't I know it. God, we sound mega old, don't we?"

I laughed again. "If that's what the kids are doing nowadays, I'm kind of glad I'm getting old."

"Yeah. Although, I admire how open they all are. I mean, it took me until I was at uni to get as comfortable as they are about sex. They're just not shy about anything. And even though I think it's all a bit much, it's nice to see how accepting of each other they are. No matter what sexuality anyone is, there's never any judgement between them. And no shaming, either."

"That *is* a nice change."

"I'd better run, my toast is getting cold here. Have a fun day with

Lucas, won't you?"

"I'm not going to have a fun day with Lucas! I'm location scouting."

"Uh-huh. All alone with Lucas at a winery for the day. Whatever will the two of you get up to?"

"Ha-ha. His aunt will be there. In fact, she'll probably be the one showing me around. I expect I won't even see Lucas at all."

"You're going to his family's grand old estate. It'll be just like when Lizzie visits Mr Darcy at Pemberley."

"No, it won't! This isn't bloody *Pride and Prejudice*. He's not interested in me."

"That's what Lizzie thought."

"Enjoy your toast, Kal!" I shouted at her, and stabbed at the "end call" button.

Blimey. We weren't some destined love story. Lucas was with Holly and I was …

I was …

What was I?

It was going to be fine.

There were more important things at stake than my highly repressed emotions towards Lucas. He might not even be there. He might have been unexpectedly called back to Sydney and I could just deal with the aunt and never have to talk to Lucas again. Exactly. And if he was there, well my best defence was to simply act like a professional. Because that's what this trip was, it was about my work as a location scout. A real, proper, location scout.

Finally buoyed by this thought, I found my mood brightening

as I began passing the first visible grapevines and signs pointing to winery cellar doors along the Castlereagh Highway as I entered the Mudgee district. It was autumn, but the leaves were still lush and green, with the first hints of red tips appearing on the trees. I knew I was entering the town outskirts when the speed limit dropped to fifty, and I let my eyes dart around as I drove first through an industrial area, and then, following the GPS, turned down the main road into town. Middlebrook Vineyard was located on the western side of town, and as I drove through, I felt immediately delighted by the old buildings and the enormous deciduous trees everywhere—these ones already turning shades of orange and yellow and beginning to drop their leaves. There were people out and about, the main street full of shops and cafes all open for business, and I wished I had time to stop and explore.

But too soon I was driving out of town again, the speed limit increasing to eighty, my destination only a few minutes away.

Middlebrook Vineyard had an old, flaking sign heralding its entrance off the main road, which I almost drove right past and had to make a very sudden stop and a sharp turn to get into the driveway. But driving up the gravel in the mid-morning air, I immediately could see that this location might just be perfect.

The driveway snaked through grapevines at the base of a gently sloping hill, and up above, perched at the top of the rise, was a gorgeously old, sprawling Tuscan-style villa, all terracotta render, curved metal fences and creeping green vines.

I followed the signs for the cellar-door parking, then stepped out into the fresh air, gazing up at the place in astonishment. It was enormous. The kind of luxurious, old-style villa that George Clooney would own in the south of France.

"Laura!"

I'd just started up the front steps when I heard him, calling out from behind me. For a second I closed my eyes, swallowing.

You're a professional, Laura. Act like a professional.

I turned, wishing my heart hadn't just leaped into allegro. And when I spotted him, I wondered if my insides had decided to spontaneously combust.

God, he was *hot*. He'd replaced his board shorts for work shorts, his Havaianas for Timberlands. His checked shirt was rolled up to the elbows, and though his surfer hair was hidden beneath an Akubra, the stubble and deep tan amplified the sheer blue of his eyes.

How the hell had he transformed from gorgeous surfer dude to country hottie in just a few days? *Farmer Wants a Wife* would fall all over themselves trying to get him on their show.

"How are you?" he asked me, rapidly closing the distance between us.

"Fine," I squeaked, trying not to breathe in too deeply as he enveloped me in a hug. Pressing up against him was torture. Pure, blissful torture.

"So, you didn't like the photos I sent?" he asked, a teasing note in his voice. "So much so that you had to drive out here and check it out for yourself?"

I pulled back, hurriedly trying to recompose myself. "Well, this is a very professional production, and what kind of location manager would I be if I didn't do a proper site visit?"

I met his eyes and it was torment, this teasing of each other. But there was a question in his gaze as well, a curiosity.

I needed to stamp that out. "Amity insisted," I quickly added. "It was her decision to send me."

I could have sworn I saw disappointment on his face, but it was hard to tell because he turned away almost immediately.

"Right. Well, I'd best give you the tour, then. Did you want a drink or something first?"

"I stopped for coffee on the way," I said. "But is your aunt here? I should probably meet her, and there's some paperwork we'll need to go through."

"Sure. The cellar door's just opened, but apparently, she doesn't get many people in before lunch, anyway."

I followed Lucas up the steps and we entered a tasting room that had me immediately salivating for wine. There was a large stone fireplace in the corner—currently unlit—and stools fronted up to an island counter that ran the entire length of the room. Behind the bar, wine bottles all proudly displaying the Middlebrook Vineyard logo and countless wineglasses created a collaged artwork on the wall, though there were also some photographs of grapevines and people thrown into the mix. A slim woman who was perhaps in her late fifties was behind the counter, taking out wine bottles and lining them up in a row on the benchtop. If Lucas was rocking the farmer look, then this woman was doing country chic, her pink-checked shirt unbuttoned over a white top, and her grey-blonde plait falling over her shoulder. She glanced up when we entered, and when she spotted me a huge, beatific smile graced her face, which made me immediately like her.

"Hello there! You must be Laura. Welcome!"

I couldn't help but return her smile as I approached.

"Laura, this is Sadie," Lucas said, stepping up beside me. "Owner and winemaker here at Middlebrook."

"It's lovely to meet you, Sadie," I said. "Your winery here is stunning. It's even better than Lucas and Ben told me it would be."

Sadie positively beamed. "Thank you! And it's such a pleasure to meet one of Lucas's and Ben's friends. Of course, Lucas has already told me all about you."

My gaze instantly shot to Lucas, wondering what on earth he possibly could have said about me. That I was flaky? Indecisive? Irritating and cowardly?

But he just smiled at me, looking amused, and like he was in no way going to elaborate on his aunt's comment.

"Yes, er, well, I'm hoping he's told you about the film we'd like to shoot here? I mean, it's not the whole film, just a few scenes. It should only take a few days."

"There's some paperwork," Lucas added. "Waivers and things, I'm assuming."

"Well, send it this way, let me take a look," Sadie said, pulling a pair of glasses out of her shirt pocket and unfolding them. It was only then that I noticed the plaster cast covering her hand, wrist and forearm.

"So sorry about your wrist! I hope you're not in any pain?"

Sadie glanced at me in surprise and snorted. "This thing? More annoyance than anything. I can't believe I broke it, to be honest. Tripping over, of all things! You know you're getting old when you no longer just fall over, you 'have a fall' and break something."

I couldn't help a laugh escaping, and was glad to see Sadie grin.

"Still, lucky my nephew lets me wrangle him into working here. My own kids fled the nest years ago and haven't been back since."

"I don't think it's hard to get Lucas up here," I said fondly, glancing around for him. But he'd disappeared from the room.

"Quite right. He'd make an excellent winemaker if he'd commit to it. He's just got too many pokers in the fire at present, what with all these businesses he has. And now with ... well!" Sadie shook her head, her lips suddenly pursed, like she'd thought better of what she was about to say. "Anyway! Let's see that paperwork, shall we?"

I took a seat on a bar stool and fished the paperwork out of my bag. She skimmed the first few pages, nodding to herself. "All looks fine," she said. "I'll read it a bit more closely while Lucas shows you around."

"Great." I searched for Lucas again and wondered where he'd got to.

I spent the next few minutes discussing the logistics of having a film crew at Middlebrook with Sadie, and to my relief she confirmed that there was sufficient accommodation that we could utilise for a very good price (practically free).

"This really is perfect," I said, once I'd answered all her questions. "Have you ever had anyone else film anything here? I mean, this villa itself is spectacular, and I've barely seen much of it yet."

Sadie snorted, though she looked pleased with my comment. "Goodness, no! I've been playing with the idea of hosting weddings here at the vineyard, but there's a lot of competition around now. It always feels the same here—people are delighted and love the place when they arrive, it's just getting them in the door that's a challenge. We're not on the main tourist drive around Mudgee, so unless people come here looking for us, we don't get much drive-by traffic."

"What sort of marketing do you do?" I asked, my mind immediately going to the Middlebrook website that looked like it was made back in the day when websites were only six-hundred-pixels wide and still designed as "pages".

"Practically nothing," Sadie said. "I know I should do more, but I refuse to pay for some big marketing firm to come in and tell me what to do. George—that's my husband—had someone come and talk to us about marketing not long ago, and the number of things he insisted we needed to do made me want to lie down! We just don't have time for any of that—we're farmers."

I nodded thoughtfully, feeling indignant on Sadie and George's behalf. I could just imagine the type of digital agency they'd spoken to, the ones who talked about "engagement" and "evergreen content" and "cost per click". All interesting stuff, but probably not the kind of low-level marketing Middlebrook needed. Just getting the basics right was so important, but digital agencies liked to bamboozle their customers by selling them on search engine optimisation and ad spend, something those agencies could make lots of commission on.

"I know the kind of company you mean. I used to work in the marketing team at a financial institution, and the amount of money they spent on digital agencies was kind of mind-blowing. Plus, I never really saw the value in what they offered. I always thought there was much over-promising and definite under-delivering."

"Exactly! I don't want all that hoopla they go on about. I've been trying to find someone to help me update the website, but everyone I reach out to tries to sell me these big package deals that cost an arm and a leg."

"How rubbish! Websites don't have to be expensive. I could help you, if you want."

"Oh no, dear, I couldn't ask you to do that!"

"I'd be happy to, especially since you're allowing us to film here free of charge. It's honestly one of the least things I could do."

Sadie seemed surprised but touched. "Oh well, if you're sure. The website could use all the help it can get."

Lucas entered the cellar door again from further within the house, his clothes changed and his hair now wet and slicked back from his face. His sky-blue eyes gleamed brightly, and—good God— it was all I could do not to imagine him naked and in the shower, which was evidently where he'd just been.

As his eyes found mine, a smile immediately sprang to his lips. "Ready for that tour?" he asked me.

16

Middlebrook Vineyard really was spectacular. The enormous villa had been built in the eighties by the original owners, and was indeed inspired by the villas of Tuscany. The front had been converted into the cellar door, and off to the north side was the most gorgeous patio that spilled away to a view of the mountains and grapevines that was just calling for sunset drinks and a cheese board.

Everywhere we went, I took photos on my phone, mentally noting which spots I thought would work for each shot Amity wanted. It was surreal and also exciting to think that I was doing the job of a genuine location scout right now. What a life this would be—constantly visiting amazing places, trying to see how different areas could be transformed through the lens of a camera! If there was a chance, however small, that the *Trigger* job could open some industry doors for me, then maybe I really could see myself working long term in the film industry.

"Oh, this is perfect!" I exclaimed, after Lucas had led me out into a courtyard with stone archways and leafy climber vines crawling across the walls. The leaves were in the process of turning from green to red, the first couple having already fallen to decorate the flagstones. I could see the exact shot Amity needed beneath one of the archways, and I carefully took a number of photos, trying to get the lighting right.

Shaking my head, I looked around in wonder. "You must wish you lived here permanently. It's like being somewhere magical."

Lucas's eyes crinkled at that. His hair had mostly dried now, and though the majority of it was all swished back from his face, one lock was persistently falling across his temple. He tried to brush it back again. "I am living here at the moment."

"Yeah, but … I'd never want to leave."

He laughed softly and shrugged. "Most people start to miss the city pretty soon."

I shot him an incredulous look. "Really? Why?"

"The beach?"

"Right. I guess you miss surfing."

He seemed surprised by that. "Not really. I could actually live out in the country pretty easily."

We were wandering through the courtyard, across broken but still beautiful flagstones, the whole floor covered in tiny creeper vines. It honestly felt like being in a fairytale.

"Why don't you stay, then? Sadie said you'd make a good winemaker."

He raised an eyebrow, a smile playing around his mouth. "Trying to get rid of me, are you?"

"No." I felt my cheeks heating again. "But isn't this what you want? I remember you once telling me that you'd love to own a winery."

His smile grew. "True. I do want that. But as much as I love this place, it isn't mine. And there's just … *more* I want to do still before

I'm ready for that."

I nodded. "I suppose once you buy a vineyard, you're pretty much stuck there for the rest of your life. What does ..." I almost choked on the name, but made myself say it, "Holly think about the idea?"

He frowned, looking off into the distance. "I don't know. She's more of a city person. I doubt she'd ever want to move to the country."

"Oh." Another awkward silence.

A thousand questions danced on my tongue.

"Come on," Lucas suddenly said, as if nothing at all was wrong. "I'll show you the winery."

I frowned at him. "I thought this was the winery?"

He shook his head, amused. "This is the house and the cellar door. The winery is where we actually make the wine."

"Right. Well, then. Yes, I'd love to see that."

A winery, it turned out, was a kind of huge, insulated warehouse. It was filled floor to ceiling with enormous wooden wine barrels, all lying on their sides and stacked carefully in these huge metal frames, each one with dates and letters scrawled across the front indicating the contents. A small office was located at the back and the whole place was coolly temperature controlled, and had a kind of yeasty, old-wine smell throughout.

"Wow," I said, taking in what must have been hundreds of barrels of wine filling the space.

"We've just finished a vintage," Lucas said, surveying the barrels with pride.

I wasn't sure what that meant, so I just nodded as if I understood.

Lucas shot me a grin. "You want to try some?"

"What—out of a barrel?"

"Yeah. Not the brand-new stuff, but some of the older stuff."

Without waiting for my answer, he walked over to an upright barrel nearby and picked up two tasting-sized wineglasses, along with a long glass straw that looked like it belonged in a science laboratory.

"Did you help make the wine?" I asked, suddenly curious.

"Not this year. I've been learning, though. Sadie and George are both winemakers, and they've taught me bits and pieces over the years. They actually met while both working at a winery in Croatia many years ago."

"Croatia? I didn't know they even made wine there."

"I didn't either, but that's just because they hardly export anything to Australia. The wine there is fantastic, according to Sadie. Did you know that zinfandel is originally from Croatia? Even though most people associate it with California."

"Right." I nodded thoughtfully, wishing I was slightly more of an expert on wine topics. I mean, if we were talking about Croatia in the context of the filming of *A Game of Thrones*, I'd be all over that conversation, but wine varietals were not my forte. Not to say I wasn't open to learning about it. Especially if Lucas was the teacher.

Lucas led me over to a particular wine barrel at the bottom of the rack that didn't have another one above it. He took the cork stopper out of the top, then inserted the glass straw thing. It came out full of a dark, cherry-red liquid, which he deposited between the two wineglasses before handing me one.

I took a sip. It was surprisingly good.

"This one will be bottled in the next few months," he said, smelling his wine before sipping it. "What do you think?"

"I like it," I replied honestly. "Is this zinfandel?"

"Shiraz," he said.

"Right. I totally knew that."

He grinned. "Don't worry. I spend most of my time here pretending to know what I'm talking about."

I laughed, feeling relieved, and turned, planning to get a photo of the winery, but instead my phone slipped out of my hand and clattered to the floor beneath the stack of wine barrels. Embarrassed, I quickly kneeled down to retrieve it, but in my haste to pull it out and stand again, I caught the back of my shoulder on something sharp sticking out of the rack.

"Ouch," I gasped, flinching away as I stood up, and also managing to spill the rest of my wine on the ground. "Oh—shit, sorry!"

"It's fine," Lucas dismissed the wine now seeping into the concrete—based on the smell in here, that was a common occurrence—and moved immediately to my side. "Are you okay?"

"Yeah, I think …" I trailed off, trying to peer at my own back. There was a definite stinging feeling across my shoulderblade, and if I wasn't mistaken, it was starting to feel a bit wet.

"Shit. You're bleeding. Badly." Lucas suddenly looked very alarmed, or concerned, I couldn't tell which.

"Ow. Yeah, I think I cut myself."

Ten points to me for stating the obvious.

"Come with me. There's a first-aid kit in the office," Lucas said, and I followed him down to the back of the winery, my shoulder stinging more and more as we walked.

Lucas seemed flustered as he rummaged around on shelves and in cupboards, and I tried not to smile while watching him. I mean, sure, I was possibly bleeding to death right then, but I didn't think I'd ever seen him look so rattled. It was kind of adorable.

"Aha." He stood up, producing a first-aid kit from beneath the desk.

"Great, um ..." I peered over my shoulder again, as if wondering how I was going to bandage myself. Lucas seemed to come to the same conclusion.

"Here, let me." He moved around the desk until he was standing behind me, and I tried to ignore the prickling sensation across my skin. I felt frozen, my breath catching, wondering if he was about to touch me.

But nothing happened.

Confused, I glanced over my shoulder at him. "You're not squeamish, are you? Or afraid of blood?"

"No," he said, although he sounded a bit uncomfortable. "It's just ... well, you might need to take off your top so I can have a look at it."

"Oh."

I met his eyes and wondered if I looked as alarmed as he did.

I quickly glanced away so he wouldn't see the heat creeping up my neck. With my back to him, I pulled off my t-shirt, pressing the fabric to my front as if this might make me somehow less topless. The cool air in the building made goosebumps instantly shiver to life across my bare skin, and I was breathing too fast, I knew I was. This felt so ridiculously intimate, alone together in the dimly lit back office.

Neither of us moved for a moment, and I knew he was staring at my near-naked back. I wished I'd put on a nicer bra that morning, something with delicate lace and tiny straps. But the functional white one worked best under my t-shirt, and at least it was fairly new.

Oh God, why wasn't he doing anything?

It felt like an eternity that I stood there, hyper-aware of him behind me, just staring at me. This shouldn't be weird—he'd seen me in a bikini before, hadn't he? Or actually, hmm, come to think of it, maybe he hadn't. I'd seen him in nothing but board shorts before—a sight that had made a semi-frequent appearance in my dreams of late. But now that I thought about it, I didn't think he'd ever seen me so scantily dressed.

I sensed him move closer, feeling the soft hush of his breath across my shoulder. And then his fingers swept lightly across the nape of my neck, pushing my hair across to the opposite shoulder, and I stopped breathing entirely.

There was no way he couldn't have clocked my reaction. With my senses so hyper-attuned, I heard him swallowing behind me, heard the moment his own breath hitched. And then he cleared his throat and stepped away again, as if realising that he was supposed to be doing something slightly more medical with me.

"It looks pretty bad," he said, his voice rougher than usual. "I mean, not *too* bad. But not great."

"Brilliant," I managed to say, regaining the use of my lungs in the process. "I've always wanted a back scar."

I heard him huff a laugh, and watched out of the corner of my eye as he pulled a wad of tissues out of a packet from the desk. "I don't think it'll scar. I'll try to make sure it doesn't."

I swallowed as he stepped towards me again, bracing for contact. Ever so gently, he dabbed the tissues on my back, wiping away the blood I could feel was trickling down my shoulderblade.

"Can I move this?" he asked, and I realised his fingers were resting lightly on my bra strap. Unable to speak, I simply nodded.

I tried to think of something else, anything else, as he slipped two fingers beneath the strap and began pushing it down over my shoulder. My skin was so sensitive that I couldn't help shivering as the strap cleared my shoulder bone and then moved further down my arm. I closed my eyes, a thousand fantasies crashing behind them, and fought with myself not to gasp.

His fingers disappeared from my skin, leaving goosebumps in their wake. I heard the zip of the first-aid kit being opened, and could see in my peripheral vision his hands rummaging around inside, checking the labels on various small white packets. He found one, tore it open and then he moved back towards me.

I held my breath.

"This might sting a bit," he said quietly behind me, so close that I could feel his breath on the nape of my neck.

I did gasp then as the antiseptic wipe touched my shoulderblade, sending needles of pain into my cut skin.

"Sorry," Lucas said softly, but I shook my head. I was just trying to breathe, not because of the pain but because he was standing so close behind me that I could feel the heat emanating from his body and smell the pine-and-sandalwood scent of the soap he'd used in the shower. I felt extraordinarily bare, even though I still had a bra on, and I knew every single tiny little hair on my back would be standing on end.

Gently, so gently, he brushed the antiseptic over my skin, the sensation now feeling cool and numbing.

"Is this okay?" he asked, his voice still soft.

Again, I couldn't seem to speak, so I just nodded, trying to focus on breathing.

"It looks pretty deep here," he said, his fingers brushing lightly over my skin, just below the cut. "I'll put some wound-closing strips on it, then a dressing on top, okay?"

"Okay," I managed to say.

He worked in silence then, carefully cutting small strips of bandage. He moved close to my back again, and I froze, closing my eyes, as I felt his fingers on my skin once more, his warm breath on my neck. Gently, he taped me back together, and I craved every brush of his fingertips, every press of his hands to my body. If only he'd keep touching me, I'd cut myself over and over again.

There was the rustling of another packet being opened, followed by the scissors. And then he pressed something large and soft to my back, and with careful, soft touches, taped it down on my skin. Finally, he smoothed the edges.

"Done," he said quietly.

For a few seconds, I didn't move. My body was screaming for him to keep touching me, my breaths coming too fast, my *heart* beating too fast. There was no way he could not have noticed.

I unfroze. Slowly, I turned around to face him.

He hadn't moved away. In fact, we were standing so close to each other. I was still pressing my t-shirt to my chest, as though trying to hold myself together, and his eyes were full of something intense, something I didn't understand.

"Thank you," I whispered.

We kept staring at each other. His breaths were also coming fast, I realised.

The urge to kiss him hit me with so much force that I almost couldn't resist it. My bare shoulders felt touched by a phantom breeze, so much so that I shivered.

Lucas parted his lips slightly. I didn't know if he was planning to kiss me or was trying to say something.

One second went by.

Two seconds.

In, out. In, out. My breaths were ragged.

Three seconds.

The distance between us seemed to be closing.

143

My ringtone blared out into the room, unnaturally loud and echoing in the quiet space.

Lucas and I jerked apart, spell broken. I hurriedly pulled my t-shirt back on, ignoring the still-wet blood on it, and answered the call.

"Hello?" I knew I sounded extremely flustered.

"Hey. Are you in Mudgee yet? How's the site visit going?"

It was Will. For a while there, I'd completely forgotten what I was meant to be doing.

"Yes, I'm here," I said, finding my voice again. "The winery is great. Perfect, actually."

"Awesome. You've got photos, right? And video?"

"Yes and yes."

"And there are enough rooms for us to stay there for a few nights?"

I met Lucas's eyes, knowing he could probably hear what Will was saying. Lucas shrugged and nodded.

"I think so. I was going to check on that next."

"Cool. Give me a call if you have any questions or need a hand with anything."

"I will. Thanks, Will."

I ended the call, feeling rather hot. When I peeked up at Lucas, his eyes skated away from mine and I was sure I could see a flush of red creeping up *his* cheeks.

"I can find you a spare shirt inside, if you want," he said.

"Oh! Sure. I mean, thanks. That would be great."

I glanced at him again but his expression was now closed and unreadable, his eyes already on the door.

"Come on, then," he said.

We walked in silence back to the house, a sizeable distance

between us as though we were scared of what might happen if we strayed too close together.

17

Lucas led me into the main house, and I waited awkwardly in the kitchen while he disappeared to find something for me to wear that wasn't adorned with blood. The house was quiet, Sadie being in the cellar door, and looking around I tried to find any signs of Lucas in the room. But the house was a patchwork of Sadie and George, full of the clutter of a lifetime living here, and nothing of their nephew stood out.

"This is the best I can do, I'm afraid," Lucas said, returning to the kitchen and holding out a white linen button-up shirt.

"Is it …?" I trailed off as I took the shirt, my eyebrows raised in question.

"It's mine," he said quickly. "Doesn't fit me anymore. Sorry—I didn't want to go rummaging in my aunt's bedroom, and I suspect you probably wouldn't want to wear anything of hers, either."

"You're right," I said with a laugh, feeling ridiculously delighted that Lucas was giving me something of *his*. In all honesty, my first thought was that he might get me something of Holly's, and that definitely would have made me feel weird.

Lucas showed me where the bathroom was, and I exchanged my bloody top for his white shirt, rolling the too-long sleeves up to my elbows. And, dear God, it *smelled* like him. For a moment I just stood there, my nose buried in the collar, feeling all kinds of ridiculous bubbly feelings in my stomach. I closed my eyes, reliving the feel of his fingertips on my shoulderblade, and suddenly I was gasping, imagining what might have just happened. That when he'd finished bandaging me, I'd turned around and he'd kissed me. That I'd let my shirt drop to the ground and pressed my body against his. That his hands had skated along my back and undone my bra, pushing the other strap down and taking the whole thing off. That I'd climbed up his body and wrapped my legs around his hips. That he'd laid me down on the desk and—

My eyes flew open and I glared furiously at myself in the mirror.

This was wrong. Lucas wasn't mine. Couldn't be mine. Even if I quite desperately wanted him to be.

Throwing open the bathroom door, I plastered a sunny smile on my face as I went back into the kitchen.

"All done! Thanks for this," I said cheerily, trying to convince myself that I hadn't just been fantasising about having rampant sex with Lucas in his aunt's winery.

"Here, I'll chuck your top in the wash."

"You don't need to—"

"It's fine. It'll dry here in the sun in no time."

I couldn't help smiling as I watched Lucas disappear back down the hallway, this time with my bloodied t-shirt in his hand. I heard the sounds of a washing machine being programmed, then he was back in the kitchen again.

"Shall we?" He gestured to the door. "I'll show you the dairy."

We walked in silence towards the dairy, which was located over the hill and quite a way from the main house. I tried to counter the awkwardness by taking photos of the landscape as we went, even though I knew none of these spots would be good for filming, but it at least gave me a good reason to once again remind myself that I was here for work.

The dairy was a former cowshed that had been turned into adorably rustic accommodation rooms, which ranged from a couple with bunk beds to a few with huge king-sized beds. There was a kitchenette and a large lounge and dining area in the centre, plus four bathrooms spaced throughout, and it could accommodate up to twenty guests.

"I can't believe you're going to let us stay here!" I gushed, looking around the rooms with genuine excitement.

"You'll have to ask everyone to give us five-star reviews," Lucas said with a grin.

"That I can definitely organise. Has there really been nobody staying here yet?"

"Nope. It's still not quite finished—Sadie wants to get the porch painted and some landscaping done before we have anyone booking it. Your group will be the trial run, so you'll have to let her know if anything is missing or anything needs changing."

I nodded. "I'll tell everyone to report back."

I crossed to the windows in the central living area and looked out at the gorgeous view. The dairy was built away from the winery and the cellar door, with its own driveway branching off the main one. From the window, I could see out over two of the blocks of grapevines, their leaves preparing for the autumn fall.

"So, how long do you think you'll stay working here?" I asked Lucas, turning to find him watching me.

He crossed to the window as well, standing close enough for me to be able to smell that pine-and-sandalwood scent on him again, and I quickly turned to face the window.

"Just until my uncle gets back, so another month maybe."

"And then?" I asked. "What do you think you'll do after that?"

His hand came up to rub the back of his neck, a habit I was quickly recognising to indicate his stress or uncertainty about something.

"Honestly? I think I'm still working that out. I'll go back to Sydney, get back into things with my old clients. But since the bar …" He trailed off, shrugging.

"I loved your bar. You were definitely the best bartender in town, though don't tell Kalina I told you that. Would you open another one? Maybe a permanent one?"

He shook his head. "It was too much. There were some things I really enjoyed, like talking to customers who were actually interested in what they were drinking—"

"Like me?" I asked with a cheeky grin.

He looked at me sideways, a smile playing around his lips. "It was always a highlight when you came in."

That sent a ridiculous warm glow through me, and I nudged his shoulder with my own. But I didn't pull away afterwards and neither did he. We kept speaking, our shoulders and arms pressed up against each other, both of our gazes fixed firmly out the window like we couldn't see what was happening. I knew it was wrong, standing so close to him like that. But I couldn't seem to pull away.

"But the bar life is not for you?" I asked softly, the humour gone.

"I don't think so. I …"

Again he paused, and I waited for him to continue.

"I'm thinking of studying viticulture," he finally said. "Maybe running my own vineyard one day."

"That sounds awesome," I said, trying to ignore how close together we were.

"Yeah." He frowned, seeming almost surprised himself. "That's the first time I've actually said it out loud. It's something that's been at the back of my mind for a while, I guess."

"You should do it. I can imagine you running your own winery. Plus, Sadie thinks you'd make a great winemaker."

"Does she?" He glanced sceptically at me.

"Yeah. She told me just before."

Lucas laughed softly. "This place reminds her of the winery she used to work at, where she met George, apparently. The view out of this window is just like the one they had from their housing quarters across the vineyard."

"They lived together?"

"With about ten other workers, yeah. They were all internationals doing study placements at the time. Sadie and George were the only two Aussies, and they didn't get along at first. Hated each other, so Sadie says."

"No way! How'd they end up together, then?"

"They used to play pranks on each other. Can't remember the specifics, things in each other's beds at night and that sort of thing. But then one day, Sadie went too far with a prank and everything got a bit out of hand. George came close to walking out on the job, but then Sadie gathered up hundreds of these yellow flowers that grew on the property and placed them on the grass outside his window, spelling out something corny like, 'I'm mean because I like you'. Took her half the night to do it, and she was terrified they'd blow away. But when George saw it in the morning, he must have forgiven her and then they were together."

"Aww! That's adorable! What a way to win someone over."

"Yeah." Lucas was grinning wistfully, as if he could see the flowers himself. "There's nothing like a big romantic gesture to show someone how you feel."

"I take it you're in favour of the big romantic gesture, then?"

He shot me a cheeky look. "Certainly. Sometimes it's the only way to go."

I rolled my eyes, nudging him with my shoulder again.

"So, how about you?" he asked. "What's next after this locations job?"

My smile faded at that. "I don't know," I said honestly. "I thought ..."

"Yes?"

I laughed softly, shaking my head. "I don't know what I thought. That this job would lead into a whole new career? I think I was deluded."

"Can it still not?"

I sighed. "Maybe, I guess. I think I was hoping that it would just feel right and natural and I'd just straightaway think, yes, this is what I'm meant to be doing with my life! But," I shrugged again, "I just don't know. I'm not sure I'm really getting that feeling of rightness."

"You'll work it out," Lucas said. "I think sometimes we have to remind ourselves that you don't need to only have *one* career during your life. You can change and try different things as many times as you want. Of course, you'll probably never be rich that way," he added with a laugh.

I gently bumped him again, our arms rubbing against each other. "Who needs lots of money, anyway? As long as you're happy, that's all that matters."

Lucas didn't reply, and after a moment I looked up at him. He was staring out at the vines, his brows drawn together in thought. But then he seemed to shake himself.

"You should see this place at sunset," he said, stepping away. "You weren't planning to drive back to Sydney again this afternoon, were you? You should stay here tonight. There is another guest bedroom up at the main house."

I watched him as he moved through the room, my eyebrows raised. "You want me to stay the night?"

"If you want to." He stopped moving and turned to face me, meeting my eyes from the other side of the room. "That way you can try all the wines here as well and not have to worry about driving."

I blinked, my thoughts suddenly going into overdrive. Lucas wanted me to stay? But in what capacity? We were just friends, right? We could only be friends. He was with Holly!

There couldn't be more to the invitation besides just friendship. Maybe he was keen to become better friends with me and nothing else.

Except ... what had happened in the winery office had felt like so much more. And just now, standing with our arms touching. Was that what *friends* would do?

Could I stay the night in the same house as Lucas without anything happening between us? Or would that be like playing with fire? If I spent the evening here, I wasn't sure I could trust myself to stay in my own bed. And would Lucas stay in his?

But that was silly. He couldn't possibly be thinking that. He had a girlfriend, for God's sake!

I should say no. Absolutely. Just go, get in my car and drive back to Sydney right now. It's what I'd been planning to do.

Except ...

"Okay," I said, a smile, uncontrolled, slipping across my lips. "That sounds like fun."

For a moment we stared at each other, and I wondered what he was thinking. If his thoughts about tonight were going into overdrive like mine were.

"Good. Shall we get lunch first?" He nodded towards the door. "I'll show you around town and we can grab some stuff for tonight— Sadie will love it if we cook."

"Okay," I said, excitement building and that smile refusing to leave my face as I followed Lucas back out of the dairy.

I had no idea what I was doing. But there was this incredible feeling of warmth blossoming in my chest, that very feeling of *rightness* that I'd just told Lucas I didn't feel with my job. *This* was where I was meant to be. Here, with him.

I could just imagine how the afternoon would play out. We'd go into town together and he'd show me around, gently pushing each other and laughing as we strolled beneath the trees. We'd stop for lunch at some gorgeous cafe that specialised in local produce, then we'd go buy the most amazing farm-fresh ingredients ready to cook tonight. We'd return to Middlebrook and I could help man the cellar door in the afternoon, serving customers and letting Lucas tease me about how little I knew about wine. The evening would begin with drinks in that gorgeous courtyard, watching the sun set over the hills. Then we'd be in the kitchen together, music playing, Sadie happily watching as we went about cooking dinner for us all. And then we'd stay up late, sitting on the couches around the fire, sharing a bottle of wine. Sadie would retire early and Lucas and I would stay up late, just talking. Neither of us would want to go to bed because neither of us would want the night to end …

I was so caught up in my imaginings that I barely noticed when Lucas suddenly stopped dead. We were almost back at the cellar door, and a red Hyundai was just pulling into the carpark. Before I had time to turn and see what was wrong with Lucas, I clocked the girl stepping out of the car.

Holly.

"Hey, babe!" she called, a huge perfect-white-teeth smile aimed at Lucas. And then she noticed me and her smile slipped. "Laura? What are you doing here?"

I watched as her eyes dropped to take in the shirt I was wearing and saw her face transform with confusion.

"I was just leaving," I quickly said, noticing that Lucas's face had closed down again, that same unreadable expression there that I'd seen earlier.

I forced a smile. "Just here getting location photos," I added. "For the film I'm working on—we're planning to do some filming here." I held up my phone, like I was presenting evidence to a judge. "But, erm, I'd better get going now."

"Holly," Lucas finally said, his voice sounding oddly flat. "What are you doing here?"

"Surprising you, obviously!" she said with a laugh, moving around to pop open the boot of her car. "I took today off work and thought I'd come up and spend the weekend here. We can go to that awesome new restaurant you were telling me about for dinner tonight! Won't that be great?"

I stared mutely as Holly pulled two large weekender bags out of her car boot. And suddenly, I felt a bit ill.

"Laura—" Lucas started to say, but I waved him off.

"Don't worry about it. I should really get back to Sydney, anyway. I've got heaps on tomorrow. You enjoy your evening, okay?"

And with that, I strode quickly back to my own car, my eyes feeling hot and my throat tight.

"What's going on?" I heard Holly asking, before I slammed the driver's door closed, encasing me inside.

As fast as possible, I started the car, threw it into gear, and within

154

moments I was driving away, forcing a cheery smile and a wave towards Holly and Lucas, before navigating back to the main road.

I made it almost all the way through town before I had to pull over and let the tears flow.

18

S aturday bloomed grey and flat, and I stayed in bed until midday. A thunderstorm had ripped across the Sydney sky last night, and I'd been alone at the apartment, my thoughts constantly replaying my half-day with Lucas. Thinking about him touching my bare skin as he patched the cut on my back. About our arms pressed together while we talked about our lives.

My eyes drifted to his white shirt, now lying in a heap in the corner of my bedroom. I'd spent a ridiculous amount of time with it pressed to my face last night, smelling it. But it was far safer to leave the thing in the corner, where I'd flung it once I'd become totally disgusted with myself.

I was just contemplating if I could stay in bed all day when my phone rang, my sister's profile picture lighting up the screen.

"Hey," I answered, trying to sound awake.

"Laura, are you at home?" Elle asked, her voice urgent.

"Er, yes. Why?"

"I need to come around. With Marrika. It's—" There were some muffled thumping noises, and I definitely heard someone saying "Oww!" quite plaintively. "What's your address? You're near the Corso, right?"

"Sort of. Elle, what's going on?"

"I'll," more muffled sounds, "explain when we get there. Text me your address."

Before she hung up, I heard Elle saying, a distance away from the phone, "Come on, Mare! You need to get up!" And then the bleep of the call ending.

Feeling much more awake and slightly alarmed now, I texted Elle my address then jumped out of bed.

I managed a quick, three-minute shower, and had just finished dressing in jeans, t-shirt and a hoodie when the apartment door buzzed.

Throwing it open, I was presented with two contestants from *The Bachelor*, drunk after a Rose ceremony gone wrong. At least, that was how Elle and Marrika looked. They were both dressed like they'd been out partying the night before, in tiny skin-tight dresses with stiletto heels carried in their hands along with their tiny clutch bags. Elle appeared to be holding Marrika upright, and she didn't look too happy about it.

"Aren't you guys cold?" was the first thing I said, demonstrating my advanced age to the youngsters.

Elle just barged her way inside, made a beeline for the couch and dumped Marrika onto it. Then she stood upright, rolled her shoulders and looked around my apartment.

"Well, this is nice!" she said, like I'd just invited her over for a cup of tea.

Thinking of tea, or rather coffee, which was likely what the two girls needed, I went and flicked on the kettle.

"Well, it's about time you came to visit," I said, turning to face Elle and crossing my arms. "And as lovely as this is, *what* is going on?"

Elle huffed one of the most dramatic sighs I'd ever heard then dropped into a beanbag, sprawling out on it like she wasn't wearing a mini-dress and wasn't now giving me a view of her underwear.

"Marrika is having a crisis, that's what's going on!"

"So I can see."

I decided Marrika could probably do with a huge glass of water, so I fetched one and moved over to the couch. She wasn't unconscious, she was just staring up at the ceiling like her soul had left her body. Looking at the black tear-stained lines of mascara down her face, I wondered if maybe it had.

"Here," I said kindly, handing her the glass.

She took it absently, and showed a high level of coordination by drinking half of it while still lying horizontal.

"How about a tea or coffee? And have you guys eaten anything? Do you want some toast?"

"Mare should definitely eat something," Elle said, looking like she was about to fall asleep in the beanbag. "After all that bourbon she drank."

I eyed Marrika again. "Are you going to throw up?" I asked her.

She moved her head slowly left to right.

"Do you want some toast? With peanut butter? Or jam? Or both?"

For a long time, she didn't move. Then she nodded minutely.

"Okay. I'll get that. You guys just hold tight."

I set about making toast for both Marrika and Elle, and three large strong coffees, all the while glancing at the two party girls who were now prostrate in my living room. I had no idea where Kalina or Ben were, but I was pretty sure I'd heard them both leaving the apartment at different times this morning while I'd still been in bed.

I brought the toast and coffee over to them, then sat on the other couch with my own coffee.

Marrika managed to slowly sit up, looking a bit like a zombie, and bit into her toast. She looked so forlorn, and so much like she was barely tasting what she was eating, and immediately I knew exactly what was wrong with her and how she felt.

It was how I probably looked when Jack broke my heart.

Elle sat up in her beanbag with an exaggerated groan, like she'd just been asked to mop an entire basketball stadium.

"Soooo," I said, drawing out the word. "Who is he?"

Clearly realising that her friend wouldn't be forthcoming with the answers, Elle took the lead.

"Marrika's been dating a guy who's a total fuckface."

"A fuckface," Marrika echoed feebly, her voice sounding as pitiful as a kitten who'd spilt its milk.

"We were out in Darlinghurst last night and she *saw* him, out with this other chick."

I looked at Marrika. "Were you meant to be exclusive?"

"Yes!" she said, with more energy than I'd seen thus far. "We've been together for *ages*."

"Three months," Elle added, in a way that implied this was a very great length of time indeed. "They even went away together for a weekend."

"It's that stupid bitch from psych class," Marrika said, her voice now venomous. "She was always flirting with him, even when she *knew* he was mine."

I waited for Elle to provide some clarification.

"Mare's doing her last semester of uni. The guy's her tute teacher."

"Marrika!" I couldn't help scolding her. "You're dating your teacher?"

"He's a student, too. And he's not *old* or anything."

"He's kind of old," Ella added in a low voice to me.

"Yeah, but I thought I was the only student he was seeing. Then I saw him out with the stupid bird girl and now I hate him."

"The bird girl?" I repeated, eyeing Elle again.

"She wears bird earrings," Elle explained.

"They're stupid," Marrika said.

"I thought you liked them?" Elle shot her a surprised look.

"Not anymore."

I heard a key jangling in the front door, and then Ben was entering the apartment, looking far fresher than I felt in damp board shorts, sandy feet and carrying a surfboard under his arm.

"Oh, hey," he said, clocking the three of us sprawled in the lounge room.

"Ben, this is Elle, my sister. And her friend, Marrika." I gestured at them in turn.

Elle didn't bother shifting from her position in the beanbag, which meant she was now casually flashing Ben her underwear. And Marrika, who had given up on her toast and lain back down on the couch, just limply lifted a hand in the air to wave at him.

"Hi," Ben said. "It's nice to meet you." I watched his gaze take in Elle, then awkwardly dart away. He hung his surfboard up on the hooks on the wall, and I was pretty sure I could see a red flush creeping up his face.

"So, *you're* the roommate," Elle said, with the same level of interest she'd show a lion that had just presented itself in front of her. "I wish I could say I know all about you, but Laura hasn't told me anything."

"Ha-ha," I said to her, deadpan.

"Er, yeah. Hi," Ben said again, looking like a rabbit caught in headlights. He didn't say much else, he just shuffled off into the bathroom, his face redder than I'd ever seen it.

"He's cute!" Elle said loud enough that Ben probably would have heard her, turning to me with a grin.

"He's off limits to you, Missy." I glared at her. "*My* roommate and all."

Elle just grinned. "Anyway. Where were we?"

"Marrika was telling us about bird girl who stole her teacher."

"I hate her," Marrika whispered, with all the cold calculation of a serial killer.

I sighed. "Look, girls. Unfortunately, a lot of guys are fuckfaces. And girls can be, too. All you can do is control your own actions, and make sure you're *never* the one stealing someone else's boyfriend. You need to treat others the way you, yourself, want to be treated."

"And just don't get involved with anyone in the first place," Elle added. "Guys are for sex or friendship, never both."

I frowned at my sister, wondering at the similarity between her and Kalina. It was odd, hearing Elle spout almost exactly the same life philosophy as my roommate, even though the two of them had never met.

Elle and Marrika stayed for another half an hour, before Elle decided it was time they headed home. They *had* pulled an all-nighter, drinking in the city until five this morning. But instead of going straight home, they'd caught the ferry to Manly and had been lying on the beach all morning.

Once I'd helped Elle get Marrika into the Uber and waved them off, I returned upstairs to ponder my own advice and the hypocrisy of it. I'd just advised them to never steal someone else's boyfriend, yet that was exactly what I'd been planning to do yesterday. If Holly hadn't turned up, I was one hundred percent sure I would have done something unforgivable with Lucas. I would have become the other woman. The home wrecker. The bitch.

I would have been no better than bird girl.

19

I couldn't stop thinking about what might have happened with Lucas in Mudgee. How I might have stayed the night and we might have stayed up late drinking together. How if Holly hadn't turned up then anything could have happened. And then I'd imagine Holly as miserable as Marrika, and I'd feel horrified. How could I even be contemplating doing anything with Lucas? He was Holly's boyfriend. And I never, ever wanted to become a home wrecker.

My thoughts were so preoccupied that I was barely paying attention to what Kalina was saying when we went out for a late breakfast on Sunday morning.

"—see either of you anymore."

I snapped back to attention and watched Kalina adjusting her wide-brimmed hat and sunglasses like she was a movie star.

We were sitting at a half-hidden cafe that was out the back of a street-clothing shop in Manly. Rollers Bakehouse was a fairly local secret, situated, as it was, in a dingy laneway. The main thing to give it away was the near-constant line of die-hard regulars who flocked there weekly for their mouth-watering range of creative croissants baked fresh each morning.

"What was that?" I asked, trying to act like I had bad hearing rather than that I hadn't been listening.

"I said I barely see you or Ben anymore. It's starting to get weird."

I put my coffee cup down and readjusted my perch on the tiny stool. "Well, we're all working full-time now. Plus, *you're* the one who's never around in the evenings."

"Yeah, but you guys aren't around in the mornings. I miss Ben's breakfasts."

I laughed at that. "Well, if you also want to start getting up at four-thirty you can see us in the mornings. Not that either of us bothers with breakfast that early."

Kalina rolled her eyes. "Yeah, right. That is not happening."

"I do imagine you need your beauty sleep. What with all the night activities you and Owen must be getting up to."

Kalina sighed happily, treating my words earnestly. "You know, I've never been so happy to be monogamous. Seriously, Laur, Owen and I in bed together is legit amazing. Although, I probably shouldn't say 'in bed' since that wouldn't be all that accurate."

"Oh my God, if you've had sex on the kitchen bench at the flat, I don't want to know. Sorry," I added to the old man who'd just sat down and was now gaping at us from the next table.

"We've had sex everywhere, Laura. *Every*where."

"Ew. You'd better be joking right now. Or at least be cracking out the disinfectant wipes afterwards. Sorry," I added again, as the man hoisted himself back up with a grumble and moved to a different table.

Kalina just smiled, a definite non-response, and took a huge bite of her pistachio, almond and hommus croissant. Once she was done chewing the thing like *it* was the next best thing to Owen sex, she lifted her coffee cup and surveyed me over the top of it.

"Truly, though," she said. "I think I've become boring."

I snorted, keeping my eyes on my own eggplant, oregano and feta croissant as I took a hugely satisfying bite of it. When I finally looked back up at Kalina, she had a worried frown on her face.

"Oh, you're serious. Why do you think that?"

"Because I work every day and hang out with my boyfriend every night. There's no more ... mystery."

"Oh, the travesty of having a healthy, functioning life."

Kalina threw a pistachio at me.

"What are you so worried about?" I asked her. "You make it sound like things are great with Owen."

"Oh, they are. And work is great, too. I guess it's just weird that everything is, well, great."

I grinned at her. "Sounds like somebody thrives on drama."

"I do not! But I mean, a *bit* of excitement wouldn't go astray."

I was too busy devouring my croissant to respond, and across the table Kalina surveyed me over her coffee cup again, this time with the look of an interviewer about to nail their prey.

"So," she said. "How is *your* sex life going?"

"It's not going anywhere," I answered flatly. "I'm too busy focusing on my career at present."

Based on the horrified expression that crossed Kalina's face, you'd think I'd announced that I planned to give up soft cheeses.

"You can have a career *and* sex at the same time," Kalina said. "Isn't that one of the best things about your new industry? You'll always be working with new people, which means a near-constant rotation of different people to sleep with."

I snorted. "That does seem to be the norm, I think. Oh, so get this." I leaned in, conspiratorially dropping my voice. "The other day, I walked in on Phoebe Winters getting it off with the makeup artist in one of the dressing rooms!"

"No! Really? I didn't know she was gay."

"Me either. But there they were."

"Wasn't she dating the actor she did *The Fronds* with?"

I shrugged. "Maybe. You know, I don't think anyone's really just gay anymore. It's all about being pansexual."

Kalina's eyes widened. "Is this like what we were talking about last week? You wanting to get it off with a girl?"

"Shh!" I hissed. "I don't … I mean … I don't know. I'm still thinking about it."

Kalina snorted. "Well, alcohol helps. If you want to get experimenting, then I'd suggest getting drunk first."

"That sounds like a terrible plan. What am I going to do, get drunk on set then crack on to Phoebe Winters myself? I think I'd be instantly fired."

Kalina laughed. "You're thinking too much about it, Laur. You just need to relax and have fun. Like when we were in Byron Bay and you slept with Truth."

"Yeah, but that was like a holiday fling! And I didn't have to work with him."

Kalina stared at me for a moment, tipping her head sideways like she was attempting a magic-eye puzzle. "Maybe there's another reason you're not banging anyone else right now. A very Lucas-sized reason."

"As if!" I said too loudly, glancing around like I thought we might be overheard by someone who cared. "That is *not* the reason at all."

"Really? Because Holly's got her knickers in a knot thinking that there's something going on between the two of you."

"Has she?" I felt irrationally pleased by this before reminding myself that that was not a good thing.

"Mm-hmm. But, Laura, you need to be *careful.*"

"Why? There's nothing going on between Lucas and me."

Liar, an inner voice said. I wondered if my cheeks were turning red.

"Exactly. You're so keen to make sure nothing is going on between the two of you, but meanwhile Holly is digging her claws in. She *really* wants things to work with Lucas. Like, a lot. Even before she started grilling me about you, she was saying how she's thinking of moving in with him."

Well, that felt like a punch to the guts.

"But they've only just got back together! Surely, Lucas wouldn't move that fast."

"I don't know if he's on board with the plan, but Holly certainly is. And she can be persuasive. I've seen her at work. When that girl wants something, it's a little scary."

"There's nothing I can do about it," I said, starting to get rather hot and uncomfortable. "Lucas has chosen her."

"But that's the point, Laura. You never gave him a choice. As far as he knows, you still don't want to be anything but friends with him. How can he choose you if he doesn't even know you want him?"

"I'm respecting his relationship choices! If he didn't want to be with Holly, he'd break up with her. End of story."

Kalina narrowed her eyes at me. "This is different, Laura. You've spent so much time pulling away from him, how's he supposed to know you're suddenly interested? You need to tell him before it's too late."

"Can we stop talking about this?" I snapped. "I don't want Lucas, I want to experiment with being pansexual, okay?"

Kalina pursed her lips together. For a second, I thought she'd press the point, but then she just nodded. "Okay. If that's what you want."

"It is," I said, and defiantly took a huge mouthful of croissant.

Facebook Alert
Friend request: Holly Kovarnic wants to be your friend.
> Accept?

New Email
Subject: Call times for tomorrow
Trigger filming day 16 (Monday).
Location: Mosman house (see address below)
Call times for all crew and actors as per below:

Locations: 4.45 am

Hair and makeup: 4.45 am

Wardrobe: 5.15 am

[message clipped]

Amazon Shopping
Recommendations based on your recent browsing history:
Out of the Closet! My Queer Awakening: A Memoir
> Add to cart?

20

I threw myself back into work the next week with as much enthusiasm as I could. I was even getting quite good at convincing myself that when my alarm went off—usually around four in the morning—that *yes, I really wanted to get up that early!*

Once I arrived on set, it was easy to distract myself with work tasks and chatting with crew members. And even though the days dragged and a standard work day was between ten to twelve hours long, I still found it fascinating whenever I got to watch the filming in action.

Phoebe and Charlotte both acted as if I hadn't walked in on them making out last week, which impressed me and also made me wonder if maybe that wasn't a big deal at all. Like, yeah, it was totally normal for crew members to hook up with each other while on set, without any negative consequences. Maybe it *was* normal. Maybe I was the weird one because I wasn't hooking up with anyone else here.

That being said, things were becoming rather flirty between Rory and me. Not that we ever seemed to have much time to chat, but on more than one occasion I'd caught him watching me, and when our eyes met he'd give me a wink or a cheeky smile. And I admit that I'd also winked at him on more than one occasion, and I just might have given him a lingering once-over, making it very clear that I was appreciating what I saw.

And it had nothing to do with what Kalina had said to me on the weekend, or the fact that I was trying to push thoughts of Lucas out of my mind. I was single. Rory, I knew, was single. And while he might not be playing into my pansexual considerations, still it didn't hurt to have a little fantasy on the side, did it?

I'd spoken with Amity and Will on Monday and shown them all the photos and footage I'd taken at Middlebrook. They'd both seemed delighted with them, and had agreed that it would be the perfect place to shoot those particular scenes. I then got to play real location manager again as I coordinated our shoot dates there with Sadie (and I got her to email the contracts back to me, which I realised I'd left Middlebrook without). I spent a few hours uploading the Middlebrook photos into StudioBinder, setting out each one alongside its respective scene, and also sorted out the accommodation arrangements and put together travel directions for the crew.

Once my locations work was finished, I found myself absently watching the filming, idly checking the time and wondering if the shoot today would run over, when Celeste pulled me aside.

"Laura, can I have a word with you?" she said, drawing me away from the filming and into the kitchen.

"What's your availability like over the next six months?" she asked me once we were out of earshot.

I blinked at her, surprised by her question. "Well, it's wide open, currently," I answered honestly. "I haven't got anything planned after this."

Celeste's face lit up. "Excellent! In that case, I have a job offer for you."

"Really?" Oh my God, this was it! Career location managing, here I come!

"Of course! You know, Amity told me about the winery you've sourced for this project, and how impressed she was by your initiative. Sounds like quite the coup, getting it at such a good price, as well!"

"Oh, it's really Ben we should thank, since it's his family connection …"

Celeste held up her hand. "Not to worry about that. We all call in as many personal favours as possible in this job. It's just what you have to do, and you're doing it, which is great."

"Thanks. So, what's this new job offer?"

"It's a new series we're filming out in the Kimberley desert. A much bigger production, and you'd be the junior location manager onsite. It'll be long, hot days and a lot of sand, but it's going to make for great TV. Four- maybe five-month contract out there, starting in June. How does that sound?"

For a moment, I had no idea how to respond. My first thought was, *Which one is the Kimberley?* I desperately wanted to look on Google Maps, but was too embarrassed to admit that I couldn't recall where exactly in Australia that was. And the rest of my thoughts were oscillating between excitement and scepticism. Another film job—yay! In the desert—not so yay. A second film production—new career, here I come! But more possible delays and dubious start times from a rather vague producer—possibly not so good.

"That sounds interesting," I eventually said. "I'd need some more information, though. When do you need to know by?"

"Sure, sure!" Celeste waved her hand. "No need to answer right now. I'll have Stephen, my production manager, email you some details. Just don't take too long thinking about it, will you?"

"No, of course. I'll let you know as soon as I can."

Despite Celeste's promise to send me more information, it was Friday afternoon before I discovered an email from one Stephen White on my phone, with contract details about the next production.

It was an outback thriller that would be made into an eight-part TV series, with filming taking twelve weeks in the desert. The pay, I was disappointed to see, would be the same as what I was getting now, but I supposed I was still junior enough to warrant that. There were also flights and share accommodation included, though if I wanted to return to Sydney for any weekends during filming, I'd have to pay for that myself.

If I saw the job as an opportunity to jump-start my career in location managing, then it was a good one. A larger production meant meeting more people, making more contacts and hopefully rolling this job over into another one. For a while, I let myself daydream about jetting across the world to exotic locations, driving out to hidden villas in Spain or secret forests in England to find exactly the perfect location for a movie shoot. What would it be like to become a proper location scout!

And yet, part of me was hesitant to accept the job. It was one thing to work on a film while still living at my apartment in Sydney, but quite another to fly to the other side of the country and live in the desert for months. And there was this inexplicable feeling in my gut that I'd be losing something if I left Sydney, even if my rational mind couldn't identify what it was.

Perhaps because I'd spent Friday afternoon questioning Will

about all aspects of the post-production process, he invited me back to the Mosman house on Saturday, where he, Amity and Rory would be reviewing footage and making rough cuts of the scenes we'd been filming so far. I hadn't realised before, but Amity, Will and Rory all were living currently at the house, since Rory was usually based in Melbourne, and Amity and Will found it easier to simply live onsite of their main film location. Plus, they were obviously staying for free, since the house was Celeste's—though not her primary residence, I'd learned.

"See here, this controls the exposure," Rory told me, indicating the dial on the old camera he was letting me play with.

"And you can use the gimbal with this, as well?" I asked, my eyes skimming over the vast amount of camera gear that was covering the dining-room table.

"Yeah, it still works with this one. Although, you wouldn't want the camera in manual mode if you're using that. I'll show you."

We were having an enormous amount of fun, Rory and I, playing around with all the camera gear. At least, I was having an enormous amount of fun. It was entirely possible that Rory was simply entertaining me while Amity and Will went through the dailies out in the living room.

I watched as Rory clamped in and connected the camera to the gimbal, which was basically a frame that a cameraman could hold that would enable you to film on the move without having jerky footage. Once it was ready, he let me have a go at it, and I moved slowly with the camera through the house and out into the front garden.

"It's so smooth! I love it. Although, it's quite heavy." I shot Rory a look over my shoulder, where he'd joined me on the front porch.

"Yeah. Gives you an arm workout, that's for sure."

My eyes dropped involuntarily to the curve of his biceps beneath his t-shirt, and when I looked up at him again, he was watching me with a crooked smile on his face.

"So, you're from Melbourne, I hear?" I sat down on the carved wooden bench on the porch, carefully placing the camera and gimbal down next to me. The afternoon was warm and still, and autumn leaves made a rainbow scattering across the front garden. Rory moved to sit on the porch railing opposite me, his back in the sun.

"Yep, not that I'm there all that often. In all honesty, I haven't spent more than a couple of months there in the last two years."

"Wow, that little? Is that just because you're always travelling for work?"

"Yeah. After this job, I'm heading out to the desert for another project with Celeste."

"Get out! Is that the *Burn Me* show? Celeste's offered me a job on that, as well."

"Nice! It should be a good production. And it'll be nice to see more of you."

I raised an eyebrow. "Do you want to see more of me?"

He grinned. "I've certainly enjoyed our interactions so far."

Before I could respond, our conversation was drowned out by the ridiculously loud roar of a car engine hooning down the street. We both turned to watch as the bright-yellow Mustang with the black racing stripe down the bonnet zoomed past, crackles and pops and bangs all emanating from the engine.

"That guy!" I said, letting my disdain drip through.

"Tell me about it," Rory said. "Every single bloody weekend, he drives that thing up and down at least ten times. I think he does it purely to piss us off."

"He probably does! Do you know how many times now I've had to go over to his house and bribe him to keep his music down? I've probably given him more whisky than he can drink in his lifetime."

"Really?" Rory started laughing. "Because I've been going over there almost every weekend giving him cases of beer to try to keep him onside."

"You have? No way! So, we're just supplying him with copious amounts of free alcohol, all for being a dick."

Rory shook his head. "It still blows me away that there are people like that in the world."

"Hopefully, he'll get what's coming to him."

"Which is?"

I thought about it for a moment. "I'm not sure. But if ever karma needed to pay a visit to someone, it's that guy."

Rory nodded, and said quite seriously, "Maybe his dick will fall off."

I burst out laughing. "I thought guys didn't wish that on anyone?"

He shrugged. "For that guy, I'd make an exception."

We grinned at each other.

"At least we haven't had to jump his fence again," I said, remembering my second day on the job.

"I thought for sure he was going to spot us."

I laughed at the memory. "Part of me can't believe I actually made it over the fence!"

"You climbed with ease."

"Only with your help."

He was still smiling at me, and I loved the way it reached up into his eyes.

"So, have you got anything on tonight? Or do you want to stay and watch a movie with us?" Rory asked, his lips curving invitingly.

"It'll be some art-house thing that Amity's chosen, and I can't say those two won't talk the whole way through it. But we'll get pizzas and drink wine, as well."

I returned his smile, delighted to be invited to spend time with the gang. "Sure. That sounds like fun."

"Come on, then." Rory jumped down off the railing and held his hand out to me. "Let's go inside and get a drink."

I placed my hand in his and let him pull me up off the bench. For a second, we stood there, a replication of when he'd pulled me up off the grass all those weeks ago. But since then, every flirty wink and lingering look stood between that space and now, and the way we looked at each other was so charged with anticipation that I *knew* movie night was suddenly loaded with potential.

The movie was a Portuguese film that I'd never heard of. And even though it wasn't really my thing, I loved how Amity, Will and Rory discussed the film while it was playing, pointing out different camera angles, lighting techniques or different special effects. At one point, Will apologised to me for them ruining the film, but I just laughed and told him not to worry as I'd already been forewarned. In truth, I actually loved listening to them. I felt like we were at film school together, and it made me wonder about what other opportunities there could be for me in the film business. Maybe location scouting wasn't the only thing I'd enjoy. Maybe after the desert project, I could enrol myself at film school, really turn this into a whole other career.

By the time the film ended, I was feeling pretty chilled out. Probably aided by the three bottles of wine we'd all shared. Plus, Rory was next to me on the couch. Although we weren't physically touching, I was hyper-aware of every movement he made, every shift of his body next to mine. On the couch beside us, Amity and Will were having no such prudishness. Will had his arm draped over the back of the couch, and Amity was snuggled into his side, as if this was the most normal thing in the world for two friends to do.

"So, Laura," Rory began softly while Amity and Will were engaged in their own conversation. "Have we turned you off working in the film industry yet?"

I laughed, but twisted to face him on the couch, pulling up one leg so I was sitting sideways and could keep Amity and Will out of my peripheral vision.

"No way! I've loved today, getting to watch you guys work on edits and learning about the cameras. You know, I used to make these home movies with my sister when I was younger, and I loved the editing part best. I'd get Elle to lip-sync to a song, then edit together a music video for it."

"I used to make movies as well with my cousins, though ours were usually short horror films. They were the ones who had all the film gear, so every Christmas when we'd go visit them we'd make movies together."

"And that's when you found your love of camera work?"

He laughed. "No, actually, I always insisted on being the movie star. It wasn't until high school that I realised I was kind of shit at acting, but that working behind the scenes was way more fun."

"And now you get to film movies all the time?"

"Movies and TV shows. I do the odd corporate contract when I need to."

"Ah, that's just like Ben. He said he does a lot of corporate work."

Rory shrugged. "They pay well. But the film and TV industry has really taken off lately. With all the streaming companies now funding local projects, there's lots of work going around. It's a good time to be working in the industry."

His words made me glance over at Will and Amity, who were getting very cosy on the couch. All of these people were making careers out of film and TV production, and I realised that I did genuinely feel impressed by their lifestyle.

Imagine getting to work all day on such creative projects? And being part of a team that was literally *making* something cool. Even on their weekends, feeling that drive to keep working on the project because you were just so passionate about it.

"I do love being a part of this. But surely, there's heaps of competition? I mean, it's such a cool industry, there must be so many people wanting to get involved."

Rory nodded. "It can be tough. And that is a downside—the competition. Because of that, the pay isn't great, since there's always someone willing to do the same job for cheaper."

Now I laughed. "Way to really sell it to me."

He laughed too. "Just being honest. But this is the way to get into it, working for someone like Celeste. And if she's already offered you another gig, then that's a big thing."

I chewed on my lip, thinking about it. On the one hand, it *was* a fun industry and there was a lot that I did love about the job. But could I live with that constant uncertainty of not knowing if I'd be employed next month? Of always wondering where the next job was coming from? I didn't even have any specialist film-industry skills, unlike Rory and Ben. They could get jobs almost anywhere when things were tight. But I couldn't imagine corporate companies having a great need for junior location managers.

"We're going to bed," Amity abruptly announced.

I looked around in surprise. Amity and Will were both getting up from the couch, and Amity was watching us with a mischievous grin.

"You're welcome to stay, Laura. Don't stay up too long, you two, now will you?"

And with a strangely suggestive eyebrow raise, she and Will disappeared up the stairs to the area of the house I'd never been.

I turned back to Rory with a grin. "Is she implying what I think she is?"

"I believe so. You up for it?" As he spoke, his fingers brushed along the back of my shoulder. The lightest of invitations.

I bit my lip.

"So ... Amity and Will are staying *together* tonight, right?"

"Yes. And we can also stay. If we like."

I let my eyes skim over him, taking in the delicious way his t-shirt clung to his muscular chest and felt a sudden giddy rush go through me. *Yes, please! Sex with Rory!* Luckily, I'd shaved my legs and dressed in rather nice underwear this afternoon before coming to the house, because obviously it was always wise to be prepared for any occasion. And clearly, *this* was the sort of occasion I'd had in mind.

I let a slow smile dance on my lips. "Why don't you take me upstairs, then?"

Rory matched my smile. "That I can do."

He stood up and held his hand out to me, like a gentleman. I took it and let him pull me to my feet. For a moment we stood close together, hands joined, total deja vu. I leaned forward slightly, expecting him to kiss me, but instead he squeezed my hand and then led me towards the staircase.

Up we went, then we were in a hallway. There were about six doorways leading into different rooms, most with doors ajar and darkness within. At the end of the hallway was the only closed door, light seeping out from the small gap at the bottom.

I had no idea which bedroom Rory was planning to sleep in, but we headed in the direction of the one lit-up door, which I assumed had to be Amity's bedroom. But as we passed one, then two, dark open doorways and still kept walking towards the closed door, I suddenly became confused.

And then we were outside Amity's closed door, and Rory was lifting his free hand, reaching for the door handle, and my entire body seemed to freeze.

21

"Isn't this ...?" I quickly gave the hand I was holding a swift tug backwards before he walked in on them. Christ, maybe he didn't realise this was Amity's room? Or for some reason, Amity and Will were now in the room Rory usually slept in?

He paused, his hand still hovering inches away from the door handle, and turned to me with his eyebrows raised.

"Aren't we ...?" he asked, indicating with his head the door beyond.

Aren't we what?

And then it clicked.

Oh my God ... he thought we were having a foursome. He thought this was a gang bang!

There was an awkward moment when we both just stood there staring at each other, and I felt like I could see the thoughts flying back and forth between us.

Me: *What on earth are you doing?*

Him: *Is this not what we had planned for tonight?*

Me: *It's certainly not what I had planned.*

Him: *So ... you're not up for group sex, then?*

Me: *No, I'm definitely not up for group sex. We all work together!*

Him: *So? Amity and Will are my friends and we do this stuff all the time.*

Then a thought occurred to me: was this what Amity and Will were expecting? Was that why Amity gave me that suggestive look as they left the lounge room? I mean, it didn't *feel* like a "come join us for group sex" kind of look. It felt more like an "I'm off to have sex— you should too, in your own bedroom, with your own guy, away from us" kind of look.

Oh God. I knew they were all pansexual, though, didn't I? Was I meant to have expected this?

The silence stretched on as Rory and I stared at each other—me in shock, him looking slightly confused. Then he seemed to make a decision and moved away from the door, back towards me.

"Sorry," he said softly, standing close. "I wasn't sure ..." He left it hanging.

"That's okay." I quickly backed away from the door. "I just ... wasn't expecting that. Can we ...?" I cast my eyes at the open doorways, wishing I knew which room was Rory's. Wordlessly, he ushered me into one a few doors away from Amity's room, and we closed the door behind us. Rory flicked on a lamp.

I breathed a sigh of relief and eyed him warily.

"Is this better?" he asked with a cheeky grin, but I was feeling a bit rattled and wasn't sure how to react.

I mean, who would just assume that we were having a foursome? Shouldn't there have been a discussion? Some ground rules? Maybe some written consent forms?

But Christ, maybe that was how it always worked? Maybe I was the weird one for not just going with the flow. If only I'd realised, I could have taken Kalina's advice and drunk a whole lot more.

"Are you okay?" Rory's smile slipped away. "Sorry, again. Look, we don't have to do anything if you don't want to—"

"I want to," I said quickly, almost aggressively. I mean, I wasn't going to let something like a little foursome confusion ruin my night, was I? How long had it been since I'd had sex with anyone? Exactly.

I just needed to block out that weird hallway encounter and we could get on with things. Taking the lead, I pounced on Rory, throwing my hands around his neck and crashing into him/kissing him a bit more forcefully than needed. He got over his surprise well enough and then we were kissing and smooshing our bodies together and awkwardly fumbling with buttons as we tried to undress each other.

But as much as I tried, I couldn't stop replaying what had happened, and I couldn't prevent my eyes from constantly straying to the door.

Were Amity and Will going to walk in? I mean, if they'd been expecting us and we failed to show in their room, would they take matters into their own hands and come join us? What the hell would I do if Rory and I were getting into the sex and then suddenly Will was standing next to the bed, fully nude?

But that was silly. Surely, Amity and Will weren't quite that forward. And Rory didn't seem to think we'd be expecting them. At least, I assumed he didn't.

Why the hell didn't these bedroom doors have locks on them?

Rory and I were properly getting into things on the bed and I tried to pull my thoughts back to the present. This was fine, I told myself. We were having couples sex tonight, not group sex. Each couple in their own room. The misunderstanding had already been cleared up.

God, at least I hoped it had been. Despite the porn I'd recently watched, I didn't think I was quite ready for a lesbian adventure.

"Can you smack me?" Rory asked huskily in my ear.

Excuse me?

I blinked myself back to the present. Up until that point, I'd been operating on auto-pilot, letting Rory take the lead, and we'd just started having some rather vanilla missionary-style sex. But maybe he wanted some hokey-pokey?

"Er ... what?" I asked.

"My butt—I want you to smack it," he purred in my ear, as if that was a totally normal sexual request.

"Right. Sure," I said, giving him a tentative little smack on his left butt cheek.

"Harder," he whispered, kissing my neck.

I whacked him again, the firm *slap* ringing out in the room, and he squirmed in delight.

"Again," he said.

Christ, how hard was he expecting me to hit him? Although I felt a bit weird, I started whacking his butt over and over again, getting into a kind of rhythm along with his thrusting. He was certainly enjoying it, but to be honest, I wasn't getting anything out of this activity. If anything, it was starting to make my palm sting.

"Can I do you from behind?" he asked, stopping suddenly.

"Yes," I quickly agreed, if only so I could stop slapping him.

We shifted around on the bed, he got going again, and I was just breathing a sigh of relief when I felt a stinging slap on *my* bum.

Whooooa. Hang on a second.

Had he seriously just slapped me? Asking to be slapped was one thing, but just going ahead and slapping someone else's butt? Wasn't that a bit rude?

His hand landed on my butt cheek again, this time harder, and I flinched in shock.

"Actually, can you not do that?" I said, freezing up a bit.

"Sorry," he said, and then his hand started stroking my bum in little soothing circular motions over the sting.

I relaxed again. That was much nicer. In fact, it was far better than missionary vanilla sex. It was like … neopolitan. Nothing too adventurous, just slightly varied.

I was relaxing and arching my back and enjoying the stroking along with the rhythm he was getting into, when I realised his hand was moving somewhat astray. I mean, it was still definitely on my butt. But not so much the cheeks anymore. His fingers were heading …

Oh dear God.

His fingers were making moves towards my butt crack.

I froze again, and maybe he interpreted that as anticipation because his fingertips were definitely moving into the chasm.

I cleared my throat loudly, coughing slightly.

"You have such a nice arse," he said, his voice all gravelly. "Have you ever had someone play with it before?" As if to clarify his question, his thumb started gliding right down my butt crack, heading straight for—

"Let me do you!" I said, launching myself forward onto my stomach, doing a great job of simultaneously uncoupling us and squeezing my butt cheeks together in a definite *now closed* manoeuvre. "Slap you, again, I mean!" I quickly added, rolling myself ungracefully over.

I was certainly not sticking a finger in *his* butt.

Without giving him much time to react, I pulled him back on top of me, and began merrily slapping away on his butt cheek like I was the drummer in a marching band.

He seemed to enjoy that, and as his breathing became more

ragged, he slowed a bit and pulled up to look at me. "Do you want me to—"

I gave him another firm whack on the bum. "This is good. You finish."

I could be like the Dalai Lama with my generosity. I had a sudden vision of myself being all zen and free-love like, saying to my lovers, "You do you."

I pulled him back down so we didn't have to make eye contact, and then found an interesting spot on the ceiling to stare at while I helped spank him over the finish line. I actually found that I rather enjoyed the aggressive slaps while he finished and I gave him a final hard slap for good measure once he'd fallen still. Perhaps there was an inner dominatrix in me, just waiting to come out.

But before I could explore that possibility, a sudden thought struck me. Was this going to make things really awkward come Monday morning at work, especially since Monday was our first day on location in Mudgee?

At least when I saw Lucas again I wouldn't have to be upset by the fact that he was currently sleeping with Holly. Because now I was sleeping with someone else, too.

22

It's okay. It's fine. There's no reason to panic.

Just because there I was, standing in the carpark of the Middlebrook Vineyard cellar door, attempting to erect a ten-foot gazebo by myself, didn't mean this would result in disaster.

Sure, the wind was not cooperating. And sure, there were some rather dangerous long poles involved that could definitely impale someone like a javelin. But I could do this. No problem. After all, it was my job.

"Need a hand?" someone called, and I heard footsteps jogging up behind me.

Well, thank fuck some nice member of the crew finally had seen my dilemma!

"Yes! Thank—" My voice tangled in my throat when I glanced over my shoulder and saw it was Lucas jogging towards me.

"Oh, er, you don't have to—" I started to say, but the wind latched onto the gazebo then and attempted to yank the whole thing out of my hands like a sail.

While I was busy yelping, Lucas grabbed the other end of it and together we managed to wrangle it back to the ground and get the anchoring stakes pinned down.

Finally, I could breathe. After what had been one of the most hectic mornings—waking up at four-thirty, driving with Ben to Mudgee, then arriving here and straightaway morphing into location-manager work mode—I suddenly found myself standing still, my mind having gone almost blank as to what I was meant to be doing next.

Can Lucas tell I had sex with someone on Saturday night?

Oh God, where had that thought come from? It didn't matter, obviously, if he could or could not tell. Not that he could. That would be weird. And besides, he'd probably been having sex with Holly on Saturday night anyway, a thought that simultaneously grossed me out and made me look him up and down, as if I could assess whether or not this was true.

"You okay?" He frowned at me.

"Fine! Just, er, got a lot of work to do."

"Do you want a hand?"

"No! I mean, no, don't worry, that's not your job, it's mine." I laughed musically. Perhaps it was maniacally. I was too wired to be sure which. "Er, don't you have things to do? Like, wine stuff?"

He shook his head. "Cellar door's closed today. I'm only here to keep an eye on this rowdy film crew who's shown up."

He grinned, clearly joking, but I just felt ridiculously flustered.

"Oh, ha-ha! We won't be rowdy."

I couldn't look at him. I just couldn't. I didn't know why.

Apparently, the universe felt it vitally important to contradict me, because in that moment Amity stepped out of her car and gave a great whoop of excitement before cupping her hands around her mouth and shouting, "Location shoot is here, bitches!"

"Is that one of the actors?" Lucas asked.

"No. That's the director."

He cast me a look that said he thought I had to be joking.

I cleared my throat. "Is Sadie here? Not that she needs to be *here* here, just, you know, wanted to see if she was around?"

"She's in the main house having breakfast with Holly," Lucas replied.

I did look at him then, hoping he was kidding. He was not.

"Oh! Right. Holly's here, too?"

"Yeah," Lucas said, a slight frown on his face. "Is that alright? She's taken the week off work, and well, wanted to come up here, I guess."

"*Great!*" Oh, I was extra cheery now. "How great for her. And for you, how great, spending the week together."

Lucas was looking at me like I was deranged. "Yeah. It's great."

"Cool. Well, I'd better go and ..." I nodded my head towards the three cars that were just pulling into the car park, and before Lucas could say anything else, I made a great show of ushering the cars into some suitable parking spaces. I was so busy trying to block Lucas out, hoping he'd go back up to the house and not keep watching me, that I barely even noticed that one of the cars was now ejecting Rory from the driver's seat.

"Laura, hey!" he called to me, jarring my already struggling brain.

Smack my butt.

Shit. Best not think about that.

"Hi there! How are you?" I called brightly, trotting over to him like we were just regular old colleagues and hadn't had sex two days ago.

"I'm good." He emphasised his statement by lifting his arms and rolling his shoulders, causing his t-shirt to ride up and reveal a delicious swathe of male abdominal muscles. Hmm. Had the sex been good or bad? Suddenly, I couldn't remember. "Glad to be out of the car, finally!"

"Yeah." I snapped my eyes up to his face. "It's a bit of a drive!"

He grinned. "Guess what? I've got something for you."

"You do?"

Oh crap. What had he got me? If it was flowers I'd just have to pretend not to see them and run away. But no, guys didn't give girls flowers after having sex with them! That would be seriously old school.

Although if chocolates emerged, I'd probably have to take them and *then* run away. I mean, there was never a bad time to receive chocolates, was there?

"Here."

It wasn't flowers or chocolates. He was holding out a black, slightly battered-looking camera bag. "I was going to sell this on eBay, but thought you might want it. Play around with it for a few days, see if you like it and let me know."

I took the bag from him, opening it up to reveal a Canon camera that seemed way more high-tech than anything I'd used before.

"This is great! Does it do video, as well?"

"Yeah, it does. I shot some of my first movies on that thing."

I smiled with delight. "How much are you selling it for?"

Rory returned my smile. "Well for you … Hmm, a hundred bucks?"

I shoved him playfully on the shoulder. "Get out! That's way too cheap."

He shrugged. "I just like knowing it's going to a good home. But test it out first. You might not like it."

"Oh, I'm pretty sure that I will."

"Yeah. It's a good camera."

I had the biggest wash of warmth through my chest and I couldn't help throwing my arms around Rory in a big hug. He wrapped his arms around me, pulling me in, and if we hadn't already had sex then that hug would have been definitely inappropriate for colleagues. I mean, you wouldn't do a full-body mash with hips touching with someone you weren't having sex with, would you?

I pulled away. "I'm so excited! I can't wait to start playing with this."

"Yeah. And this is a great spot to be practising."

Rory looked around, as if taking in the grapevines and the gorgeous cellar door for the first time. I followed his gaze, that big smile still on my face.

It was only when I saw Lucas, in the process of turning and walking away, that my smile faded. Maybe it was my imagination or maybe it was the particular hunch of his shoulders, but I had the distinct impression that he'd been watching my interaction with Rory.

How he would have interpreted that hug sent a wash of unease through me.

The rest of Monday passed in a blur. I spent all morning running around helping set up equipment, showing people where to go, assigning bedrooms and running into town for last-minute essentials. Filming kicked off in the afternoon, with a sunset scene up on the hill, then we broke for a quick dinner back at base camp, which was essentially just the gazebos in the cellar-door carpark. Katie, the production assistant, was in charge of organising all our meals, and tonight it was Thai food ordered in from town. We then moved on to a night shoot in the courtyard off the cellar door and I spent a good part of that time trying to find and silence the many frogs that had become Amity's bane.

I didn't see Lucas or Holly at all for the rest of the afternoon, which I thought kind of odd, but Sadie was around and I was relieved to have her as my point of contact instead of Lucas. It made sense, really, since the property was hers, so who better to ask if we could move certain things to facilitate the film crew? And Sadie was in excellent spirits during the whole shoot, and seemed particularly keen to watch what Ben did for work and speak to him during all the breaks.

By the time Amity called it a wrap, it was well past eleven and everyone was exhausted. People fled to their respective lodgings—some driving back to their hotels in town, while most trundled off to their rooms at the dairy. I had to hang back and clear up the set, to make sure we weren't leaving any rubbish lying around or leaving anything valuable out overnight. By the time I finally made it to the dairy and flopped into my own bed, I could hear a chorus of snores coming from the many bedrooms.

That was day one done, I thought, relief flooding over me as I lay there waiting for sleep. Not only had I barely had to see Lucas, but things weren't weird with Rory, either. My last thought before I drifted into slumber was a quick prayer to the universe that the next two days could go as professionally and boy-interaction free as the first.

23

Base camp was buzzing early on Tuesday morning, with the actors getting their hair and makeup done, wardrobe steam-ironing costumes, and Katie fetching coffees for everyone. Well, not *everyone*. The other low-level employees and I had to get our own.

Filming commenced at nine, this time way down in one of the grapevine fields. I had to hang back at base camp to keep an eye on everything, because even though the cellar door was closed, there was still the odd wine tourist who drove hopefully up the driveway, seeing all the cars here and thinking perhaps it was open.

I'd just sent another car back down the drive when I heard the sound of the cellar door opening behind me. I glanced around, expecting to see Sadie, but instead felt a weird kind of clenching in my chest as Holly emerged from the building.

Argh, why did she have to have such nice hair? She looked like she was auditioning for a Pantene commercial!

I tried to pretend I was very busy with many important things to do, but stabbing frantically at my phone didn't seem to fool her.

"Hey, Laura!" she called, skipping down the steps in her platform sandals, her midi-dress swinging about her legs. How could she not be cold? I was wearing jeans, boots and a puffer jacket. Granted I was starting to get a bit sweaty ever since the sun rose overhead, but still. It definitely wasn't summer.

"Oh hi, Holly!" I feigned surprise. "What are you up to?"

"Wow, this is exciting!" she said, moving around and eyeing all the gear lying around. "You must be loving working on a film."

"Yes," I said after a pause. "I am. It's cool."

"It's amazing how many people are involved in making a movie, isn't it? I've got to get a small film done for one of my projects, but that will be a much smaller production than this."

"Right," I said, not sure what else to say.

"So, where is everyone?" Holly finally stopped snooping through all the gear and turned to face me with a radiant smile, as if we were fabulous friends having a grand old chat. I had to remind myself to try to act friendly towards her. The poor girl had no idea that her very presence was sending weird stabbing feelings through my chest.

"They're filming down that way." I gestured in the direction of the crew, trying my best at a friendly smile.

"And am I right that the director is that young girl with the rainbow hair?"

"Yeah, that's Amity."

"Wow! That's so impressive."

"It is. She's really talented."

I didn't bother adding that her grandmother was bankrolling this project. Because Amity *was* talented. Not that I had any other directors to compare her to.

"What's she like?" Holly asked.

"Amity? She's really nice. Really level-headed and patient. And open-minded. She doesn't judge anyone and she seems to genuinely like everybody."

Holly sighed happily, as if I'd just described her dream movie star. "Do you think you could introduce me later? I've got so many questions I'd love to ask her."

"Er, sure. We're doing another night shoot tonight, but we'll be breaking for dinner around five."

"Perfect! I'll come find you around then."

Holly waved at someone over my shoulder, and I glanced around only to feel my heart clench yet again. Lucas was approaching us, looking all farmer-hot again, in boots, jeans and a checked flannelette shirt, sleeves rolled up to the elbows, open over a tight white t-shirt.

"Hey, babe!" Holly called happily.

His eyes darted between the two of us, a slight frown on his face. "Hey. How's everything going?"

"It's great," I said, right as Holly answered, "All fine."

We glanced at each other and I felt immensely awkward.

"What are you guys doing today?" I quickly asked. "Got some work to do?"

"Yeah," Lucas replied as Holly simultaneously answered, "Nope."

Holly's gaze shot to Lucas, her face dropping in shock. "What? You're working?" she said, sounding horrified by the thought.

"Well ... yeah. I might as well."

"But I wanted to go into town. I thought we'd go wine tasting or something?"

Lucas looked a bit caught out, and I found myself hanging on this conversation like it was some juicy scene from *The Bold and the Beautiful*. I just needed a bowl of popcorn and I'd be all set.

"Today? I really need to stick around here and help Sadie out."

"But the cellar door is shut. What else is there to do?" Holly said, glancing at me as if I should agree with her. "I mean, there's only so long you can stare at a shed full of barrels, am I right?"

Holly grinned, and I forced myself to give a supporting token laugh, even if her words were reminding me of what happened the last time I was alone with Lucas in that very shed full of barrels.

His fingers on my back. Sliding my bra strap down my arm.

His warm breath on my neck.

Luckily, I was saved from being drawn further into this conversation by Katie, who was jogging up the driveway towards me.

"Laura!" she shouted, sounding completely out of breath. "Will asked … if you can … hang on." She doubled over, breathing heavily, and I grabbed a bottle of water out of the main stash and handed it to her.

"Thanks," she said, taking a few huge gulps. "That was further to run than I thought. Anyway, I meant to say, Will has asked me to ask you if you can go to the hardware store and buy all of this stuff."

She handed me a scribbled list of about five items, which ranged from specific light globes through to electrical extension leads.

"Sure. Urgent?"

Katie nodded but also gave a shrug. "Soon. He said we'll need it for the next scene they're planning to do after lunch."

"Got it. I'll go now. Although someone needs to stay here and keep an eye on things."

"I'll stay. I've ordered lunch already, so I've got to wait for the delivery now."

I nodded, and turned to find Lucas and Holly standing not far behind us, talking quite intensely in hushed voices.

Leaving them be, I dug around in my pocket for my car keys, but then stopped and swore when I realised my car had been parked in by a silver Toyota. It had to be one of the actors or one of the crew members who was staying in town, since it wasn't there yesterday.

"Do you know whose car that is?" I called to Katie, pointing at it.

She shook her head. "Sorry."

"Bugger. I'm not sure—"

"Do you need a lift?" Lucas was suddenly right beside me.

Oh God. No. Yes. Yes but no.

Not from you.

"Er, I don't think …"

"Ooh, I'll come too!" Holly was on my other side. "Where are we going?"

"Um …" I cast my gaze around, searching for an alternative. Any alternative. But all the crew members were far away in a field, and I didn't even know who had parked me in.

"A lift would be great," I said to Lucas, realising I didn't have any other options. Then I explained to Holly, "I just need to go to the hardware store—it won't be exciting—"

"No worries, I'll just come in and grab a coffee! I'm dying for a proper one."

I glanced at Lucas, hoping he might object and tell Holly to stay behind. But he didn't.

"Let's go, then," Lucas said. "My car's up by the house."

And so we all trooped up there together, Holly grabbing Lucas's arm and giving it a squeeze, while I pretended not to be watching them.

I mean, this shouldn't be weird. Why would it be weird? Lucas and I were friends. We'd been in the same car together before.

I just hadn't been in the same car with Lucas and Holly together.

When we arrived at the dark-blue four-wheel drive, Holly went immediately to the front passenger seat and I slid obligingly into the back. And then Lucas was in the car, too, and the doors were all shut, and I felt distinctly aware of just how close we all were in this small, confined, quiet space.

Well, this isn't weird. No, not weird at all.

I mean, it was fine. Holly had no idea that Lucas and I had an interesting history. As far as she knew, I was just Ben's flatmate.

"So, Laura." Holly turned around in her seat to look back at me as Lucas accelerated out of Middlebrook's gate and onto the road. "What's it like living *and* working with Ben?"

"It's fine. We're pretty good friends."

"*Just* friends?" Holly waggled her eyebrows, suggestively.

The idea that Ben and I were anything more was so ludicrous that I found myself meeting Lucas's gaze in the rear-view mirror, both of ours wide and shocked. And we both burst out laughing.

Holly huffed and crossed her arms, glaring now at Lucas. "What? Why is that so funny?"

"Sorry!" I wiped away tears from my cheeks. "But no. Ben and I are just friends and that's it."

"But you went all the way to Byron Bay to find him!" Holly turned in my direction again, genuinely confused.

"Well, yeah." My eyes slid to Lucas's in the mirror, then quickly slid away. "Because he's a friend. And my flatmate."

"Hmph. I just figured there must be more between the two of you."

"Me and *Ben*? No. No way."

I laughed again, which fizzled out awkwardly. Lucas appeared to be gripping the steering wheel rather hard.

"Laura doesn't do relationships," he said, his eyes not straying from the road.

"That's a bit of an overstatement!" I retorted a bit too tetchily. Directing my attention to Holly, I explained, "I've been taking some time out for me after getting divorced from a *very* long-term relationship. And, you know," I looked at Lucas through the rear-view mirror, "maybe I am ready for something more serious again."

Lucas's eyes darted to the mirror again, and I glared back pointedly at him.

Ha! Let's see what he makes of that.

"That is *so* sensible, Laura!" Holly said, turning in her seat and giving me a warm, positive smile. "I think everybody needs to take time to really know themselves before they're ready to commit to anything long term. My year in London taught me so much ... but also showed me exactly what I'd left behind."

She turned her smile to Lucas, reaching out and twining her fingers through his where they rested on his lap. I watched, in slightly horrified fascination, as he gave her hand a quick squeeze, then extricated his own to put back on the steering wheel.

"I didn't know you were in London," I said. "So, was that just after you broke up with Lucas?" I couldn't help it. I really couldn't.

But Holly just laughed lightly. "Yeah. Biggest mistake of my life, leaving this one. But like I said, I needed to work out who I was. Just like you."

"Hmm, not *quite* like me," I muttered.

Lucas was looking at me in the mirror again, and I wondered what he was thinking.

"Well, either way," Holly continued, "I think us being apart for a while did the world of good. We're so much stronger now for it."

Lucas didn't say anything, but his knuckles did seem rather whiter than necessary. And then he was parking the car on the street, and I realised we were outside the hardware store.

"There's a coffee shop just up there if you want to grab a coffee," he said to Holly, pointing to a corner cafe about a hundred metres away.

"You're not coming?" Holly asked.

"I'll help Laura find the stuff she needs. I've been here heaps."

A jolt of something that felt like triumph shot through me at that, and I had to carefully control my face so Holly wouldn't see my maniacal grin.

"Sure, babe. You want anything? How about you, Laura?"

"Me?"

Oh, well that threw me. Holly wasn't supposed to be *nice* to me. Still, if she was offering ...

"Oat cap, thanks."

"Yeah, I'll have a coffee, too, thanks," Lucas said.

I frowned, not feeling victorious anymore, and quickly clambered out of the car, perhaps closing the door more forcefully than necessary.

As Holly walked off towards the cafe, I jogged across the road and entered the hardware store, not bothering to wait for Lucas. He caught up to me almost immediately.

"So. What do you need?" he asked.

I handed him the list.

He read over it, nodding. "Easy enough. This way."

I trailed him through the store, and it was only once he'd led me to the light-globe section and we'd found the correct one that I couldn't help blurting out the thing that had been bothering me ever since the car.

"Why did Holly move to London for a year?"

He considered the light globe in his hand for a little while, then put it back on the hook before he turned to me. "She got offered a job over there."

"Oh. So, why didn't you just go with her?"

"Because she didn't want me to."

I frowned at him. "Because she wanted to be single?"

201

His expression darkened. "Something like that."

"What do you mean, something like that? What other reason is there?"

"It's not …" He sighed. "To be honest, the guy who offered her the job … well, she ended up moving in with him."

My jaw dropped. "So, all that talk about finding herself …?"

He shrugged. "I don't know. I don't need all the details of what she did or didn't do. I just know that she lived with that guy for a while. And now she's back."

"And you just *forgave* her? For leaving you for someone else?"

He shot me a scowl. "Who said I forgave her?" Then he turned and started walking off down the aisle, his shoulders stiff, but I wasn't letting him get away so easily. I ran after him, catching up and keeping pace as he began searching for the next item on my list.

"Well, you've obviously forgiven her if you're back together with her."

"Obvious, is it?" he scoffed. "You know what else is obvious? You and that cameraman."

"Who, Rory?" I blurted, surprised by the sudden change in topic. "We're just … friends."

"'Course you are," he derided. "You're just friends with everyone."

"What is *that* supposed to mean?"

"What do you think it means?"

"I think it means you're being a dick."

And with that I strode ahead, eyeing off the rows of bathroom taps as if I definitely needed to buy one for the film production.

"Hey!" Lucas caught my arm, pulling me around to face him. He had a huge smile on his face and that teasing gleam in his eye. "Bit touchy, aren't you?"

"You're the one suggesting that I …"

"What?"

"That I sleep with everybody I meet!"

"I didn't say that."

"You implied it."

"I thought you weren't ashamed about sleeping with whoever you wanted to?"

"I'm not!"

"Well, then." He raised his eyebrows.

"Oh, for—" I punched him on the shoulder. Hard.

He rubbed his arm but he kept grinning.

"Anyway, we weren't talking about *me*. We were talking about you and Holly."

"And why is that?"

"Because I don't understand why you're back together with her!"

Narrowing his eyes, he leaned towards me and asked in a low but deadly serious voice, "And I'm interested to know why you care."

We stared at each other then, me glaring at him, him kind of looking amused and curious.

"I guess I don't," I finally said, throwing my hands up and turning away. "Why would I? It's your business. You can do whatever you want."

"And yet you seem particularly angry at me."

"I'm not!" I shouted, rounding on him again.

He just raised his eyebrows with a grin, as if to say I was proving him right.

"Oh, you're so … annoying!" I shoved him again, quite forcefully.

He laughed at that, stepping back but otherwise seeming unbothered by my physical assault. "Nobody can annoy you unless you let them."

"I disagree. Some people are just so annoying that there is no possible way they could not annoy you."

"And I'm that annoying, am I?"

"Right now? Yes. Yes, you are."

He laughed again, and I realised that while we'd been arguing he'd managed to find the next thing on my list and added it to our basket.

Shooting me a sly look, he said, "It's funny how much fun annoying you can be."

"Well, that's exactly why I'm here, for your entertainment." I held my arms out wide, like an actor waiting for applause.

By the time we found the rest of the items, paid for them and made our way back to the car, we were still needling each other. Only now we seemed to have moved on to the topic of last summer and the many miserable dates I'd been on.

"She didn't tell you!" I said, nodding at Holly as she handed me my coffee.

"She did." Lucas grinned, getting into the driver's seat. "Kalina told me all about your Tinder dates. Although, I could always tell they were bad based on your face and how long it took before you'd be in my bar. It was like you preferred to be in Los Perdidos than anywhere else."

"Oh, don't flatter yourself!" I said as I managed to do my seatbelt one-handed while holding my coffee cup aloft. "I was there for the free drinks, that's all."

"Yeah right." Lucas shot Holly a grin. "Laura spent a *lot* of time warming up the bar seats in Los Perdidos when she was apparently meant to be out on dates."

"Is that so?" Holly asked, turning to frown at me.

"You're exaggerating. I didn't spend *that* much time in there."

"I could have engraved your name into one of the bar stools."

"Hey, that stool *was* the most comfortable! I'm sure of it."

"I think you'd just managed to imprint it with the shape of your butt."

Despite the fact that he was now driving, I leaned forwards and smacked him on the arm. Quite hard again.

But as I sat back in my seat, Lucas and I both laughing, Holly turned towards me again. And the look in her eyes made the happy glow in my chest immediately fizzle.

It was the look of betrayal. Of shock. That instant when something clicked into place and you just *knew*.

I swallowed a sudden lump in my throat, feeling cold and ... guilty.

Holly had worked out that it wasn't Ben I was in love with.

She knew it was Lucas.

24

I felt drenched in guilt.

How could it feel so right when Lucas and I were together, teasing each other, laughing, and yet be such a bad thing at the same time?

Was I the only one who felt that pull of more than friendship between us? I had to be. Because he was with Holly. So, the way we'd been acting in the hardware store, the teasing, the punching, the annoying of each other, was just ... what? Friendship? Was that all it could be?

I made a point of avoiding both Holly and Lucas for the rest of the day, something that was easy to do since I barely saw them after we returned from our trip into town. The remaining car trip had been a bit frosty, and when we'd arrived back Holly had stormed off into the main house, clearly upset, and Lucas had followed her. I'd just returned to base camp, tail between my legs, and made a conscious effort to focus on work and nothing else.

In the afternoon, filming resumed in the fields and I remained at base camp watching over the gear. With not much else to do, I took the opportunity to get out the camera Rory had given me and have a play with it. I snapped away, taking photos of the grapevines with their autumnal leaves just starting to fall; of the cellar door with the sun behind it; of the beautiful courtyard with some tasting glasses set upon the wrought-iron table.

I remembered Sadie lamenting her marketing efforts, and began to have ideas for how best to promote Middlebrook. Refreshing the website was a good start, and building up a social media following was a must. But creating a newsletter would be the most valuable, giving Sadie a means to communicate directly with known customers, and the content for it would practically write itself. Already, I could think of at least ten interesting newsletter topics, and I barely had any knowledge about wine myself.

Before I knew it, I was sitting at the trestle table at base camp, my laptop out, putting together a marketing plan for Middlebrook Vineyard. I hadn't done anything like this since my PR company days, and yet as I worked through timelines and brainstormed ideas for special events, I felt a deep spark of excitement begin to grow inside me.

We had another evening shoot on Tuesday night, and I briefly saw Holly hanging around during break time, talking with Amity. She seemed to be in high spirits, talking and laughing and having a good old chat with our director, so I decided she couldn't be too concerned about whatever she thought she'd witnessed between Lucas and me. Which was great. Lucas probably had reassured her that there was nothing going on between us.

Filming finally wrapped for the day not long before midnight, and I practically fell into bed shortly after, utterly exhausted.

But barely had my eyes closed before my alarm was going off again. These long hours were gruelling, yet I couldn't complain today; it was the last day of our location shoot in Mudgee, and I knew from talking to Will last night that we were running to schedule. There were only two scenes left to shoot of the Mudgee scenes. There'd been talk last night of going into town to celebrate once we were done, so everyone was in not just a good mood but an efficient one, as well. The sooner we got the work done, the sooner the drinking could commence.

After the shoot began up on the hill behind the winery, and I was once again manning base camp, I went to find Sadie in the cellar door. The winery was open today for customers to come in and try wine; however, Sadie already had told me that she didn't expect anyone until at least eleven. Since we'd all be leaving Mudgee early tomorrow morning, and everyone would be busy this afternoon, I thought it a good opportunity to talk to her about my marketing ideas for her vineyard.

I was glad to find Sadie alone, no sign of Lucas or Holly about. She was behind the bar, drying wineglasses and lining them up, giving no indication that her broken wrist was bothering her.

"Knock, knock!" I called as I walked inside.

Sadie turned and gave me a broad smile. "Laura! How is the filming going?"

"It's going really well. Everything's on track to finish this afternoon, and then we'll all be packing up and you'll get your winery back tomorrow."

Sadie waved a hand. "Oh, it's been a blast having you all here! I've popped out a few times to take a sticky beak at the action. Although it's all quite slow-going, isn't it?"

I laughed. "Yep. It can take days just to shoot one scene. Especially when the actors forget their lines or the director isn't happy with the lighting."

"Ah well, it's all a bit of excitement really. I'm looking forward to telling everyone who visits in the foreseeable future that we've been used as a location for a movie!"

"And once the film's out, you'll be able to really promote that fact. Actually, that's what I wanted to talk to you about—I've been having a think about how I can help you with your marketing here."

"Oh goodness, have you really?"

"Of course. I've put together a bit of a proposal for you. Have you got time to take a look now?"

"Absolutely!" Sadie seemed delighted. "Until someone shows up for a tasting, I'm as free as a bird."

I sat down at the bar and opened my laptop, spinning it around so I could show Sadie what I'd put together. She fished her glasses out of her shirt pocket, slid them up her nose then leaned in to take a look.

"First up is giving your website a revamp," I began, showing her the images I'd mocked together of a newly designed site using an easy WordPress template and some of the images I'd taken yesterday.

Her mouth practically fell open. "You did this?" She sounded far more impressed than she needed to be. "This is amazing! It looks so much better."

"It's just a mockup, but if you like the design then I can get started on a new site for you."

"Is it expensive?"

"No, not at all. The template itself is the main cost, but it's only seventy-five dollars and that's it."

Sadie's eyes widened. "That can't be it. I have to pay you for your time, of course!"

"No, you don't need to. I'm just happy to help."

"Oh, no, no. I insist. We'll work something out. But keep going for now, this is exciting!"

I showed Sadie the other things I'd mocked up—a newsletter

template along with some suggested content ideas. An Instagram and Facebook account and how easy it would be to maintain them. Plus, I explained she could easily have paper forms and signs sitting right here in the cellar door, so people could simply write down their email addresses while they were here and be added to the mailing list, or know what the Middlebrook handle was to follow them on social media.

"And you're sure I'll be able to manage this all by myself?"

"Absolutely. Once it's all set up, there's really not that much time needed going forward. You'd only need to send a newsletter every one or two months, and the social media posting doesn't need to happen more than once a week. It's really just there to present a brand image, so when people search for Middlebrook they find recent information."

"Goodness, you make it all sound so easy!"

"It should be. Marketing should be fun. I love it myself, and I'll always be around to help you if you get stuck with anything."

"This is very impressive. Are you doing the marketing for this film, as well?"

That threw me a bit. "Oh—no. No, I'm just the location manager."

Sadie frowned, taking off her glasses and returning them to her pocket. "But if you love marketing so much, why aren't you doing that for work?"

I scrunched up my nose. "Marketing is ..." I waved my hand at my laptop, which still had the newsletter mockup on it. "Not this. The marketing jobs I've had in the past have been really different. This is ... well, I guess it's freelance stuff, really."

"Well, why don't you do that, then? I know at least ten other wineries here in Mudgee who could do with exactly the same refresh as you've just shown me."

I blinked at her, my mouth opening and closing but no sound coming out.

"Well, something to think about," Sadie said, smiling kindly at me. "Lucas knows a good thing or two about running his own business, if you need some pointers."

She gave my hand a squeeze with the one not currently in a cast, and turned to pick up another wineglass to polish.

"Right," I finally managed. "Yes, that is something to think about. And in the meantime, I'll get going on this, shall I? You sure you're happy with the website design?"

"Absolutely. I think you've nailed it. Let me know when the money's involved, and I'll pay for whatever you need to make it happen."

I spotted a mini-bus making its way up the driveway amidst a cloud of dust, carrying what had to be Middlebrook's first group of wine tourists.

Nodding to Sadie, I grabbed my laptop and went back outside to base camp. As I stood there, looking around at the beautiful rolling grapevines, inhaling that clean, crisp country air, I suddenly imagined this becoming my life. Of travelling around to different wineries, setting them up with marketing plans and helping them update their images. I'd always wanted to travel for work, and being a location manager on a film set had seemed like an ideal job for that. And yet ...

Did I want to spend months of my time out in the desert, spending long hours standing around on the peripherals? Or did I want to make up my own path, start my own business and possibly spend time travelling around to wine regions?

Sadie's words had opened a door somewhere in my brain, shining a light on a possibility I'd never even considered before.

Maybe I could return to marketing under my own terms. Do the things I enjoyed and forget the things I didn't. Freelancer, business owner. I didn't know if the idea thrilled me or terrified me.

25

Filming wrapped in the late afternoon, and after Amity gave a short speech thanking the crew for making the shoot awesome, everyone seemed to be in high spirits. The pub idea was abandoned—mainly because nobody fancied being a designated driver—and so while most of the crew began packing away the gear, Katie and I headed into town to procure pizza and booze.

Thank God the dairy was well away from the house, because I wasn't sure how Sadie would feel about her brand-new accommodation being used as a party venue. But nobody was the particularly rowdy type, I reasoned, and besides, the actors and some of the crew who were staying in town had disappeared back to their hotel, so it wasn't *that* big of a party.

Someone had brought out portable speakers, and soon we had music pumping in the common area. I thought we might have overdone it with the amount of beer and wine we'd bought, but everyone was drinking and the pizza was going down a treat. I was flying high on the success of the shoot as much as anyone, plus my mind was still buzzing with the ideas Sadie had planted there that afternoon. In fact, I barely realised how much time had passed until I glanced out of the window and saw it was dark.

"Ben!" I threw my arms around him when he walked over to me. "I feel like I haven't seen you in an age!"

"Yeah, been up at the house," he said, patting me on the back. "Thought I should spend a bit of time with my aunt before we leave. How many drinks have you had, Laura?"

I waved my hand in a broad, dismissive gesture. "Oh, a *few*. That white port over there is really nice. Have you ever heard of white port before? I hadn't. We got really upsold at the bottle shop. Apparently, it's a specialty around here."

Ben laughed. "Maybe you should have some pizza with it, though, yeah?"

"Pizza, smeesha! What's that German saying? *Zwei bier sind auch ein schnitzel.*"

Ben raised his eyebrows, looking flabbergasted. "And that means?"

"Two beers are also a schnitzel!" I shrieked, giggling at my wittiness and also surprised I still remembered my one German sentence.

Okay, so I was pretty drunk. I didn't know if it was the lingering sleep deprivation from the late nights and early mornings, the giddiness from having successfully managed a proper location shoot, or the fact that everyone was in high spirits, but both Katie and I had been getting stuck into the white port (I wasn't sure anyone else fancied it) and my glass seemed to be forever full despite my best efforts to drink it down.

Besides, it wasn't like I was the only drunk one in the house. Chris, the second cameraman, currently was wearing a mop on his head and doing a Cindy Lauper rendition.

"Laura!" Amity came up to me and gave me a big hug. There was a lot of hugging going on, I realised. Everyone seemed to be enjoying hugging each other more than usual.

Amity smiled. "Did I mention how perfect this place has been? You're such a star for finding it."

I smiled back. "Well, it's probably more thanks to Ben, since it's his family's winery." I glanced around, meaning to include Ben in our conversation, but found he'd moved off and was now talking to someone else.

"Do you want to see some of the dailies?" Amity asked. "They're looking amazing."

"Yes! I'd love to see them!"

I followed Amity over to the couches in the corner, where Will was sitting with his laptop, going through the footage from today.

"Wow!" I breathed, watching the gorgeous shots of Phoebe walking through the grapevines.

"Yeah," Amity agreed, also sounding awed. "Rory and Chris have done a great job."

"What have I done?" Rory was suddenly sitting down on the couch beside me, and we all smooshed up together to try to see the laptop, which was now on Amity's lap. I was squished between Rory and Amity, and it might have been all the alcohol I'd drunk, but I found it very comfortable being pressed in between them.

We continued watching the dailies, joking and laughing about certain bits that were definitely unusable, and I barely noticed how much time was passing until we got to the end of the footage and I looked up and realised the four of us were the only ones still up. The music had been turned down slightly, and I could hear snores coming from one of the bedrooms down the hallway.

I also realised that we'd all been getting very cosy on the couch. Rory had his arm around me, and I had my back snuggled into his chest. I also had one of my legs up over Amity's leg, which she didn't seem to either mind or notice, because she had her hand firmly planted on it, as if holding it in place.

That's when I realised the atmosphere had intensified. And I was definitely feeling all drunk and languid and warm, because when Rory started kissing my neck I tipped my head, silently asking for more. And I watched as Will leaned in and kissed Amity right beside us, and then her hand was making little circles on my thigh and Rory's hands were stroking up my shoulders, and all I could think was that this felt *amazing*.

I might have gasped or moaned, because Amity broke away from Will and turned to look at me. She bit her lip, a slow smile playing across her mouth and her eyes darkening as she watched Rory kissing my neck. And then I felt him gently turning my head, and my lips met his, and it was all the more erotic knowing that Will and Amity were watching us. I felt Amity's hand squeeze my thigh, as if egging us on, and when Rory's warm hand slipped under my t-shirt and across the bare skin of my waist, I moaned and arched my back.

I barely had time to think about what was happening. I didn't know if my drunken mind was quite keeping up with processing things. Or maybe it was having spent so much time working on a film that I was mixing real life with the fantasy world we were creating. But when Rory broke our kiss and I turned back towards Amity, suddenly she was leaning in and her lips found mine. Her mouth was softer than Rory's, her tongue somehow more delicate. And maybe it was the fact that Rory was pressing into my back, his lips on the bare skin of my neck again, but I honestly didn't think I'd ever been so turned on.

I was kissing Amity. I was kissing a girl. And behind her, Will was kissing her shoulder, and Rory was behind me, and oh my God *this* was how foursomes got started!

I'd never imagined it could be so erotic. I guess I just kind of imagined that foursomes would simply be two couples having sex in the same room, possibly on the same bed. But then, wouldn't that be a bit crowded? And what if the bed was really bouncy? God, imagine if one couple managed to bounce the other couple right off.

A door slammed in the hallway and the four of us broke apart guiltily. But with a bite of her lip, Amity stood up, holding her hands out for both Will and me. I took her hand, pulled Rory up behind me, and then we were all giggling and moving down the other end of the house, down to where our four bedrooms were.

Without discussion, we all piled into the furthest one, closing the door behind us. I could still faintly hear the music playing out in the lounge area, but I knew it would act as a good buffer, even though we were far away from the other sleeping crew members.

Was this even real? I felt definitely drunk and definitely liquidy, but also totally alive and exhilarated and only just seeming to realise that I was about to participate in a foursome.

The others had to have instinctively known I needed a bit of hand-holding here, because they were all there paying attention to me. Rory was behind me again, his firm body pressed up against my back, hands on my waist and lips on my neck. Will was suddenly in front of me, leaning in, an eyebrow raised questioningly. I nodded my head, and then Will was kissing me, rough stubble grazing my chin. I sensed rather than saw Amity come up behind Will, her hands snaking around his hips. And when he growled a moan against my mouth, I knew her hands likely had slipped inside his pants.

Oh my God, this was *hot*. Foursomes were amazing, I decided. I was breathing fast, I had two hot guys kissing me, two pairs of male hands roaming over my body. Good God, but why had I never done this before?

Will broke away from our kiss, leaving me gasping as he kissed his way across my cheek. And I felt Rory's lips leave my neck and then … okay, then Will and Rory were kissing. Which was still hot, I guess. Except that their hands were now finding each other and I felt a bit like a flattened pancake pressed in between them, or like the forgotten bit of cheese between two slices of man-sized bread.

But it was fine. I just had to get back into the game. I ran one hand up Will's side, the other reaching back to squeeze Rory's thigh. And maybe Amity realised I'd become a squashed flat cake, because she was reaching for me, pulling me out from between the boys.

Amity kissed me again, her feminine arms coming up around my back to pull me into her. Her breasts pressed into mine, and her hips bumped up against mine, and although I closed my eyes and tried to enjoy the sensations, I felt my stomach turn a bit cold.

This didn't feel as good as when a Rory or Will kissed me. I liked the largeness of a man, the broadness of Will's chest, the feel of the bulge in Rory's pants. Amity was all narrow ribs and delicate soft skin, and somehow it just didn't seem to be working for me.

I turned my head, glancing back at the boys to see what they were doing, and wondering why they weren't coming over here for us. I mean, foursomes were mainly about the girls, right? That's what my porn research had suggested. But Will and Rory seemed to have completely forgotten that there were two girls in the room. They'd pulled off their shirts, and Rory had his hand down Will's pants, and they were kissing each other like there was no tomorrow.

"Do you like watching?" Amity whispered in my ear, moving behind me and turning me so I was facing the boys. She kissed my neck, and if I imagined it was a guy kissing me it was almost good. But then her hand started snaking across my abdomen towards my pants and that's when my foggy brain seemed to catch up with me and time slowed down.

Fuck!

As if in slow motion, I watched Rory and Will kissing and moaning and grabbing at each other like I wasn't even there. And Amity's delicate fingers were heading towards my waistband, and they were so different to a wide, broad male hand, and suddenly I felt my stomach bottom out as I realised what was going to happen.

Rory and Will were going to have sex with each other, weren't they? Which meant ... was I going to have sex with Amity?

Christ, I didn't know how to have sex with a girl! It was one thing to maybe close my eyes and let her touch me, but was I going to have to touch her? The thought of touching another girl down *there*, the thought of using my mouth ...

Oh God. I didn't want to do this. This wasn't how I'd imagined a foursome would go! I thought it would have been me and Rory and Amity and Will, maybe me and Will and Amity and Rory, but either way I'd assumed it would go *boy, girl, boy, girl*! Not *boy, boy, girl, girl*! Argh!

Kissing Amity while I had strong male hands on me was one thing. But having sex with Amity was on a whole other level, one that I abruptly realised I wasn't ready for.

"I—sorry." I tore away from Amity, not able to meet her eyes. "I've drunk too much."

And then I was stumbling out of that room, right as Will was pushing down Rory's pants, and the last thing I saw as I closed the door behind me was Amity's forlorn face watching me as Will roughly grabbed Rory's naked butt, the two boys pressed together mouths and bodies.

I made it into the closest bathroom and locked myself in. My stomach was swirling with adrenaline, or perhaps just swirling from too much booze because then I was leaning over the toilet and suddenly vomiting my guts up.

Christ, I thought, as I sank down onto the cool tiles, my stomach hollowed out. That was a very narrowly avoided disaster.

Facebook Alert

Cath Baker added 32 photos to the album "Queensland"

Cath Baker commented:

Graham showing me up on the bicycles!

Trish Stephens commented:

You were fine after we fished you out of that bush 😂

Graham Baker commented:

She needs a four-wheeler next time.

Elle Baker commented:

Who are you and what have you done with my parents?

New Email

From: Stephen White

Subject: *Burn Me* production update

Dear crew,

We have a new estimated production start date, two weeks later than initially anticipated. (Reminder: This is still a start ESTIMATE.) Please see attached for your updated schedule and contract.

New Message

From: Elle Baker at 6.58 pm

Yo sis! Can Mare and I crash on your couches this Sat?

26

The next morning I woke with a start, mercifully without a hangover, no doubt thanks to purging my guts up before going to sleep. I remembered leaving the bathroom and tiptoeing back to my own bedroom, hearing the sounds of people having a very good time coming from the end bedroom. I wasn't sure if I was glad that Rory, Will and Amity had continued on without me, or a little put out by that fact. Still, I'd had no desire to return to the bedroom, and so after barring my own door with a chair on the inside, I'd fallen into bed and passed out.

Now, I scrabbled around for my phone, knowing it was early because there was no sunlight coming in around the blinds. There were birds singing their morning song, though, and a check of my phone confirmed it was just before sunrise.

I could sleep in. I should, considering we weren't filming today and so didn't need to get up this early. But I felt jittery and antsy and like I really didn't want to shuffle around the kitchen getting breakfast if Amity, Will or Rory were going to be there. So, I got up.

As I pulled on my jeans, my eyes fell to the camera sitting atop my duffle bag and I had the brilliant idea that I should get some sunrise shots of the winery to use on the website. And so, while everyone else was still asleep in the dairy, I tiptoed outside into the cool pre-dawn air.

The stars were still visible in the sky. I took a moment to stare up at them, at how vast the world suddenly seemed, making me feel so small. The country sky was breathtaking compared to the city sky, even with the sun on its way up and the horizon lightening with every moment.

Feeling energised, I zipped my puffer jacket right up and made my way towards the darkened main house.

It was so peaceful here in the country dawn. Quiet wasn't the right word, because the sounds of nature were everywhere; birds singing their sunrise chorus, frogs getting in a few last croaks. But there were no human sounds. No cars driving by, or TVs blaring. Despite knowing that there were people tucked up in the buildings around me, I felt like I might as well have been alone in my own personal slice of heaven.

Slinging the camera strap around my neck, I began capturing the world awakening. The first light on dew-dampened leaves. Mist rising from the grass as warmth crept over it. A spiderweb beaded with crystal-bright water droplets. I captured it all.

And when the sunlight cast its first rays across the main house, I noticed the lights were on inside and I skipped towards it. Sadie was probably up, making coffee or tea, and I could show her these photos and ask if she'd had any more thoughts on her newsletter. I was in such a positive mood as I jumped up the steps that it took me a moment to comprehend what I could see through the window.

It wasn't Sadie in the kitchen. It was Holly and Lucas.

I'd been about to reach up and knock on the door, but instead I froze, hidden in the lingering darkness outside, while the kitchen lights blazed from within.

Holly was sitting on a dining chair, pulled slightly away from the main table. Her glorious mane of blonde hair fell around her shoulders, like a stylistic version of bed-hair. But that wasn't what caught me and pinned me to the spot. It was the fact that Lucas was *kneeling* on the tiles before her. He had her hands clasped in his, his expression earnest.

Although I couldn't see her face, her body was unnaturally still. And then her shoulders heaved like she was laughing and she threw her arms around his neck, pulling him in towards her.

I stumbled backwards, blinking rapidly. Horrified by what I'd seen. Horrified that here I was, spying on them at such a moment.

At such a moment!

I spun away and began running back down the steps. I ran and ran until I was around the other side of the cellar door, the main house blocked from view, and I could breathe again if only my chest wasn't cracking shut, compressing and crushing and strangling my lungs.

I couldn't breathe.

I couldn't see.

I couldn't think.

Tears were falling down my face, my heart pounding, and I hunched down on the ground, wrapping my arms around myself.

Only one thought was getting through.

You're too late.

Again, deja vu. Standing outside, looking in. Seeing things that should be private. Witnessing the end of my world.

Why hadn't I said something sooner? Taken Kalina's advice and told him how I felt. At least given him the chance to choose between Holly and me. Instead, I'd stuck my head in the sand and ignored the fact that he was back together with her. This whole time I'd been trying to focus on work, trying to ignore him, his feelings for her had been blossoming. And I'd just stood back and let it happen.

There was no denying what I'd just seen. No other reason why a man got down on bended knee before his girlfriend.

I'd just seen Lucas proposing to Holly. And she'd said yes.

They were engaged. Which meant …

There was nothing here for me. *He* was not for me.

Game over, Laura.

27

The next few days vanished in a haze of hard work and denial. Once Ben and I returned from Mudgee on Thursday morning, I found myself locking everything I'd seen in a tidy little box and shoving it to the back of my mind. In one respect it was easy, because Mudgee felt like a world away. Back in Sydney, back filming at the Mosman house, I could carry on with my job and pretend like nothing had happened. Pretend like I hadn't seen Lucas kneeling on the ground before Holly, her hands held in his, that serious, earnest look on his face.

In Sydney, things were exactly as they were. And really, nothing *had* changed, had it? Lucas and I were nothing more than friends. Exactly what I'd been insisting we were for months. I just felt like perhaps I should never see him again and that would be the best thing for everyone.

There'd been no announcement from Lucas about his new engagement, and I was too cowardly to ask Ben if he'd heard anything. Maybe they wanted to keep it quiet for now, or maybe they wanted to tell their families in person first. Whatever the case, I felt grateful that nothing was being said and I could live in denial for a little while longer.

Still, I had the new website to work on for Sadie, something that *was* giving me immense joy to do. Even when I was back on set at the Mosman house on Friday, I found myself thinking through the Middlebrook marketing plans and working out what I could fit in that evening. It was such a good distraction that I didn't even feel weird being around Amity, Will or Rory. All of us had gone straight back into professional mode, as if the last night in Mudgee hadn't even happened, and I found it easy to pretend that it hadn't. Just like what I'd witnessed in the kitchen on Wednesday morning, what happened between the four of us felt as though it was a whole world away.

By Saturday, I'd finished the new website design for Middlebrook and was working on the marketing playbook for Sadie—basically a guide for what she should be doing and how often—when Kalina came barging into my bedroom.

"Kal!" I practically fell off my bed. "Did you even knock just then?"

Kalina narrowed her eyes at me, clearly taking in my trackpants and unwashed hair.

"You're depressed," she announced.

"What?" I glanced down at myself. Okay, sure, that chocolate stain was new. As was the three-quarters eaten block of Cadbury on my bedside table. But still. I was working, and I needed the sugar fuel. "No, I'm not," I told her. "I'm just busy."

She folded her arms and leaned against the doorframe. "I've barely seen you since you got back from Mudgee. Something happened up there, didn't it? Ben's got no idea, and I can't ask Holly because she's still away. What's going on?"

I pursed my lips. So, Holly hadn't had a chance to tell everyone she was engaged to Lucas yet? It was only a matter of time and then

Kalina would know.

Kalina sighed. "Come on. Let's go out for a drink."

I glanced at my watch, startled to see it was gone four-thirty. "I'm still—"

"No excuses! We've barely done anything together since you started work on that film. Plus, I'm not seeing Owen tonight for the first time in ages. And as much as I appreciate how busy you are, I'm having a crisis of my own."

My head snapped up at that. "You are? What's happened?"

Oh God, I'd been a bad friend, hadn't I? Here I was, all wrapped up in my own problems, and something was up with Kalina and I hadn't even noticed.

Kalina just gave me a look. "Come have a drink with me and I'll tell you."

She spun around and left the room and I sighed, knowing I'd need to follow.

An hour later, Kalina and I (freshly showered) slid into a booth at The Blonde Pony, the dive bar in Manly she used to work at. Evidently, she was still on good terms with the bartenders because two beers arrived in front of us free of charge.

"So," Kalina said. "Mudgee. You, Lucas, Holly. Spill."

I sipped my drink, wondering how to even answer that.

"There's nothing there," I eventually said, staring at the foam slowly dispersing in my glass. "I thought Lucas maybe felt something for me … but he doesn't. There's nothing." I looked up, letting Kalina see the misery on my face. "I saw him proposing to Holly."

Shock rippled across Kalina's face. "*What?* Are you sure? I don't believe that. He wouldn't be so stupid!"

I huffed a humourless laugh. "You don't just get back together with an ex if you're not sure about them. This isn't the grand Laura and Lucas love story. It's the Lucas and Holly love story. I was just a side act. Not even that. The half-time jester."

Kalina put her hand on my forearm. "Laur. That's not what you are. I've seen the way he looks at you. The way he—"

"Don't," I begged. "I need to stop thinking about him. It's done. There's nothing for it."

Kalina withdrew her hand, and I could see her chewing her lip, as if trying really hard to restrain herself from saying more. I knew what she wanted to say. What she probably was entitled to say.

I warned you to talk to him sooner.

And she'd be right. God, how I now knew she'd been right. I never should have sat back and watched Lucas's love for Holly blossom anew. I spent so long telling him that I just wanted to be friends, that of course he believed it. How many times had I pushed him away? And now I'd pushed him right into Holly's arms.

It was a bitter sadness, realising I'd lost him.

"Anyway," I said, willing the tears not to start. "I don't want to talk about this. Tell me about you. What's this crisis you're having?"

Kalina shifted in her seat, looking a bit sketchy. "I kind of just said that to get you to come out. I'm not really having a crisis. Maybe more of a panic that everything seems to be going *too* well. Is that a thing?"

I snorted into my drink.

"No, really! I mean, I really like my job. It's intense but it's also satisfying. And things with Owen are just so … easy. He's one of the most laidback people I think I've ever met. Plus, he's smart. He tried explaining what he does for work to me the other day, and it was like he was telling me he could see The Matrix."

I smiled at Kalina. "I'm really happy for you. If there's anyone I know who deserves to be happy, it's you."

"But that's just it. I feel like this has all happened so quickly, and there's something I'm missing. Like, I haven't even realised yet that I've lost something."

"What would you have lost? Aside from not being able to sleep with lots of random people anymore."

"Oh, I don't care about that. The idea of sleeping with anyone now who isn't Owen feels weird. But maybe that's it. It's not the random sex I miss. It's the *fun*. The sense of adventure that used to go along with things."

I laughed. "I think that's why people go skydiving, Kal."

She looked horrified. "That is something I will *never* do."

"Well, maybe that's the trade-off. You gain stability and happiness in your life and let go of some of the fun. Plus don't forget, a lot of the time it *isn't* fun. How many times have we gone out, hoping to meet someone to hook up with, only to find it's the bloody desert out there?"

"Oh yeah. It's easy to forget that, isn't it?"

"And, being spontaneous isn't always the best idea," I added darkly, remembering the almost-foursome I'd had in Mudgee mere days ago. Sure, none of the others had made me feel weird about it, but they could have. It could have ended up being a huge clusterfuck.

"Okay, *what* is going on here?" Kalina gestured at my face. "What are you keeping from me?"

I briefly considered not telling Kalina about the foursome, but decided that some stories were better off shared. And by the time I finished talking, Kalina was in near hysterics.

"You just left the room?!"

"I had to! I was about to throw up!"

Kalina doubled over, laughing so hard she had tears streaming down her face. "Oh my God," she finally managed to say. "That has got to be the funniest thing I've ever heard!"

"It's not funny, it's mortifying! The only slight upside is that they all seem totally fine with pretending the whole night never happened."

"So, you wouldn't want to try it again? Foursome two-point-oh?"

"God, no! I think I've satisfied my curiosity in that regard. And as much as I like the idea of being all open-minded and attracted to anyone, I've realised that I'm really just attracted to men. Straight men."

Kalina patted me on the shoulder. "I'm glad you've worked that out."

"Oh shut up. I probably already knew that. But," I shrugged, "I guess it was worth a try."

Kalina grinned. "So. You've done some sexual exploring. Tried your hand at a new career. What are you going to do next, Miss Laura the Explorer?"

I opened and closed my mouth a few times.

That was the question, wasn't it? What *was* I going to do next?

I hadn't mentioned the *Burn Me* job offer to Kalina, I realised. I supposed I'd deliberately not said anything to her, because I knew she'd be upset. I knew *I'd* certainly be upset if Kalina announced she was moving away for work for a few months. Yet, if I wanted to have a career in the film industry, that was the next move, wasn't it? I'd take the job offer, live in the desert for a while, and then see if I could springboard that into another job. That was how I'd get my career started. My career as a location manager.

But there was no point in saying anything to Kalina until I was totally sure. And I wasn't sure. Not yet. In fact, thinking about it kind of made my insides squirm around, which was probably why I'd pushed it to the back of my mind.

"I suppose I'm about to be unemployed, single and alone," I said instead. "Yay for me." I took a comforting gulp of beer.

"Well, the employment side of things I can't help you with. As to being single and alone … Look, I just have to say it. It's not too late to tell Lucas how you feel."

I cast her a dark look.

"I'm serious!" she pushed on. "As much as I like Holly, I like *you* way more. And Lucas, I can tell you right now, has been waiting for you for months."

"He has not!"

"He has! He might be back together with Holly, but that's only because he thinks you're not interested!"

"That's ridiculous."

"It's not, Laura. You need to tell him. What have you got to lose?"

"What, then?" I slammed my beer down on the table. "Am I just supposed to walk up to him and say, 'Oh hey, now that you're with Holly, I've decided I'd like to give it a go with you'?"

"No! Tell him you're in love with him!"

"I can't do that! Not just … I mean …"

Hmm.

Suddenly an idea sprang into my mind, a remembered conversation I'd had with Lucas weeks ago.

There's nothing wrong with a big, romantic gesture to prove to someone how you feel.

Oh God. I needed to do something like that, didn't I? Just like Sadie did when she was trying to win George over. I needed to spell out that I loved him in flowers outside his window. Except I

232

couldn't do exactly the same thing. I'd have to modernise it a bit. Like, organise a dancing flash mob or pay for one of those sky-writer planes to spell it out in the clouds.

And, okay, so ethically I wasn't really that keen on potentially ruining the happiness of another woman. But on the other hand … if Lucas *did* choose me, then it wasn't really meant to be with Holly, was it? It wasn't like I was going to seduce him and trap him into ending things with Holly. All I'd be doing was giving him the choice between us.

I blinked a few times, and realised that Kalina was staring at me with wild anticipation written across her face.

"I'm not—" I began, but a wild scream cut me off.

"Lauuuurrrra!"

Kalina and I both jumped, though then we were being squished up into our booth as Elle and Marrika slid in next to us, cocktails in each of their hands.

"Ellie! I didn't think I'd see you until much later tonight."

She shrugged. "We like to start early. But why are *you* here? Aren't you too old to be out drinking in Manly?"

Too old? Blimey, my younger sister had some cheek. Still, I couldn't deny the fact that while Kalina and I were in jeans, t-shirts and sneakers, Elle and Marrika were dressed like they were off to a New Year's Eve dance party in Darling Harbour.

"Hey," Kalina said warningly. "We're not old, we're experienced."

Elle giggled. The younger girls clearly had one up on us in the drinking stakes, too.

"We live here in Manly, remember?" I nudged my sister. "This is totally our local."

"Well, we love Manly, too!" Elle enthused. "It's our new favourite going-out spot."

Brilliant. I supposed I could expect them to crash on my couches frequently, then.

I eyed Marrika across the table. She was scowling down at her phone and looking distinctly like she was *not* having a fun night.

"Is she okay?" I asked Elle quietly.

Elle pulled a sympathetic face in her friend's direction. "We saw *his* car just down the road. Mare is still pretty … annoyed about it."

"Ah." I nodded.

"What's this?" Kalina asked, looking confused.

"A guy Marrika was dating who turned out to be dating other people," I supplied.

"We weren't just dating!" Marrika slammed her phone down on the table. "We were in a *relationship*. He's a fucking fuckface."

"Oh, juicy!" Kalina turned to Marrika. "Tell me more."

"He's an arrogant douchebag. You know he's got a *Where's Wally* tattoo on his butt cheek? And he drives the douchiest yellow Mustang with a stupid racing stripe down the bonnet. He thinks he's a rally driver, but he's really just some lazy-arse shit who still lives at his parents' house!"

Alarm bells were going off in my mind. How many guys could there possibly be in Sydney driving yellow Mustangs who also had *Where's Wally* tattoos on their butts?

"Where does he live, Marrika? Is it in Mosman?"

Marrika glanced at me in surprise. "Yeah. How'd you know that?"

"Oh my God. I know exactly who you're talking about. Have you got a picture?"

While Marrika scrolled through her phone gallery to find one, Kalina and Elle both were eyeing me.

"Who is it?" Kalina asked.

Marrika handed me her phone.

"It's *him*!" I squealed. "It's Shouty Sex Man!"

"*What?*" Marrika screamed right as Elle said, "*Who?*"

"He lives across the back fence from where we've been shooting the movie in Mosman. And you're right, Marrika, he is a fucking fuckface!"

Marrika still looked disturbed. "Why do you call him Shouty Sex Man?"

"Because he's a mean dickhead and he … erm …" Hmm. Best not mention all the women he'd been having wild sex with in his living room. "He walks around naked in his back garden."

"Ew!" Elle said.

"Such a dick," Marrika muttered.

"Well, if he's here in Manly, let's go find him and make his night awful!" Kalina said, her eyes lighting up with excitement. "Come on, Laur, this is exactly the kind of fun I need!"

"I don't want to see him!" Marrika cried, horrified.

"But don't you want revenge?" Kalina implored. "I'm sure you do, Laur, after the way he yelled at you."

"Revenge is an excellent idea, but only if Mare is up for it," Elle said in concern.

Marrika bit her lip, seeming uncertain.

And then the idea struck me.

"Girls, I've got it!" I said, practically jumping up out of my seat. "Elle, Marrika, do you know exactly where his car is parked?"

"Yes," Elle said slowly.

"Right. I know how we can get back at him without having to actually *see* him. Finish your drinks, ladies. We're going on an adventure."

28

I led the gang back to my apartment, Elle and Marrika practically dancing along the street as we went. Kalina tried to get me to divulge the plan as we walked, but I didn't say anything until we were back at the flat, standing around in the kitchen like it held all the answers.

"Okay, ladies," I began, addressing them all like I was the group commander. "Now, men like ..." I held my hand out to Marrika.

"Kyle," she supplied.

"Shouty sex men like Kyle care the most about *one* thing. Can anyone guess what it is?"

"How many women they've banged?" offered Kalina.

"Having people worship them?" said Marrika.

"Where's your booze?" asked Elle.

"It's in the cupboard there. Shouty sex men like Kyle care about their *status symbols*. Such as their fancy sports cars, which they can pick up said ladies in and have bystanders on the street admire them."

"Yeah," Marrika said. "You know how many times he wanted to have sex in that car? And it's so tiny and cramped."

"Oh my God! Laura, are you suggesting we get crowbars and smash his car to shit?!" Kalina looked like she wasn't sure if she was excited or mortified by this idea.

"No! Nothing so *obvious*. We're not criminals, after all." I let a slow smile creep across my face. "What we're going to do is more of a *delayed* sabotage. Something that won't leave any visible damage but that is going to fuck up his car so bad that no woman will ever want to set foot in there again."

Kalina and Marrika glanced at each other, clearly perplexed. Elle poured some Frangelico into her mouth directly from the bottle.

"Drum roll, please!"

While Kalina and Marrika provided a very satisfying benchtop drum roll, and Elle just kind of clapped the Frangelico bottle a few times, I moved with pomp to the freezer, pulled it open, and with a flourish removed a suspiciously soggy but otherwise quite frozen white paper parcel.

"Ladies." I smiled triumphantly at them. "We're going to prawn his car."

I was expecting a more positive reaction to my announcement, to be honest. Maybe some gleeful squealing, a few high fives. A triumphant waltz wouldn't have gone astray.

Instead, Kalina scrunched up her nose, Marrika gaped at me like I'd said I was resurrecting the dinosaurs, and Elle just burped then sniggered.

"Oh, come on!" I put my free hand on my hip. "Haven't you heard of this before?"

"I don't get it," Elle said.

"How do we get the prawns in his car?" Kalina asked. "And won't he see them lying on the back seat or something?"

"They don't go in the car, they kind of go in under the bonnet. It's easier to show you on an actual car."

"And then what?" Elle asked.

"And then, as they rot and get all manky and stinky, that smell is going to get into his air-conditioning system and pump rotten prawn smell all through his car. He'll have no idea where the smell is coming from, but once it's there, no amount of car detailing will get rid of that stench."

There was a beat of silence and then Marrika burst out laughing. "That's awful! But so good!"

Kalina was nodding sagely. "Ah yes, it's just like leaving prawns in someone's curtains."

"Surely, that's illegal?" Elle asked, not at all sounding concerned if it was.

I shrugged. "Probably. But does a smell count as damaging a car? And how will anyone know how the prawns got there? Maybe they just crawled in there by themselves and died. *That's* a force of nature."

"Prawns don't crawl into cars!" Kalina laughed.

"Don't they?" I asked her, totally deadpan.

"Okay," Kalina said. "I'm in."

"Me too!" Marrika squealed, sounding delighted.

"Well, if the gang has spoken," Elle said, putting the Frangelico lid back on.

I glanced between them all, a gleeful smile on my face. "Girls. Let's go fuck up his car!"

Alright, so what we were doing was *probably* illegal.

I was sure it was vandalism and damage to private property and probably some other random word in there like *battery*, a term that I honestly had no clue what it meant.

We slunk back into Manly, keeping to the shadowy pathways like the deviants we were. I carried the prawn parcel in a Coles shopping bag, very aware that it was beginning to defrost and praying like hell that none of the prawn juice would soak through and get on my jeans. Because then I'd have to burn them, like serial killers did after they disposed of a body.

The car belonging to Shouty Sex Man was not difficult to locate, being the only bright-yellow car on the street—probably in the whole of Manly, in fact. The only problem was that it wasn't exactly parked in a quiet street. A few buildings away, there was a small cafe that was operating as a late-night wine bar, and people were sitting out on the pavement, in full view of the yellow car and the women currently skulking towards it.

"Shit," Marrika hissed. "What do we do?"

"Just act normal," I said, trying my best to remember how I usually walked.

Kalina, who'd frozen for a moment, now seemed to be walking unnaturally, and I realised she was swinging her right arm at the same time as her right leg.

We all drew level with the car, and since none of us had offered up any plan of attack, after a brief hesitation we walked right on past it. In fact, we walked right past the wine bar, drawing the attention of a number of men sitting out front (at least, Elle and Marrika drew their attention with their short dresses and high heels), and we kept on walking until we reached the end of the road and could duck behind a tree.

"Well, that was successful," Elle said.

"There are too many people watching." Marrika peered out from behind the tree to eye the tables and chairs on the pavement. "Someone will call the police and we'll get arrested!"

"They'd have to know what we're doing to call the police," I said. "What we really need is a *distraction*."

I met Kalina's eye and she quirked her eyebrow at me. As one, we turned to look at Elle and Marrika. Elle put her hands on her hips and narrowed her eyes.

"What?" Marrika asked, looking between us all.

"You guys are dressed more … eye-catchingly than we are, so you'll need to create the distraction," I explained. "Kal and I will circle around the block and approach again from the other end. Once you see us near the car, you create a distraction up here to draw the attention of everyone out the front of the wine bar. Kal and I will do the prawning while nobody's looking."

"What kind of distraction are we meant to create?" Marrika's voice rose several octaves in clear panic.

"Don't worry, Mare," Elle said calmly. "I've got an idea."

"Excellent. Kal, let's move."

Two minutes later and the plan was a go. Kalina and I moved up the street once more, trying as much as we could to look casual and not suspicious—something that seemed easier once I'd pointed out that Kalina was *not* walking normally and she'd self-corrected.

"Slow down," Kalina hissed, as we approached the car, and there was no sign of our distraction materialising.

We both slowed, and I tried to telepathically tell my sister to get a move on.

"Come on, Elle," I said under my breath. And then, feeling inspired, I pretended my shoelace was undone and stooped down to retie it.

Ahead of us, people were eating and talking at the wine bar. I wasn't sure anyone was paying us that much attention, but enough people were facing our way that we'd definitely be spotted if we started doing something suspicious around one of the cars.

A pair of headlights cruised past, lighting us up like startled cats.

"We'll have to abort," Kalina said. "Elle and Marrika are clearly—"

But whatever it was Kalina was about to say was cut off, as at the other end of the street there came a high-pitched squeal of brakes, a woman's scream and a loud thump.

I stood, my eyes going wide. "Oh my God!" I gasped, seeing what looked like my sister standing next to—or perhaps lying on top of—the bonnet of the car that had just driven slowly past us. "Elle's been hit!"

But Kalina grabbed my arm before I could rush towards my sister, instead pushing me sideways towards the yellow car.

"That's the distraction, you muppet! Get prawning!"

"What? But—" I could barely peel my eyes away from the scene at the end of the street. Elle was leaning over the bonnet, yelling at the rather startled driver, who was climbing out of the driver's seat, while Marrika was in near hysterics beside her. But then I realised that all the patrons at the wine bar were watching as well—some even had jumped out of their seats and looked like they were making their way over to the scene of the apparent accident.

"Come on!" Kalina hissed, yanking the bag of prawns off my arm. "Let's get—argh!"

She'd opened the bag and the smell had erupted.

Luckily I hadn't been standing too close, so I was able to suck in a lungful of mostly fresh air, before plunging my hand into the bag and getting promptly stabbed by a sharp prawn spike.

"Fuck!"

Kalina was retching. In fact, I wondered if she was about to vomit on Shouty Sex Man's car.

Marrika and Elle were still screaming at the end of the street, but I knew we couldn't rely on them for long to keep up the charade. Holding my breath, I more cautiously grabbed a few prawns and began stuffing them into the gap between the bonnet of the car and the windscreen.

"Kal!" I said nasally, still without breathing. "Come on!"

Rather bravely, Kalina reached for a prawn, got it under the car's hood, and then turned sideways and retched again.

I was just going for another rotten prawn, when I realised a couple was walking up the street towards us. Fear shot through my stomach as I thought it might be Shouty Sex Man returning to his car.

Shit! Would he recognise me?

But as they came closer, I could see it wasn't him. Still panicking, I dropped the bag of prawns, kicked it slightly under the car, then began rubbing Kalina's back like she was just needing a quiet spew out here in the street.

"What are you doing?" Kalina gasped, but I quickly hushed her.

"Shh, it's okay," I cooed loudly. "Just let it all out."

I threw the couple one of those apologetic, you-know-how-it-is looks and hoped they'd just walk on by. As they drew level, the woman gasped, her hand coming up to her nose, and the man muttered, "That smell!"

"She's got gastro!" I called after them as they hurried away.

"Laura!" Kalina elbowed me in the stomach.

"Ow!"

I was distinctly aware that we needed to wrap up this operation before the police were called on Elle's behalf, so I grabbed the prawn bag off the ground and with one last furtive look around to make sure we still weren't being watched, I stuffed two more prawns under the hood.

"Okay. Let's go."

Kalina, it seemed, had anticipated me, because she was already halfway down the street.

Trying to look as casual as possible, and hoping that Elle or Marrika were keeping an eye out for us, I twisted the prawn bag around to trap the remaining smell and walked as fast as I could away from the scene of the crime.

The four of us were in high spirits when we rendezvoused back at the flat. Kalina was alternating between laughing and retching as she frantically tried to scrub the prawn smell off her arms in the kitchen sink, while Elle and Marrika had put on some music and were doing a kind of victory dance around the beanbags.

"That was the best thing EVER!" Marrika crowed, gleefully high-fiving Elle.

"Who knew Laura had some good ideas in her?" Elle shot me a cheeky grin.

"Now we just need to—*ergh*—for Laura."

"What was that?" I eyed Kalina where she was hunched over the sink.

"I said." She stood up, pausing to wipe water across her mouth. "That now we just need to sort out *your* love-life, Laura."

"You don't need to—"

"WHAAAT?" Elle was suddenly right beside me, victory dance forgotten. "What's going on with Laura's love-life?"

"Nothi—"

"She's been in love with this guy for *months* but doesn't have the guts to tell him."

"Oh." Elle looked pityingly at me. "She *has* always been a bit shy."

"I have not! And that's not it at all—he has a girlfriend! No, he has a *fiancée*." I couldn't help a shudder as I said this, almost as if I was saying *he has a terrible disfigurement to his face.*

"He *possibly* has a fiancée." Kalina scowled. "But that's even more reason why she needs to act now."

"What are you going to do, Laura?"

"Yes, what are you going to do?" Marrika echoed Elle, both girls right beside me and staring at me like goldfish.

"Nothing! Something! I don't know. I need to flash-mob him or something."

"You need to flash him *what*?"

"Not *flash* him. Do one of those flash-mob things where one person starts dancing then everyone from the crowd rushes to join in and suddenly everyone's doing the 'Thriller' dance."

Elle's eyes were still wide. "And how's that going to help?"

"Oh, I get it," Marrika said. "But instead of the 'Thriller' dance, it would be some romantic song, right?"

"Exactly!"

"Well, there are four of us," Kalina offered. "But you're going to owe us big time if you expect us to do some choreographed dance out in public."

Elle snorted. "Forget dancing in public. We'll just do the modern-day version of a flash mob."

"Which is?" I questioned, not bothering to hide my scepticism.

"A TikTok."

Despite my initial protestations, there soon was general consensus about making a TikTok video, no doubt helped by the varying levels of intoxication in the room, the still-high spirits from the recent car prawning, and Kalina and my secret fascination with TikTok, a platform that until now we had managed to avoid joining. I also wasn't too bothered by this turn of events, since it would get Kalina off my back about confessing my feelings for Lucas, and I was one hundred percent sure that Lucas didn't have TikTok, so there was no way he'd ever see the video. And so it was that after a brief discussion around song choice (Taylor Swift's "You Belong With Me" was a hot contender), we settled on the sexier and slightly less teenage-feeling "Never Be the Same" by Camila Cabello.

"We should film her kneeling on the bed in just a white shirt like that," Kalina said, as we all crowded around my laptop watching the music video.

"God no! I don't want him to think I just want sex!"

"Let's put her in a red jacket like Camila's wearing, with the collar pulled right up over her face."

"Yeah! I have a jacket just like that!"

"*No!* I'll look ridiculous!"

It was amazing how passionate I was getting about what I wouldn't do, considering I had no intention of Lucas ever seeing this.

"Let's just film her lip-syncing in a range of different outfits, then we can splice it together." Elle, who had appointed herself director, decided.

"What about us?"

"You guys can be backup dancers."

"Awesome!"

I was so glad Ben wasn't home.

We raided first my, then Kalina's wardrobes (Kalina's provided far better outfits than mine), and soon we were back in the lounge room and I was holding up a hairbrush like it was a microphone.

"And, action!" Elle said, pressing "play" on the music and holding up her phone to film me.

Wearing the closest thing we'd found to a ball gown, I lip-synced the chorus as best I could, but struggled not to laugh when I caught sight of Marrika strutting around behind me, a red blazer wrapped around her head and shoulders. I kept it together until I spotted Kalina wearing a sparkly skirt upside down and doing some kind of pantomime like she was stuck in a glass box.

"Be serious, guys!" Elle implored, but it was to no avail. As we cycled through outfits in different variations of outrageous, our movements became more exaggerated, and then I could barely breathe from laughing and we were all rolling around on the floor together with tears streaming down our faces.

"Oh my God," I managed to gasp. "I'm not sending him *that*."

"Why not?" Marrika managed to get her giggles under control. "At least if it all goes horribly wrong you can pretend it was a joke."

"Elle?" I sat up, suddenly serious as I clocked my sister intently bent over her phone. "What are you doing?"

"I'm splicing it together. You know, it's not *that* bad."

"Don't you dare put it on TikTok!"

Elle rolled her eyes. "As if. It has to come from *you*."

Mollified, I sank back onto the floor.

"This has got to be one of the weirdest evenings I've had in a long time," Kalina said.

I turned my head to look at her, and realised she was smiling happily at the ceiling.

"Have we satisfied your need for a bit of excitement, then?"

She turned her head and grinned at me. "Definitely."

29

In the days following the prawning of Shouty Sex Man's car, I felt like the adrenaline high stayed with me. And sure, the smell of overripe prawn did remain on my hands for longer than I would have liked, but it was far more than that. It was the sense of being in control of something. Of coming up with a plan and executing it successfully. Of being the one in the driver's seat for a change.

The last week of filming went smoothly, the final scenes shot at the Mosman house. There were a few earlier scenes that Amity wanted to reshoot, but even so, we had everything wrapped up and finished by Thursday afternoon.

And just like that, the shooting of the feature film *Trigger* was complete. Friday had been a hold day, a backup day in case we ran over, but with everything neatly tied up, Amity announced that we'd have a wrap party, instead. There were still months of work ahead for Amity and Will on the post-production and editing, but this party would be the last time the whole crew and the actors would be able to get together before everyone moved on to their next projects. I'd heard that Phoebe had landed a role in the next *Thor* movie, and was flying up to the Gold Coast on Monday to commence filming, while Troy was off to Melbourne, where he had a part in a new Stan

TV series.

Although some of the crew members had new jobs in film or TV lined up, most were going back to their regular jobs while they waited for the next film contract to come their way. Ben was back to freelancing for corporate clients; Charlotte, the hair and makeup artist, was returning to the hairdressing salon she usually worked at in Glebe; and Oliver, Ben's boom operator, was going back to his casual retail job at JB Hi-Fi. It seemed that even for those who regularly worked in the film industry, the jobs were sporadic and hard to get.

"Have you decided about the job in the Kimberley yet, Laura?" Celeste asked, cornering me near the drinks table at the wrap party. "I need to know today, otherwise I'll have to find someone else."

"Celeste." I gave her my warmest smile. "I want you to know how grateful I am that you gave me this amazing opportunity to work on *Trigger*. I've really enjoyed working here so much, and with all the wonderful people." Best not mention that I was rather disillusioned to start with, but that was neither here nor there now.

Celeste's gaze was discerning. "But you've decided not to take the next job?"

I felt my stomach drop. Not because she was wrong, but because I hated to disappoint her. How ungrateful did I seem? Yet she didn't look disappointed in me. If anything, she simply looked curious, and almost like this was what she'd been expecting.

"I've decided not to take it," I confirmed. "As much as I've enjoyed this, I ... well ..."

"The film industry is not for you?" Celeste's smile was kind.

"I don't think so," I said, knowing it was true. "I see how much passion Amity and Will and Rory and the rest of the crew have for this work, and I'm just not sure I have it. At least, not enough that I'd leave Sydney and abandon my life here for it."

Celeste's eyes sparkled warmly, and when she patted me on the arm it was with a knowing look on her face. "It's definitely not for everyone. Funny, then, that so many people think they want to be part of it. Still, you were a hard worker, Laura. I'd happily have hired you onto any of my next jobs, if that's what you'd wanted."

"Thank you. I'd have happily worked on many more projects for you if it weren't for all those early starts."

Celeste laughed, and I was relieved that there were no hard feelings between us; I always found leaving jobs and disappointing employers to be so tricky.

Speaking to Amity proved to be just as easy, with Amity once again proving that when it came to liberal thinking she was the queen.

"I'll miss you, Laura," she said, wrapping me up in a big hug. "And thank you so much for your help with the film!"

"Absolutely! I've had such a great time working with you all, and I am *so* looking forward to seeing the film."

Amity laughed. "Aren't we all? Actually, I secretly can't wait to get into the editing room. Filming is fun, but it's so full on! Lock me away in a dark room with a couch and a coffee to review all the footage and I'm in heaven."

"You talking about post?" Will stepped up next to Amity, bumping his shoulder against hers.

"Yeah. Our favourite part." Amity smiled up at him, and I was struck by how much they seemed like a regular couple. Despite the open relationship, or perhaps the lack of any official one, I realised that they were and probably always would be connected.

"I'll miss you guys," I said. "I've had a really fun couple of months working with you."

"I was worried you'd be dying to leave us," Will said with a smile. He cast his eyes around as if to make sure no one else was listening, then added softly, "Sorry about that last night in Mudgee. I know our, ah, *activities*, aren't quite for everyone."

Amity squeezed his arm and smiled at me, as well. "I hope we haven't scarred you."

I just laughed, albeit quite awkwardly. "No, I should say sorry for bailing. I just, erm, had drunk too much and ..." I trailed off, unsure what else to say. That the foursome hadn't been playing out the way I'd imagined it would? That watching Will and Rory have sex with each other while Amity and I got it on was not really what I was into?

But Amity just reached out and took my hand in hers, giving it a soft squeeze. "No explanation necessary," she said simply.

"Thanks." I gave her a grateful smile. "I hope you know, though— it's not you guys. It's me."

Will and Amity both laughed, and any tension that had built up around us seemed to ease.

A small commotion broke out around the drinks table, voices rising louder than the music, and I looked over to see Phoebe and Charlotte engaged in a rather heated debate.

"Oh dear," Amity said. "Poor Charlotte."

"Phoebe and Charlotte? Really?" Will asked, seeming genuinely surprised. "I thought Phoebe was hooking up with Katie."

"She was hooking up with both," Amity said quietly, so only Will and I could hear. "She's a notorious heartbreaker—didn't you know?"

"I thought Troy was going to be the heartbreaker on set," Will said. "He was definitely sleeping with Beth in Mudgee."

"Seriously?" I couldn't hide my own surprise. "I thought we

were the only ones ..."

Amity laughed. "Christ, no. That last night I don't think there was anyone alone at all."

"Huh." Well, that stunned me. Hopefully, Sadie never discovered that her brand-new accommodation had hosted so many adventures. Ben was probably the only one who missed out, staying as he was at the main house.

I spotted Rory heading up the hallway towards the front door, and quickly followed him, hoping he wasn't leaving before I could say goodbye. But when I stepped out onto the porch, I found him standing by the railing, frowning down at his phone.

"Hey," I said, giving him a shy smile when he looked up at me. "Am I interrupting?"

"Not at all." He returned my smile with at least three times the magnitude, putting his phone away in his pocket. "So, have you decided to join us in the Kimberley?"

I couldn't tell if he sounded hopeful or simply curious, but either way his expression fell when I shook my head.

"I've actually decided to stay in Sydney and start my own business."

That surprised him. "Wow. So, we really did turn you off the film industry?"

I couldn't help laughing at that. "No, you didn't. I think this was always a bit of an experiment for me. Trying on a different career. And I did enjoy it, I really did. But," I scrunched up my nose, "it's not really for me long term."

"Damn. And here I was, imagining us spending all those nights together out in the desert." His smile was both suggestive and sad.

I bit my lip and stepped up beside him, turning so I was leaning against the railing. "If there's anything I've learned about the film business, it's that you won't have any problems with loneliness no matter where you are."

"Sure I can't convince you to stay? There are so many things we could explore together." His eyes sparkled mischievously, suggestively, but all I could imagine was the sight of Will and him pressed together, Will's hands squeezing Rory's naked butt. As much as I admired them both for being pansexual, I just wasn't sure I found Rory attractive anymore.

Plus, there was also that phantom feeling of his thumb in my butt crack, sliding disturbingly towards the abyss. I tried not to shudder. Perhaps there were certain things I really *didn't* need to explore.

"I'm sure." I shot him a smile. "But feel free to enjoy all that sand in the desert for me."

He laughed. "I'm already dreading it getting into my cameras."

We both heard it then, the sound of that familiar yellow car revving its way down the road. As one we turned, expecting to see Shouty Sex Man whipping by, except that he didn't. His engine revved down, and then he was pulling to a stop barely ten metres away from Celeste's house.

The passenger door was flung open, and a young woman in a short skirt clambered out before the car had even come to a full stop. She was gagging and looked like she was about to be sick.

The driver's door opened a moment later and there was Shouty Sex Man, for once clothed and looking just as angry as I remembered, although also arguably rather ill.

"I just had it detailed! I swear!" he called to the woman.

The woman was waving her hand in front of her nose as she stumbled away from the car. "I think something's died in there!"

"Babe, please! Get back in, we'll just put the windows down!"

"I'm not—" She doubled over, retching. "Not getting back in

there!"

"Babe!" he shouted at her as she began marching down the street away from him. "Babe, come on!"

"No!" she yelled before she was out of sight.

Looking like he wanted to murder something, Shouty Sex Man got back in his car. And as he did a U-turn, I watched in delight as all the windows of the car went down and he hung his head out of the driver's side, appearing both angry and as though he was going to throw up, before he drove away.

I glanced at Rory and found him watching me, a stunned expression on his face.

"What the hell do you think that was?" he asked.

"That," I said with pure delight, "was karma."

30

The next day, I had an early-evening video call with Sadie after she'd closed up the cellar door.

I took her through everything I'd created for Middlebrook—the now completed website, the newsletter templates and the social media library I'd built up for her. I had a few other ideas I wanted to explore that would involve making some video content for Middlebrook, and Sadie loved that concept, as well.

"Now, Laura darling, we need to discuss your payment for all of this. You haven't sent me any invoices or charged me anything so far, and this can't be cheap, what you've been doing!"

"Actually, Sadie that is something I wanted to discuss with you. I don't want to take any payment from you, but I was hoping that you could write me a testimonial and let me use Middlebrook as a case study for the kind of work I can do. And if you could let me know which wineries in Mudgee that you mentioned could do with a similar marketing upgrade, that would be wonderful. See, I've decided to go freelance and start my own marketing business."

"What a wonderful idea! Of course you should do that, you've absolutely got the talent for it. Lucas told me you were very bright, you know, and that you definitely have the aptitude to do whatever you like."

"Did he?" My voice was rather strangled.

"Oh yes! We spoke about you a lot while he was here." Her eyes sparkled at me through my laptop screen, a sly smile on her face.

"He's not there anymore?"

Sadie shook her head. "He's back in Sydney now. George came home this week, a bit earlier than planned, but now we're back to being fully manned at Middlebrook. Lucas loves it here of course, but well. There was something he wanted to take care of in Sydney, I believe."

My heart sank. He was probably back to make a big engagement announcement with Holly. Get all their family and friends together and reveal it.

Despite what I'd told Kalina last week, and despite the TikTok video (which would never see the light of day), I wasn't sure I could bring myself to interfere. I needed to just be his friend and nothing more. If Holly was the girl he wanted, then I couldn't destroy that happiness for him. I just needed to get it into my head that he and I weren't meant to be.

"Anyway," Sadie said. "Back to this idea of yours. Of course I'll introduce you to my winemaker friends who are in need of a little website assistance. There are a lot of them! And I'd be happy to write you a testimonial—whatever you need. But," Sadie looked sternly at me down the camera, "I absolutely insist on paying you. I know from Lucas how hard it is running your own small business, and how you can't just get away with doing favours for friends. So, I've had a look at what I think this sort of service should cost, and here's what I was thinking."

She named a figure that made me almost choke. It was more than a month's pay from working as a location manager on *Trigger*.

"Oh, Sadie, that's too much!" I immediately said.

"Nonsense," she said. "I might be a farmer, but I'm not poor, you know. Besides, George and I have been discussing this marketing thing for a while now, and trust me this is far less than what we thought we'd be spending."

"Are you sure?" I asked hesitantly, barely daring to believe it. If I could do just two contract jobs like this per month, I'd be earning more than I used to get paid at Tiger Finance.

"Definitely. Oh, and we need to discuss a retainer, as well. I know you think I can do all this newsletter and social media stuff myself, but trust me, I'd much rather outsource it."

I laughed, and told her to let me have a think about it.

After the call, I was positively buzzing. I'd found it! I'd found what I could do with my life. I'd make my own successful career as a boutique marketer, specialising in wineries. Perhaps I could even branch out into other industries, other farming practices, too. There were so many possibilities, and when I thought about it all I felt that warm, happy glow in my chest, that feeling of rightness. Like I'd finally found the right career for myself.

But there was still one dark cloud lingering on my horizon, something I couldn't seem to shake no matter what. I realised that part of me hadn't ever really given up hope about Lucas, about him and me being together. Maybe that was part of why I hadn't been able to take the *Burn Me* contract with Celeste and go live out in the desert for months.

Because then I'd be so far away from him.

It felt so unfair that after everything we'd been through, after the realisations I'd had in Byron Bay, that we weren't destined to be together. It was as if he had a hook in my heart that I couldn't seem to dislodge.

Kalina had to have noticed my despondent mood that evening. I'd taken a hot shower and was making a cup of tea, wondering what to do for dinner, when she came home and found me in the kitchen.

"Have you spoken to Lucas yet?" she asked me immediately, flopping down onto one of the bar stools.

"I don't have anything to talk to him about," I replied, sounding just as miserable as I felt.

"Oh, come on. After we made that video for him?"

I scowled at her. "We were all drunk and being badly influenced by Ellie."

"Ellie?" Kalina sounded scandalised. "You're the one who suggested prawning that dude's car!"

"Oh, did I tell you?" I grinned at her, suddenly feeling good again. "It worked! His car is a total stink bomb and I saw a girl practically dumping him in the street over it."

"Laura." Kalina's face was rather stern.

I crossed my arms defensively. "He's engaged," I said, my voice flat.

"Who is?"

"Lucas! He's engaged to Holly!"

Kalina looked like she thought I might be on drugs. "You know, you're the only one who seems to think that."

"Well, I saw them! The last morning in Mudgee. I saw him getting down on one knee and proposing to her. They might not have announced it to the whole world yet, but they're engaged."

Kalina narrowed her eyes, leaving me in no doubt that she didn't believe me.

"It's true!" I said, glaring at her. "I know what I saw."

As though she thought she could find online proof, she pulled out her phone and started doing something on it. Probably checking

Holly's social media accounts, or trying to find evidence of what I was saying. Well, let her try. I knew for a fact that there was nothing about it online yet.

"Done." Kalina looked up at me.

"What?" I flinched. "Did you find something?"

Oh God, it was real. Holly had to have posted some announcement.

"No. I mean ..." Kalina trailed off, appearing rather ... guilty. She cleared her throat, her expression deadly serious.

Like she was explaining something to a child, she said, "If it is true, and they are engaged, then you have no time and nothing to lose. And since you've failed to take matters into your own hands, I've done it for you."

For a moment I just stared at her, wondering if *she* was on drugs.

"What are you talking about?"

"You might hate me right now, but I think you'll thank me later."

A cold, dark feeling began building in the pit of my chest. My throat was suddenly dry, my lungs forgetting how to breathe.

"Kal, what have you done?"

She smiled grimly, like a surgeon about to announce they needed to amputate your leg. "I've sent him the video."

An Antarctic snowdrift manifested in my stomach. I stared at her like she'd just transformed into the grim reaper. "You didn't."

Kalina sighed. "You were never going to do it yourself."

"DELETE IT!" I screamed, jumping forwards like we could turn back time. "Delete it before he sees it!"

"I can't." Kalina was defiant. "I sent him the actual video file. Via message. I can't delete it."

"Kal!" I wasn't sure if I wanted to punch her or strangle her. Possibly both and in that order.

"Well, if it bothers you that much, go and explain it to him! Or just go and snatch his phone off him before he has time to watch it!"

"I can't! No, wait, yes. That one!"

"You're going to tell him how you feel?" Her eyes lit up hopefully.

"No! The phone-snatching thing!"

Like a crazed bat, I flapped about the apartment, grabbing my phone and keys and racing to the door.

"I'll text you his address!" Kalina shouted cheerily as I flew out into the hallway.

31

Oh God, this drive was taking too long. What if he'd already seen it? If he had his phone anywhere near him, then he was guaranteed to have seen it. I mean, Christ, everyone lived with their phones a hand's reach away, didn't they?

But maybe I'd get lucky. Maybe he was currently in the shower and hadn't noticed the incoming message. Maybe I could call him, and keep him talking until I got there so he wouldn't have time to watch the video? But no, I didn't want to draw attention to his phone. Plus, if he'd already seen it, what the hell was I going to say to him on the phone?

Another thought suddenly struck me. What if Holly was there right now? They were probably sitting together on the couch, Netflix on pause, watching the video over and over again and laughing about it between themselves.

I found his building and managed to snag a parking space directly outside. The security door was propped open with a brick, and I ran up the three flights of stairs, barely pausing to take in my surroundings properly and register that I was standing *outside Lucas's apartment door.*

Only after I'd knocked did it occur to me that he might not be in.

It was Saturday night, after all, and he was recently engaged. He was probably out having drinks with his friends. Or he and Holly might be around at his parents' house, having a big family celebration dinner. That's probably where Ben was. They were probably doing the big announcement thing at this very moment.

I was just about to turn around and leave again when I heard movement inside the apartment. I held my breath, praying it wouldn't be Holly who answered the door, but at the same time weirdly praying that it might be *anyone else* who answered. And then the door was being opened and there he was.

Lucas.

Shirtless Lucas, as it happened.

Christ, he was *fit*.

I wasn't sure how much time went past, but eventually Lucas cleared his throat and I snapped my eyes up, realising I'd just been staring open-mouthed at his chest.

"Oh, hi there!" I said, as if I'd just bumped into him on the street and my cheeks weren't now on fire.

"Laura." There were a million different things he could be thinking right then, but none of them were apparent in his expression. "Come in."

Oh my God, he'd seen it, hadn't he? Was that why he was staring at me like he was trying to work out what the fuck was going on?

Trying not to hyperventilate, I stepped into the apartment. And oh, it was so *homey*. It definitely looked like a bachelor pad, but one where the occupant was clean and tidy and had things they were passionate about. I noticed a magnetic knife block with expensive Japanese knives on display, a fancy wine rack made out of an enormous slab of timber completely full of wine, and a guitar propped up on a stand near the white leather couch. I didn't even know Lucas played the guitar, but seeing it made me fall in love with him a little bit more.

And then I remembered why I was there.

"It was a joke," I said, turning around to face him. Christ, this would be a lot easier if he was wearing a shirt. "I'm so sorry. We were all a bit drunk. Well, I wasn't that drunk, as it happens, or maybe I was, because I'm not sure how else I could have thought that was a good idea. Anyway, a flash mob might have been better, or less confusing, or maybe more confusing because you're looking really confused."

He did look confused. He also looked clean and a little damp, and there was a delicious soapy scent to him that told me he'd just been in the shower, and suddenly I was wondering if he *had* even seen the video, or maybe I had actually got lucky and he'd been in the shower the whole time.

"Laura," he finally said, sounding slightly at a loss. "I have no idea what you're talking about."

"Oh—great! So, um, you haven't checked your phone in the last twenty minutes, then?"

I glanced around the apartment, wondering where Lucas kept his phone when he wasn't using it. But when I turned back to him, to my horror, I realised he'd fished it out of his jeans pocket and was now examining it.

"Stop! Oh my God, don't watch it! Please don't! It was a joke!"

I wanted to grab the phone out of his hand. How pissed off would he be if I plonked the whole thing in the toilet and flushed it away? Although phones were all so waterproof these days, and so enormous that I doubted it would make it around the first U-bend.

Lucas was frowning at his phone, his thumb flipping the screen up and down. My hands were poised out in front of me, like I really was about to break into the "Thriller" dance, ready to snatch the thing away at the first hint of Camila Cabello.

"What am I not meant to watch?" he finally asked, looking up at me with that same confused expression on his face.

Ignoring propriety, I snatched the phone and inspected it. A home screen so full of folders and apps met my gaze that I honestly had no idea what to do with it. Somewhere in the back of my panicked mind, I was pleased to see that his background photo was of rolling grapevines at sunset, not some chummy couple's photo with Holly. But I had more pressing concerns to think too much about that then. At the top of the screen, where notifications should pop up, there was nothing. Which meant …

I swallowed. "You already watched it, didn't you? And you're just trying to save me the embarrassment by pretending you haven't?"

Lucas shook his head, still perplexed. "I haven't watched anything. And I don't know what you're talking about."

"But didn't …" I faltered then. "Didn't Kalina send you a video?" I finished in a small voice.

Lucas stared at me with eyes so blue they made me feel like I was treading water. "Not that I'm aware of."

It hit me then. The answer was so obvious I thought I really could have strangled Kalina if she'd been within grasping distance.

She'd made it up. Of course she hadn't sent Lucas the video file. Because she wasn't a psychotic friend. But she *was* a meddler, and a pusher, and she'd made me believe she'd sent him the video so that I'd have to come over here and talk to him, and she probably knew I was going to back myself into a corner and that I'd need to give Lucas some explanations.

I swallowed. He was waiting, albeit patiently, but still *waiting* for those explanations.

263

I cleared my throat, delicately. "Oh, great! Well, I'll just go, then—"

"Laura." *Now* Lucas sounded frustrated. "What was it you thought she had sent me?"

"Oh, er, just a video. Just a silly video that we made, which like I said, was a joke and we were drunk and it's really nothing, nothing at all to worry about."

"Nothing to worry about so much that you came over here in a panic?"

His intent gaze was unnerving. I felt my face flush, and I had to look away. "Just, well, it was a music video. That's all."

"Laura." He stepped closer to me and I found myself backed up against the wall. "What was it really?"

"It was ..." God, I couldn't do this. I couldn't reveal my feelings and make everything weird and then never talk to him again. But as I stood there, my eyes resting on his naked chest, which honestly I was surprised I was managing to keep my hands off, I decided that yes, I *could* do it. Even if it ruined our friendship and Lucas just went off and married Holly anyway, I had to tell him. I had to be brave.

I looked at him, at his face this time, properly, all my armour gone.

"It was a video of me lip-syncing to a Camila Cabello song."

His eyes narrowed marginally. "And what was so bad about that?"

"It was, er, the kind of implied subliminal message in the song."

"Which was?"

I could feel my heart drumming between my lungs. He hadn't stopped staring at me since I'd walked through the door, as if he feared if he looked away I might disappear.

"I think you know," I whispered.

Lucas swallowed and I realised his breaths were as shallow as mine.

"Where's Holly?" I forced myself to say, wishing I hadn't just asked but knowing I had to.

I was expecting him to step away from me. For that shuttered look to fall across his face, and the realisation that he had a fiancée and he shouldn't be standing, half-naked, with another woman practically pressed up against the wall inside his apartment right then.

But he didn't. His gaze didn't leave mine, and he didn't step back. "Why would you ask that?"

It was my turn to be surprised. "Because she's your girlfri—your fiancée, isn't she?"

Lucas's eyes widened and that did at least send him a step backwards. "My *fiancée*? Where did you get that?"

"I … well, I saw you. In Mudgee last week. You were kneeling on the ground proposing to her."

Lucas looked like he might laugh. Actually, he did laugh, one loud, incredulous *ha*! Then he shook his head at me like I was crazy.

"Laura, last week in Mudgee, I broke up with Holly."

My world imploded.

"You … you did? But I thought …"

Suddenly I was seeing it again, that scene in the kitchen. Lucas kneeling there, holding Holly's hands. Holly's laugh right before flinging herself at him. Good God, she hadn't been laughing. That was *sobbing* I'd seen. She was being dumped!

"Oh." I finished. Then, because I was clearly a sadist, I added, "But why?"

Lucas rubbed at his neck, obviously uncomfortable. "She wasn't … I mean, I guess me and her, it was something I was trying on.

265

To see if it worked. But now I know that it doesn't. Does that make sense?"

I almost laughed. Hadn't I been doing exactly the same thing these last few weeks? Trying on a career to see if it fit? Even trying on being pansexual, which, quite frankly, was a disaster.

"I know what you mean. I guess we have to try these things to make sure, huh?"

"Hmm."

"So … what wasn't right with you and Holly?"

"Honestly? I think you know."

His words echoed mine and I felt my heart stop. Holding my breath, I whispered, "Do I?"

"Laura." His voice dropped and he stepped towards me, his expression intense. Demanding. "Why did you really come here?"

"I … came because …"

"Say it."

He wasn't going to let me squirm out of it. He wanted me to say it, and to say it first. No more hiding. No more pretending. I forced my eyes up to his. Held his gaze as I told him.

"I came to tell you that it's you that I want. That I've been in love with you for months. That you're the person I want to be with." I didn't know how I prevented my voice from cracking, but somehow I did.

He stepped closer again, closer than I thought possible. My skin was at risk of combustion from the proximity of him, the heat I could practically feel.

His blue eyes piercing my own, he said, "I broke up with Holly because she wasn't you. Because you're the one I want."

My chest was cracking open, with sparklers bursting inside me, desperate to escape. Here we were. Just Lucas and I saying such simple words that honestly made my whole world light up with joy.

And then his lips were just a breath away. But he paused, his eyes searching mine. His voice was low, rough and charged, as he softly asked, "If I kiss you, are you going to run away again?"

I could have laughed and cried simultaneously. The first time we'd kissed, months ago, it was supposed to be the end of my infatuation. I'd needed to heal, to grow, to learn who I was on my own. Now, things were so different. Now I knew who I was, and I knew what I wanted. I couldn't be further from running than I'd ever been.

My own voice was soft, husky, as flayed as I felt. Staring into his eyes, letting him see how raw and sincere I was, I said, "If you kiss me, I might never leave."

Lips soft, firm, perfect, met mine instantly. I felt the heat between us as I kissed him back, felt like my heart was going to explode out of my chest. Kissing Lucas felt like the most wonderful thing in the world. But more than that. Kissing Lucas felt so *right*.

His arms encircled me and I was finally pulled against him, finally allowed to melt into his chest. Our bodies fit together like yin and yang, and I pressed myself into him so closely that I could barely remember where I ended and he began.

I could feel tears on my cheeks and he seemed to understand because he kissed them away so tenderly. And I clung tightly to him because I never wanted to let him go.

32

He picked me up with ease, and I wrapped my legs around his hips. My hands cupped his face and I couldn't stop kissing him. But then he pulled back, just enough to look at me. And he laughed softly.

"Laura, why are you crying?"

I kissed him again and he squeezed me into him. I just wanted to nuzzle in, to hold on tight like a koala. But I could feel his lips beneath mine smiling, wanting an answer to his question.

"Because I never thought this would happen," I finally said, a sob escaping.

Still smiling, he gently put me down, but moved his hands up my back to hold me close.

"I thought you never wanted this to happen," he said, a teasing gleam in his eyes. "To be with me. I don't do casual, remember?"

I laughed, wiping the tears away from my cheeks. "I don't think I've ever wanted just casual sex with you. Not since the first time I saw you."

He pretended to look hurt. "You didn't want to have sex with me?"

I kissed him in response, so demandingly that he'd have no doubt that wasn't true. This time he didn't stop to chat. His hands were under my t-shirt, tracing shivers up my back. Pulling me against him until all space between us was erased. Telling me, with every touch, every breath, how much he also wanted me.

Gasping for air, I pulled away a little. "So tell me," I said. "Did you want to have sex with me the first time you saw me?"

He narrowed his eyes slightly. "Did I want to have sex with the weird girl who was meditating on the beach and pretending not to stare at me?"

"Hey!" I slapped him lightly on the arm. "You didn't know I was staring at you!"

His lips curled up. "I did."

"Oh my God." I could feel my cheeks flushing again and I had to look away. But Lucas didn't let me go, pulling me back towards him and kissing me again, this time briefly.

"Maybe not the first time I saw you," he teased, clearly enjoying my mortification. "But certainly soon after."

"At the wine festival? When I was drunk?"

"Hmm. Something like that."

"You perve, you. Fancying drunk girls."

"Only the ones who pretend to like wine so they can talk to me."

"Well, that's not true. Everyone likes wine."

He gave me a squeeze then, up against him. "Well, lucky I only want you."

I snaked my hands around his neck and kissed him again, this time slow and exploratory. I felt his hands soften on my back, his fingertips lightening as he traced them down the curve of my spine and over my hips. I gasped as he stroked my sides, the sensation ticklish but oh so delightful.

"Laura," he rasped against my mouth, a question in his voice.

"Take it off," I whispered.

Our eyes met for a moment, the question so much bigger. But as commanded, he grabbed my top in his hands and I stretched my arms up as he pulled it off me. We were back together instantly, the heat and passion from before immediately reigniting. In one flick he had my bra undone, and I pulled it off myself. When I pressed up against him, my bare breasts on his naked chest, my whimper was met by his groan. And I didn't know if I was shaking or he was.

"Laura," he said again, his voice raw. "You don't know how much I've wanted you. How much you've been haunting my dreams."

I couldn't stop smiling between the kisses. "It can't be as much as I've wanted you. Just the thought of you has tortured me for months."

He made a low growl in his throat that rang with pleasure. And then he was lifting me again, and I wrapped myself around him as he carried me into the bedroom.

"Is this okay?" he said, his voice ragged and his breathing rough. "I mean, we don't have to—"

"No!" I refused to let go of him. "Lucas, we have to. We absolutely do."

He grinned, releasing my legs so I could slide to the ground again. "*Have* to, you say?"

"Yes." I stared at him completely deadpan. "Now, take off your pants."

In answer, he reached up a hand to cup the back of my head, pressing his still-smiling lips to mine. His other hand came around to find the front of my jeans, his fingers lingering on the button.

With a wicked smile, he looked into my eyes. "Only if you take yours off first."

◌

Hours, centuries, eternities later, we lay wrapped in each other's arms. I felt raw and shell-shocked, but at the same time contented in a way I hadn't remembered I could feel.

Everything seemed right in the world. I felt like I'd found the place I was meant to be, and that everything in my whole life had been leading up to this moment. Dazedly, my eyes caught on a piece of fabric that sat folded on the dresser. Like a favourite item of clothing that just hadn't been put away.

"Is that?" I asked, pointing at it.

Lucas roused as if he'd been drifting off to sleep. "Your t-shirt? Yes, it is."

I smiled against his chest. "I forgot about it. What were you going to do with it?"

He hugged me against him, pressing my naked body firmly against his. "Well, I wasn't planning to give it back. I like having your t-shirt here."

I huffed a laugh. "Good, because I've still got yours. I like that it smells like you."

"What, it smells like sweaty man and BO?"

I pinched his nipple, making him flinch before he drew me against him again, pinning my arms between us. He smiled at me, his eyes so alight that I could get lost in them.

"Then again," he said. "I don't need the t-shirt anymore. Because now I've got the real thing."

I returned his smile, letting him see how happy I was. And I could see my own joy reflected back in his eyes.

"I think you mean *I've* got the real thing," I said. "And I'm also keeping your shirt."

He rolled me over, pinning me under him, and made me laugh as he kissed my neck, his hands roaming across my naked skin once again. And again I was lost, we were lost, together in a dance as old as time but as fresh and new as if just discovered.

After, we fell asleep wrapped in each other's arms. Lucas held me so close, like he never wanted to let me go. And my lips, pressed against his skin, were caught with a smile that would not leave.

Facebook Alert
Cath Baker added a photo:
Broken down!! Stuck between a rock and a hard place 😆
Trish Stephens commented:
We're coming to push you out!
Graham Baker commented:
Onwards, convoy!

New Email
From: Amity Grace
Subject: *Thank you!!!*
To all our lovely cast and crew,

Thank you so much for helping to make the last six weeks such a blast! Not only did we get the whole project filmed on time, each and every one of you was such a pleasure to work with. I'll keep in touch once the post-production is completed and we have a release date locked in for the film. Will and I are already planning a fantastic launch party, and we hope to see you all there! xxx

New Message
From: Elle Baker at 7.34 am
Guess what?! Mare said Kyle's been driving some old shitbox Toyota into uni this week! Guess he can't get that stink out of his Mustang, ha-ha-ha!

33

Six months later

I took in a deep breath, relishing that earthy, damp scent of just-rained atmosphere. It was springtime, daylight savings had just begun, and I was sitting on the patio of an Airbnb cottage overlooking grapevines and rolling hills at sunset. The door slid open behind me and Lucas stepped outside, holding two wineglasses and a bottle of Eden Valley shiraz from one of the wineries we'd visited earlier today.

I never got tired of seeing him smile at me. Every morning and every night, every time I caught him watching me, he had an expression on his face that I was sure I shared. A kind of surprised wonder that the other person really was there. That here we were, together, a proper couple. Some days, I still wondered if I was going to wake up and realise it was all a dream.

He sat down in the other patio chair, and poured out the wine.

"This cheese is amazing," I said, squishing another piece of the gooey brie onto a cracker and handing it to Lucas. "And the cheese lady was right. The blue one is the stinkiest cheese I've ever smelled."

"Well, only the stinkiest of cheeses for my lady. But seriously, I reckon I could smell that one from inside." Lucas grinned as he handed me a wineglass.

"It's the stink that adds the deliciousness."

We were both laughing as we clinked our glasses together, our eyes pinned as we took a sip.

It still felt strange that this was my life now. Just me and Lucas, travelling around together, each running our own business. Today we'd visited three different wineries—he tried the wines on behalf of his clients back in Sydney, and I met with the owners and discussed marketing options. Of the three, one had seemed genuinely interested in my services, and I hoped they would become the third client I'd managed to land so far on our South Australia trip.

My freelance marketing business was proving to be a much wilder success than I'd ever imagined. After the work I'd done for Sadie, she'd introduced me to a number of other winemakers in Mudgee, who were impressed with her new website and wanted an update themselves. Some of them, including Sadie, were now paying me monthly retainers to help out with their newsletter campaigns and social media postings, even though I'd shown them all how to do it themselves. So it was that I had created a client list that provided me with ongoing, regular work, yet still allowed me to travel around, look for new clients and generally just run my business however I wanted.

At first, I was embarrassed at the price I was charging the wineries for my marketing services, but Sadie had helped put my mind right at ease. According to her, I was still only charging a fraction of the price that big agencies did, and I was doing a better job with broader services. I was a marketing all-rounder, I had realised. Not simply good at one thing, but able to do a whole range of things. Maybe that's why I was so reluctant to get a full-time job in marketing again, working for another company. Because most companies just pigeonholed their staff into doing one particular task over and over again until you wanted to drill your eyes out. Even just thinking about running an incentives report at Tiger Finance one more time still made me feel like I was going to break out in shingles.

"So, I finally got a hold of Ben," Lucas said, biting into a piece of blue cheese on a cracker. "Oh wow," he added, his eyes going wide. "That really is strong."

I grinned at him. "I still find it funny that Ben ignores you. I mean, if *I* called him—"

"I know. He'll answer your calls, but not his own brother's."

"He must just like me better." I shrugged nonchalantly.

Lucas shot me a look, his eyes narrowed. "You wish. He just thinks I'm going to grill him about his love-life again."

"Well, *did* you grill him about his love-life again?"

Lucas picked up his wineglass and took a long, slow sip. "I may have done," he said cagily. "But that's hardly the point."

I laughed. "Well, aside from that, how is Ben doing?"

"He's fine. Good, even. From what I gather—not that he'd say anything directly—I think he's met someone."

"Really?" I squealed. Ha! So much for him swearing off women. "Oh God, I hope she's not another Amy."

We both grimaced, recalling the girl who'd lured Ben to Byron Bay and tried to steal all his money.

"I'd say not," Lucas said. "He's not dumb enough to make the same mistake twice."

We stared at each other for a moment, as if both wondering if that statement was true. I mean, I knew Ben had *said* he wouldn't make the same mistake again, but still ...

"Maybe I'll call Kal and check," I finally said.

"Good idea," Lucas agreed. He stood up, picked up the empty

cracker packet and leaned down to kiss me quickly before heading back inside.

I simply sat, turning my gaze out to where the sun was setting over the grapevines, enjoying the last of the day's lingering warmth. And then, picking up my wineglass in one hand and my phone in the other, I called Kalina.

"Soooo, how's it going down there in the valley?" she asked immediately. "Lots of wine and shagging?"

"Kal!" I couldn't help but laugh. "Is that how you greet your long-lost flatmate?"

"Yes. Do you not know me?"

I rolled my eyes, even though she couldn't see. "In that case ... well, yes, actually. I am enjoying lots of wine and shagging."

She burst out laughing.

"How about you? Bet you and Owen are loving not having me hanging around the apartment so you can get your own shagging on?"

"Hardly. Ben's still around all the time. Every time I mention you and Lucas now, he kind of scrunches up his face like he doesn't want to imagine it. Says it's too weird—like his sister and his brother hooking up."

"Aww! Poor Ben. Actually, that's what I wanted to ask you about. Has he got a new girlfriend on the scene?"

"Not that I know of. Why? Do you know something?"

"No, nothing. Lucas just reckons he's got a feeling that Ben's met someone."

"Ooh, intriguing! I'll grill him about it tonight."

"Oh God. Don't say I told you to, though!"

"Why not? You're practically part of Ben's family now, even more than me. He even told me that despite how weird it is, he's glad that

Lucas is with you now and not Holly."

"Really?" I felt touched. "I thought Ben liked Holly?"

"Hmm." I could practically see Kalina shrugging. "I think he was worried she'd do something to hurt him again."

My eyes tracked a kangaroo as it jumped through the grapevines in the distance. "Yeah. I can't decide if I feel bad for Holly or not. I mean, she got dumped, but she did the same thing to Lucas not so long ago."

"Oh, didn't I tell you?" Kalina's voice perked up. "You're going to just die when you hear this."

"What? What's happened?"

"So, Holly ..." Kalina paused, leaving me hanging in suspense as long as possible. "Is now dating Amity!"

It took me a moment of stunned silence to process this.

"Hang on ... what? How?"

"Turns out they got chatting when you were all up there filming in Mudgee. And Holly kept in touch with Amity because she wants to get some filming done for Follow the Rainbow. And now they're a couple!"

"Jesus. I thought Amity didn't do relationships."

"Well, apparently she does with Holly."

"Damn. So, Holly's even better at being a pansexual than I was."

Kalina laughed. "Either way, I don't think you need to feel bad for Holly. Turns out she wasn't done exploring her sexuality, so it was a good thing Lucas dumped her!"

The screen door slid open behind me again, and I turned and caught Lucas's eye as he stepped outside. I wondered if he'd want to know about Holly and Amity? How ironic, that we both now had gay exes.

I smiled at him. "I'd say Lucas is definitely winning."

He raised his eyebrows at me, but I just laughed and shook my head.

"Anyway, best go, Kal. Lots of love to you and the gang!"

"Have fun, lovebirds! Tell Lucas you're just dying for him to—"

"Bye, Kal!" I ended the call before she could finish whatever sordid suggestion she had. Then turning to Lucas, I gave him a smug grin. "I was just saying how lucky you are to be sitting here with me."

"Don't I know it," he said, a wicked sparkle in his eye.

And then he was in front of me, pulling me up and wrapping his arms around me, and smiling with that look on his face that I loved so much. I managed to get my wine back on the table, before standing on my tiptoes and throwing my arms around his neck, pulling him in and kissing him.

I sighed happily as we leaned back, our bodies still entwined.

"Laura," he said, his eyes dancing. "Have I told you today that I love you?"

He had, but he could never say it enough. We'd been saying it for months, since almost that first night we spent together, and still I got a thrill every time.

"I love you, too," I whispered, and kissed him again.

And with the sun setting before us, and sheep bleating somewhere in the distance, we stood pressed together, just him and me.

Happy. Home.

Together.

Acknowledgements

This book was probably the most challenging one I've tried to write to date, perhaps because there were just so many ideas and places that I wanted to include in the story!

Firstly, a huge thankyou to the Mudgee region, my second home, and to the wonderful community of people in Mudgee. The landscape, the sky, the autumn trees and of course the wineries all made for perfect inspiration for this book, and I hope my love for the area came through in Laura's visits there.

A huge thank you to all the cast and production crew on the Australian TV series The Twelve, who, unbeknownst to you all, had an author at work in your midst! Working on the show as an extra for a few days gave me some great insights into how TV shows and movies work behind-the-scenes, and a special thanks to Ellie who answered some of my questions about location managers.

Thank you to my writing bestie, Bernadette Eden, for our monthly calls and giggles! Thank you to my copy editor, Alexandra Nahlous, for once again making my book shine brighter than I thought it could. And a huge thank you to all of my family for your ongoing support and belief in me as a writer.

The biggest thank you to Linden, for being the most amazing

husband in the world, and for continuing to support my writing dreams. You're still my go-to person for plot brainstorming, and the inspiration behind all my romantic happily-ever-afters.

Finally, I'd just like to say that prawning someone's car is never a good idea, and is most likely illegal, and this author does not condone that as an activity in any way. Even if they really do deserve it.

Support an Author

Leave a Review

Even a single sentence can make a huge difference!
If you enjoyed this book, please post a review on Goodreads,
Amazon or any other book platform you might use.

SARAH BEGG lives in Sydney with her husband and a dog named Ruby. She loves to travel and has been writing fiction for as long as she can remember. She decided she was going to become an author when she was seven and realised that was a real occupation. When she's not writing, she works in digital marketing.

Follow Sarah on Instagram and Facebook
@sarahkbegg

Subscribe to Sarah's email newsletter at
sarahbegg.com

www.ingramcontent.com/pod-product-compliance
Lightning Source LLC
Chambersburg PA
CBHW020004140726
47904CB00018B/1816